Rave Reviews for
Austin S. Camacho's *Russian Roulette*

"... Russian Roulette delivers a whipsaw of a plot with more layers than a Vidalia onion.... Solid storytelling and compelling characters Don't miss it!"
 Libby Fischer Hellmann, Author of the Ellie Foreman mystery/suspense series

"Hannibal Jones is no John Shaft wannabe. He stands on his own as a welcome addition to the ranks of the fictional private eye."
Robert J. Randisi, Founder, the Private Eye Writers of America

"Russian Roulette has everything: a terrific story with great characters in vivid settings. Clear time on your calendar for this one."
John Gilstrap, author of No Mercy

"An atmospheric, entertaining read. Troubleshooter Hannibal Jones is the most engaging character to come upon the mystery scene since Patterson's Alex Cross."
 JoAnn Ross, NY Times Bestselling Author of the High Risk Series

"Russian Roulette starts with a revving engine and picks up speed till racing across the finish line. If I was in trouble I'd want Hannibal Jones on my speed dial."
Jon Jordan, Editor, Crimespree Magazine

"Camacho employs his usual rich layers of plot; fascinating characters; and plenty of action to keep the reader mesmerized in his latest Hannibal Jones installment."
Shelley Glodowski, Midwest Book Review

"I may have to add Austin S. Camacho to my list of authors to follow and catch up on after reading his latest novel, Russian Roulette. I received the book for review before I left on vacation, and I would have been perfectly happy to have all of the Hannibal Jones series with me to read."
Thomas Duff, Amazon.com Top 25 Reviewer

"Austin is one helluva writer. What Austin shows off in his novel is not just the ability to forge a sentence or a paragraph, but how to create an interesting story with a steady pace that keeps you hooked for hours at a time."
Hugh Howey, Crime Critics blog

Russian Roulette

by

Austin S. Camacho

ISBN 10: 9794788-4-0
ISBN 13: 978-0-9794788-4-0

Published by:
Intrigue Publishing
7707 Shadowcreek Terrace
Springfield, VA 22153 USA

This book is dedicated to the book sellers who have supported my budding career by presenting my novels to their customers, and allowing me to meet their customers by hosting book signings. These people are not merely business acquaintances, but my good friends.

Thank you all so much for your valuable support!

Jim Huang	The Mystery Company	Carmel, IN
Becky Froberg	Borders Express	Waldorf, MD
Leo Gordy	Borders	Largo, MD
Kathy Harig	Mystery Loves Company	Baltimore, MD
Warren Hender	Borders	Silver Spring, MD
Ann Meneses	Borders	Bowie, MD
Joe Mix	Borders	Frederick, MD
Missy Robinson	Borders	Waldorf, MD
Sandy Sinanian	Books-A-Million	Greenbelt, MD
Dave Watt	Borders	BWI Airport, MD
John Cross	Foul Play	Westerville, OH
Antoinette Cross	Foul Play	Westerville, OH
Lorenzo Andreaggi	Borders	Arlington, VA
Keyonna Brooks	Books A Million	Alexandria, VA
Dennis Bryant	Borders	Dulles Itnl Airport, VA
Ron Burch	Borders	Fredericksburg, VA
Lucy Dennect	Books-A-Million	Leesburg, VA
Dan Fister	Borders Express	Springfield Mall, VA
Ilka Fettig	Borders Express	Springfield Mall, VA
Steve Gillikin	Waldenbooks	Landmark Mall, VA
Tracy McPeck	Waldenbooks	Landmark Mall, VA
Leigh Hall	Borders Express	Dulles Town Center, VA
Kellee Walters	Borders Express	Dulles Town Center, VA
Beth Jenkin	Books-A-Million	Alexandria, VA
Jessie Marino	Borders	Manassas, VA
Steve Moose	Borders	Springfield, VA
Dustin Pfannenstiel	Waldenbooks	Manassas Mall, VA
Kathleen Richardson	Waldenbooks	Tysons Corner, VA
Chris Roach	Borders Express	Fair Oaks Mall, VA
Janet Lane	Borders Express	Fair Oaks Mall, VA
Jen Stewart	Borders	Manassas, VA
Patrick Williams	Books A Million	Woodbridge, VA
Ramunda Young	Barnes & Noble	Tysons Corner, VA
Gary Beal	Borders	National Airport, DC
Kim Carpenter	Borders	National Airport, DC
Beth Jenkins	Books A Million	Dupont Circle, DC
Mark Wachhaus	Books A Million	Washington, DC

Prologue
- Tuesday -

Eddie Miller was just a poor working stiff. He'd tell you so himself if you asked him. Lord knows he wasn't looking for any trouble. He never was. But trouble was about to find him. And as usual, it would find him when his hands were full.

Eddie lumbered out into the Safeway parking lot carrying a half dozen plastic bags, three dangling from the fingers of each hand. He could only imagine how silly he looked in his work pants, work boots, and flannel shirt, the bald front half of his head reflecting the afternoon sun like a polished pink bowling ball, and the blue plastic pods growing down out of his fingers. How could anyone look at him and see a threat?

And yet, a good ten yards from his aging red Camaro, he saw three men stalking toward him as if he were the devil himself. He recognized these men. They were dressed like he was, but just like most of the guys on the construction site, they were all wider than he was. And their hands were empty.

The three bruisers stood in an arc between Eddie and his car. The blond dude crossed his huge arms across his chest. The taller bald guy hooked his thumbs into his belt loops. Eddie stopped, but while he was trying to decide whether he should put the bags down, the black guy in the middle stepped forward so close that Eddie could smell the cigarette smoke that his shirt had absorbed in some bar the night before. He looked like Mike Tyson but he had Wesley Snipes' voice.

"You don't really think they're going to let you kill the project, do you?"

1

Eddie stood his ground and stared up into the black guy's dark eyes. He was a little scared but, hell, he'd taken an ass whooping before and if he had one coming he'd handle it.

"Look I hate the thought that I might be taking food out of anybody's kids' mouth, but damn it, they're using substandard materials. I been doing this too long to just be quiet while they pour concrete that ain't going to last. Louie here saw the same thing as me."

The black dude looked to his left at the blond. "Yeah, but Louie's keeping his mouth shut. Now, you convince me you're going to keep your mouth shut, this don't got to get ugly."

Eddie nodded. He knew where this was going. A cool breeze, or maybe something else, sent a chill down his back. He unlocked his knees and lowered just enough to place his grocery bags on the tarmac. When he stood erect again, he pushed his chest forward as far as he could and locked eyes with the obvious leader of the group. The energy passing between them forced the rest of the world out.

"You know I can't do that."

Silence enveloped them as the black guy tried to stare Eddie down. After six long seconds, the slam of a car door drew Eddie's attention. He hadn't even noticed the black Volvo drive into the parking lot and roll into a space just six cars from his.

The newcomer walked toward Eddie like an old friend. He was African American but no more than six feet tall and smaller than any of the guys crowding Eddie. He wore his black suit like it was his working clothes. Expensive sunglasses hid his eyes. He looked first at Eddie, then turned to the bigger black guy and held out his right hand. That was when Eddie noticed the black driving gloves.

"Hannibal Jones," the newcomer said. "And you are?"

"I'm Mack," the black guy said, ignoring Hannibal's hand, "and this is a private conversation. Get gone."

"Sorry, no can do," Hannibal said, tugging on the ends of his gloves to tighten them on his hands. "Eddie here, he's got places to be."

Mack turned to Eddie. "You think this little clown can protect you?"

Hannibal stepped between the men, putting his face very close to Mack's, and his voice dropped into a deeper register. "Don't talk to him. Talk to me. The law affords whistle blowers a certain amount of protection. I'm part of Eddie's protection. Now, make it a nicer day for all of us and just walk away."

Mack grinned, flashing big yellow teeth. "You really do want us to kick your ass, don't you? I won't even get warmed up on you."

Something about Hannibal's demeanor made Eddie think maybe Mack had it wrong. He took a step back, not to avoid conflict but to give the new fellow room to move if things got hectic. He sure looked relaxed, even as Mack balled his hands into fists and the other two guys slipped farther to the sides. They were grinning, just like schoolboys do when they see a fight coming. Hannibal just seemed to take it all in.

"They ain't paying you enough for this kind of grief, dog," Hannibal said. "Can't we talk about this?"

"You arrogant asshole," Mack said, squaring his shoulders. "I think you just earned yourself a beat down."

Mack, who had shifted his feet into a boxer's stance when Hannibal arrived, looked as if he intended to brush this problem aside so he could get back to Eddie. His right fist started its journey forward, straight from the shoulder, but it hadn't gotten far before Hannibal's left hand snapped out. Eddie didn't actually see the blow, but he could tell it wasn't Hannibal's fist but just the web between his thumb and first finger that hit Mack. It looked like his hand had barely touched Mack's throat, but it seemed like that was enough. Mack gurgled and his hands went to his throat. His knees buckled but before they hit the ground, Hannibal turned to Louis.

3

"Do we have to make a scene here?" Hannibal asked. "Or can we be grown-ups about this?"

Louie looked at Eddie, at his bald partner, at Mack, and then back at Hannibal. He seemed to go through some kind of decision-making process that ended with him stepping behind Mack and grabbing one of his arms. Bald guy got the idea, took the other arm, and helped Mack to his feet. The three moved off toward a pickup truck on the other side of the parking lot. As they shuffled between the vehicles, they passed a young Latin woman who was stepping out of the passenger side of the black Volvo. She ignored them, stepping with care on spiked heels toward the man in black. When she reached him, she blessed him with a smile that made Eddie wish he went to work in a suit too.

"Well, that didn't take very long," she said.

"I guess it doesn't always have to be the hard way," Hannibal answered, returning her smile. She nodded, and then turned to Eddie. The smile she gave him was not quite as warm, but he appreciated it just the same.

"It looks as if we found you just in time, Mr. Miller," she said.

"Them fellows wasn't going to bother me much, Miss Santiago," Eddie said. "I told you my story and I'm sticking to it. You don't need to worry about me."

"You are my worry until you take the stand, Mr. Miller," Cindy Santiago said. "The plaintiffs in this class action owe you a great deal, including safety, for stepping up. This man will help you stay safe. Eddie Miller, this is Hannibal Jones."

Eddie gave Hannibal's gloved right hand a firm shake. "Ain't you the fellow they call the Troubleshooter? Glad to know you."

"Mr. Jones is under contract to our firm to maintain your security," Cindy said, her shoulder-length brunette locks tossing. "He's a trusted agent for us."

Eddie nodded, but he could see that Hannibal was a good deal more to her than a trusted agent. He looked at the other man, average height and on the slender side, wearing a conservative suit, and driving a boring car. He just couldn't see what made him so special. But then, he also couldn't see the sense of power and control he had felt a few minutes earlier when Hannibal shooed away three brawlers with one quick move and the tone of his voice.

Cindy turned back to Hannibal, a twinkle in her fawn brown eyes. "Don't forget now, after Mr. Miller testifies tomorrow, you're coming with me to look at that house in Crestwood."

"Right now, why don't I help Mr. Miller get these bags to his car?" Hannibal said, turning to Eddie. "Then Ms. Santiago and I will follow you home. I want to go over some basic security measures with you."

Hannibal stooped to gather half the plastic bags in his hands but Eddie hesitated, watching Cindy's hips as she swished away toward the Volvo. J-Lo with brains, he thought, a woman who made even a navy blue power suit look seductive.

"You are one lucky son of a bitch," he said, grinning as he scooped up the rest of the bags.

* * * * *

Hannibal wasn't feeling very lucky as he pulled into his unofficial parking space across the street from his apartment in Southeast DC. It was ten o'clock by then and he was worn out. Darkness hung over his neighborhood like a warm blanket, except for the cold pool of light from the streetlamp he parked under. He got out of his car feeling as if someone had strapped weights to his shoulders.

Many of his neighbors had their windows open despite the late autumn cool, and he was pulling in snippets from three different television shows. A deep breath told him that someone was enjoying their show with overbuttered popcorn. Somehow, the sounds and smells of families relaxing in front of their TV sets had a sedative effect on him. The steps up to his stoop looked a lot steeper than usual as he trudged toward them. At the top he pushed through the common door of his building, pulling off his Oakleys and sliding them into his suit jacket pocket.

His work with Eddie Miller was not what had fatigued him. Miller lived in a sixth-floor apartment in Bethesda, just north of and indistinguishable from the District. Hannibal had verified that Miller's doors and windows were secure, instructed him to keep his blinds closed, and made sure Eddie had Hannibal's phone number beside the telephone. He was certain Miller would be fine until morning, when Hannibal would pick him up to go to the courthouse.

It was the conversation with his woman that had drained Hannibal. Cindy had received a block of stock as part of her law firm's public offering. The stock had exploded and overnight, she was wealthy. She didn't seem to notice that Hannibal, a working stiff private investigator, was not comfortable with the dramatic difference in their economic levels. Now she wanted him to help her pick out a million-dollar home.

Meanwhile, Hannibal felt at home in his low-end apartment building in a five-room railroad flat. He was part of a real neighborhood and didn't think he would desert his neighbors even if he won the lottery. He sighed and shook his head.

If he had any sense, he would be heading into his apartment, but he needed to record his hours and expenses for the day and that meant getting into his office on the other side of the hall. As he unlocked his office door his foggy mind was busy berating him for not proposing to Cindy as he had planned to do, just before he learned of her windfall.

He had gotten as far as buying a ring. He had chosen the words he would say. But by the time he had gathered his nerve she was thrilled by the news of her sudden wealth. At the time it seemed that news would overshadow a proposal. Besides, what did a rich woman need with a husband? And, what did he really have to offer her?

Now he was telling himself that the money didn't matter, that she respected him for who he was and what he did, not for what he had.

That is why he was all the way into the room before he realized that he was not alone. A man sitting at his desk was pointing a pistol at him.

"Close the door behind you," said the man in a thick, Eurasian accent.

-1-

Hannibal kept his eyes on the stranger as he pushed the door closed. He could almost feel his irises widening, adjusting to the darkness. The man behind the automatic had military-short hair. His tight, angular face looked as if someone had assembled it from a number of flat planes. The eyes were a sharp, piercing blue, like ice chips set into the ruddy face. This man would think nothing of killing Hannibal. The silencer attached to the barrel of his nine millimeter Browning Hi-power said that he might even get away after doing so.

"Remove your coat," the stranger said. Hannibal considered the situation and decided that if this fellow wanted him dead he already would be, so he had nothing to lose.

"Say please."

The stranger smiled then, a cold, hard smile, and leaned back in Hannibal's chair. "Please."

Well, the man was at least being respectful. Hannibal pulled off his coat and hung it on the coat rack beside the door.

"Now, with your middle finger and thumb lift that Sig Sauer out of its holster and set it here on the desk. Please."

This man was very calm and well controlled. A professional, not like the amateurs Hannibal dealt with earlier. That knowledge put him more at ease. He might die tonight, but not because of a jumpy gunman having a careless accident. Hannibal watched those hard blue eyes as he reached under his right arm and pulled his gun free of its holster. He placed it carefully on his desk in front of the gunman. Interesting, Hannibal thought, that he was left-handed too. With a nod, the other man turned on Hannibal's desk lamp. After a second he waved the tip of his barrel at Hannibal's face.

"They are truly hazel, just as your file said."

He would be referring to Hannibal's eyes. But what file was he talking about? Hannibal had no police record, except of course as a past officer. He had never served in the military. And not many people could get into his old Secret Service jacket. Now he was more curious than worried.

"Look, I hope you won't consider this rude, but this is my office after all. Just who the hell are you?"

The stranger motioned Hannibal into the guest chair. "I am Aleksandr Dimitri Ivanovich. And you are Hannibal Jones, the self-described troubleshooter, born in Frankfurt of an American soldier and a German mother. Six years New York City Police Department, three of them as a detective. Seven years in the Treasury Department's Protective Service. Licensed investigator in Washington, Virginia and Maryland."

"Okay, so you've done your homework," Hannibal said, unbuttoning his shirtsleeves. "Obviously you're not just some casual burglar."

"Of course not. Do I look like a thief? It is important that you know who I am, so that you will not make a foolish mistake. I am in fact a professional assassin."

"Really," Hannibal said. "Killers don't usually open up so easily. Freelance?"

"I do not simply work for the highest bidder," Ivanovich said with an air of indignance. "I work for what you would call the Red Mafiya. The Russian mob. So you see I am in my way a troubleshooter as well."

Hannibal sat forward, his mouth suddenly dry. The shadows behind Ivanovich seemed to grow taller and more menacing. Hannibal's mind raced back through his most recent cases, searching for an enemy who might be in the position to place an assignment in this man's hands. Then he considered Russians or Eastern Europeans he might have offended while doing his job. Ivanovich allowed him all the silence he needed to consider and reject every possibility.

"I give up. Who sent you? Why are you here?"

Ivanovich surprised Hannibal with a charming smile, although the gun's muzzle never wavered. "No one sent me here. I have come to your office for the same reason most people do. I need your help."

"My help? At gunpoint?"

Ivanovich lifted a photo album from under the chair and placed it on the desk. He slid out an eight-by-ten black-and-white photo and turned it to face Hannibal.

"This is Dani Gana, a wealthy Algerian, or so I am told."

Hannibal took the face in. The man was darker than Hannibal but his features were not African. He was aggressively handsome, wearing a day's growth of beard and the kind of self-possessed smirk that women are drawn to and men want to slap off any face they see it on. Hannibal would have disliked him right away if someone other than a hired killer had presented the picture. He raised his eyes back to Ivanovich.

"I won't find your target for you."

Ivanovich shook his head. "I already know where he is. I want to know who he really is, where he is from, where his fortune came from, and why he is in Washington."

Hannibal crossed his legs. "So you just want me to do a background investigation on this fellow. And no one is paying you to kill him?"

"No."

"Then what makes him a person of interest for you?"

"His relationship with Viktoriya Petrova."

Hannibal took his time standing up in order to avoid any threatening movement. He found his curiosity piqued despite himself, and felt confident that he was in no real danger as long as he didn't get too close to Ivanovich.

"There's a woman," Hannibal said. "That means there's a story. How about some coffee?"

Ivanovich nodded, his lips pressed together. He looked uncomfortable, maybe more so than Hannibal. After all, Hannibal had had guns pointed at him plenty of times before. But Ivanovich looked like a man who had rarely asked anyone for help and didn't like doing it at all.

Hannibal took the coffee carafe from the machine on the table beside his desk and headed toward the kitchen at the other end of the five-room apartment that served as his office. Its rooms formed one long space unless the pocket doors set in the walls were pulled together to separate them. Ivanovich followed. As Hannibal filled the carafe, he asked, "You have a relationship with this girl?"

"Viktoriya and I have a long history."

Ivanovich stood, stiff as a wooden soldier, in the doorway to the kitchen. He held his gun close to his ribs, pointed at Hannibal's chest. Once the carafe was full, Hannibal turned to face him. "What has the girl to do with the man whose picture you showed me?"

"They are engaged to be married."

Hannibal nodded and headed back through the apartment, passing the bed in the room beside the kitchen. "So why aren't you with her now?"

"There are times when one must lay low," Ivanovich answered, stepping around the heavy bag hanging from the ceiling in the middle room. "This is one of those times."

They continued past the small table in what Hannibal sometimes referred to as his conference room and into his office. He poured the water into his coffee maker, wondering how close the police might be to finding Ivanovich.

"Well, you must have been watching this guy for a while to be able to get that picture of him," Hannibal said.

"Yes," Ivanovich said, pulling an airtight canister from a shelf behind Hannibal and handing it to him. "I was simply observing him, but as it turned out the FBI was watching him also. I was spotted but escaped before the agent could call in backup."

Hannibal poured beans into the grinder side of his coffee maker. It was a custom blend of Kenyan, Colombian, and Guatemalan coffees prepared for him by The Coffee Mill in Rehoboth Beach. It was much better than his captor deserved. He hated the fact that the proposed case was beginning to interest him.

"So the FBI is also interested in this Gana," Hannibal said over the whine of the grinder. "Is he Russian mob too?"

Ivanovich paused at the same moment Hannibal did to enjoy the fresh aroma that the grinder ripped from the beans. Then he said, "I do not know. But Viktoriya's father was, before he died. Nikita is no longer there to protect or advise her. She lives with her mother, Raisa, now. She seemed secure there until this Gana appeared in the city two months ago and leased Raisa's second home."

"Also in the District?"

"Yes. Both are in Woodley Park."

"Nice," Hannibal said, pouring his coffee. "He must have plenty of cash to be staying up there. It sounds like your Viktoriya will be well taken care of." He looked at Ivanovich who nodded with a thin smile, so Hannibal poured a second cup.

"Perhaps." Ivanovich accepted the cup and returned to Hannibal's desk chair. "But I fear he may have come by the money dishonestly. If that is true, he could have worse enemies than the FBI. And if someone is out there who wants to hurt this man, Viktoriya could be hurt in the process. I will not allow her to be put at risk."

Hannibal stood at his desk, considering this enigmatic assassin and his request. Ivanovich was asking Hannibal to take a case he was sure he would accept from a different client and maybe from this man if they had not had this entire conversation at gunpoint.

"You really love her, don't you?"

"How could that matter to your investigation?"

"It has to do with your motives," Hannibal said. "You must be desperate to be here, talking to a black detective because you figure I can help you find out the truth about a rich African foreigner. But why would I take your case? Do you really think you can force me to investigate at gunpoint? I could walk out that door and just keep going. Or, I could call the cops and let them come in here and yank you out. Why on earth would I invest any of my time and energy into helping you stalk this girl who doesn't appear to need help or to be interested in you at all?"

Ivanovich's voice deepened and became a bit harder, as if he wanted to be very sure that Hannibal understood him clearly.

"Because, my arrogant friend, I have very competent associates watching Miss Cintia Santiago, associate at Baylor, Truman, and Ray and daughter of Reynaldo Santiago who lives upstairs from you. My associates are invisible, obedient, and deadly. If you fail to find the answers I need about Dani Gana, your beloved Cintia Santiago will die."

-2-
Wednesday

Aleksandr Ivanovich's words had echoed in Hannibal's mind all night like a continuous tape loop. The loop continued to play in his head the next morning as he gathered Eddie Miller from his apartment just before dawn. Driving his black Volvo S60 downtown, Hannibal replayed every ugly word Ivanovich had said to him. The jarring statement that at least two trusted men were watching Cindy Santiago at all times. The declaration that her telephones were tapped and that Ivanovich could even tap into her BlackBerry messages. The warning that any contact with her would endanger her and her coworkers.

He didn't need to be told that letting any of his friends or neighbors know what was going on would put them at risk. All the men who lived upstairs had helped him on cases before. Sarge, Quaker, and Virgil were always up for anything but none of them would be able to deal with a professional killer like Ivanovich. And none of them could keep a secret from the fourth man who shared the building, Cindy's father. With his Cuban temper, Ray Santiago would likely go racing right into the assassin's sights.

Worse, a firefight in the building would involve little Monte, the boy Hannibal mentored, and possibly his grandmother. Mother Washington would try to talk the killer out of the house, believing that prayer can solve any problem. Maybe she was right, but he would not risk their lives. This problem he would have to deal with on his own.

All this occupied one compartment of his brain as he drove the car he called the Black Beauty into the parking garage under the building that housed the law offices of Baylor, Truman, and Ray. He stepped out of the car and looked around for a second before signaling Miller that it was safe to get out.

"I thought we were going to the courthouse," Miller said, looking uncomfortable in a suit that Hannibal suspected only left the closet for weddings or an Easter church visit.

"You'll be safe here until court time," Hannibal said, keeping his eyes moving as he escorted Miller to the elevator.

"I don't think anybody's going to bother me this close to the trial," Miller said.

Hannibal didn't think so either. He was watching for other men. But it seemed he had guessed right. Cindy would head straight for the courthouse this morning and, with limited resources, Ivanovich's people would be with her, not staking out her workplace.

They carried little of the crisp morning air into the elevator with them, and warm, dry air greeted them as they stepped out of it. Hannibal was surprised to see lights on behind the office door and for a second he feared he had guessed wrong after all. Miller stepped back when Hannibal drew his weapon, gripped the doorknob, and pushed the door inward.

Silence and a sweet aroma greeted his entrance. The outer office was empty except for Mrs. Abrogast, who was floating fresh begonias in a shallow bowl filled with water. The office manager turned toward the door with an expression that somehow combined an unimpressed smirk with a scowl of impatience.

"Can I help you with something, Mr. Jones, or are you here to rob us?"

"My apologies, ma'am," Hannibal said, holstering his gun. "I didn't expect anyone to be here this early. I thought I'd end up waiting for you in the hall."

"Someone has to prepare this place for the all the young lions," she said, moving around behind her desk. Mrs.

15

Abrogast was one of those lovable, blue-haired, old-school ladies who never smiled but loved her charges despite her constant criticism of them. This, and her stone visage, made her the perfect gatekeeper.

"Well, since you're here, I'd like to leave Mr. Miller with you," Hannibal said.

"You do know that Ms. Santiago is not in yet," Abrogast said. "I'm the only one here."

"Yes, ma'am," Hannibal said, "but I have another case that I have to attend to. I'm pretty sure Miller here will be safe in your charge and the rest of the crowd will be in soon enough."

"You need to stop by more often, young man, and I don't just mean when it's business related," she said, fussing with things on her desk as if Hannibal wasn't worth paying attention to. "You give her more attention, or we'll find someone else for her to waste her time on."

Hannibal leaned one palm on the desk. "You are absolutely right, Mrs. A. You don't know how badly I wish I could be talking to her right now. But when you see her, give her this, OK?"

He kissed the tip of a gloved pointer finger and pressed it on Mrs. Abrogast's head. She gave him a skeptical glance and a small piece of a smile.

"That won't hold her for long, young man."

* * * * *

Hannibal's smile faded by the time he was driving north and west down Connecticut Avenue, the major thoroughfare that slices into the heart of Northwest DC. He was at the leading edge of rush hour, the sky not quite light thanks to low cloud cover, the pedestrians not quite awake. Heading toward Viktoriya Petrova's place, he had more time than he wanted to consider Ivanovich's threat against the person he cared most about in the world.

It was a big stick, maybe bigger than necessary. After all, Ivanovich was not asking him to do anything illegal or that would put anyone at risk. In fact, Hannibal knew he might have taken the job anyway if Ivanovich had asked him nicely. It was nothing that would make him even think about putting his woman at risk, and he saw no reason to leave an alarming note for her at work or make any attempt to inform her of the situation because it would only frighten her. Besides, he might be able to end the case quickly. He would start by talking with Gana; his girl, Petrova; and her mother. If the man had nothing to hide, Hannibal would know right away.

To reach the Petrova house Hannibal drove past the Omni Shoreham Hotel and down the block he called restaurant row in his mind. He had once counted twenty-five international restaurants on that one city block. Most of them pumped hypnotic aromas into the street. Crawling through traffic with his windows down, Hannibal found the scent of food changing with each breath.

He drove past stately rowhouses whose ornate architecture cast him back a century or so before trees and lawns took over and the rowhouses gave way to upscale single-family houses. These were not the contemporary dwellings sprouting like kudzu all around the Beltway, but old-school mansionettes, most of which were still inhabited by old money.

Hannibal was watching the numbers on the mailboxes. After he drove past the Petrova house, he turned the corner and parked almost at the end of the block. He was dressed for business in black suit and gloves and his ever-present Oakleys, but he didn't feel conspicuous. In that neighborhood, most people would assume he was a member of a government or private protective service, or perhaps working at one of the nearby embassies.

It was a crisp day, as if all the trees in the neighborhood were working overtime on oxygen production, and he wanted to walk the area a bit before knocking on a stranger's door. On a whim, he decided to walk toward the closer corner and stroll up the block to pass the house that backed to the Petrova residence. It also belonged to Mrs. Petrova and was leased to Dani Gana. If Hannibal got lucky he might even catch a glimpse of Gana, although he still wanted to speak to Mrs. Petrova first.

A brown suit caught his attention as he walked. It was wrapped around a man holding a camera. The camera's lens was big enough that the man had to support it with his spare hand. He was leaning against a brown Saturn wearing New Jersey plates, itself more out of place on that block than Hannibal's Volvo. The longer Hannibal looked at the man, the less he seemed to belong there. He was trying to be casual but was watching for something at the other end of a steep driveway. If Hannibal was judging the distance to the man's position correctly, the house he was watching was the Petrova rental property. That was enough to make Hannibal want to know more.

He could walk straight down the sidewalk to greet the stranger, but instead he crossed the street. Soon he was standing behind the man, separated by a narrow strip of asphalt. The white, modified split-level house stared down from its perch surrounded by a variety of foliage. A tall bank of hedges offered the house some privacy. Hannibal wondered if Dani Gana could have done anything to warrant being stalked by paparazzi.

The stranger with the camera let any random sound yank his attention to the left or right. When he looked uphill through the hedges, he lifted the camera to his eye, as if using the lens as a spotting scope. Could this be the man Ivanovich saw watching Gana?

Hannibal waited for a taxi to pass before stepping into the street. He walked at a normal pace, not trying to conceal his presence, yet the stranger looked startled when he heard Hannibal's voice beside him.

"What are you doing here?" Hannibal asked.

The stranger's head whipped around and his right hand slid into his jacket as if he were looking for something. "Get away from here. I'm authorized. I'm INS." He pulled out a badge but Hannibal ignored it. He looked at the man's suit, his shoes, and the quality of his haircut. He was soft around the middle and his sandy brown hair was just a little too long. His shoulders were slight for a man Hannibal's height.

"No, you're not," Hannibal said.

"Sure I am. Now beat it. I'm following a suspect."

Hannibal glanced at the fake badge and wondered if "special agent" Ben Cochran had used his real name on it. Having seen the real thing so many times, he didn't have to stare long to see this badge was made from a much cheaper metal. Not that it mattered, since nothing about this man's style, appearance or approach felt like a real INS agent.

"You're not immigration and you're not FBI. So who are you?"

Cochran hesitated for a moment, then lowered his hand and put his badge away. "Who said I was FBI?"

"A guy I know, but he must not have gotten a good look at you." Hannibal watched Cochran's eyes wilt.

"OK, look, I'm really a private detective."

Hannibal leaned back against the car, side by side with Cochran. "Wrong again. That's my gig and I know every private op licensed to work in the District." It was a casual lie, but he had little fear of contradiction.

"So you're watching Gana too?" Cochran asked. Hannibal smiled and Cochran took that as his answer. "I'm from out of town. I'm here helping a friend who wants to know who Gana really is. Damn, I hate being stuck in the Ramada day after day, but I told my pal I'd help him out, you know? I'll give you five hundred dollars if you'll just…"

The sound of an engine starting spun Cochran around toward the house. A black Mercedes had pulled out of the garage and was idling in front of the house. When the driver got out, all Hannibal could see was dark skin and a dark suit. The driver went to the door, walked a woman to the passenger side, and opened the car door for her. Then the man walked around to the other side of the car. As the driver was about to open the car door, Hannibal heard a click beside him.

"Got it," Cochran said. At the other end of the driveway, the driver's head snapped up. He had heard the camera. The thin eyebrows on that dark face pushed together and Hannibal felt a wave of hate roll downhill. Still unseen, he walked a few feet down the street and crossed, keeping his pace casual.

Cochran, on the other hand, giggled in a high-pitched voice and yanked at his own car's door handle. He placed the camera on the passenger seat, got in, and slammed the door.

Cochran and his car were slow. He got it started and was just pulling into the street when the Mercedes roared down the driveway. Cochran yanked the wheel to the right but not fast enough. The right quarter panel of Gana's Mercedes creased the little Saturn, cracking a headlight and forcing it over against the curb. Both drivers jumped out of their vehicles, but Cochran held a camera while Gana held a knife.

-3-

Hannibal wasn't sure what he expected from his first good look at Dani Gana, but this was not it. Black marble eyes were set deep in a polished teak face, only a bit darker than Hannibal's, with features that reminded him of a Lebanese neighbor he once had. Black, straight hair lay facing forward and hanging over the edge of his forehead. Rage widened his eyes, clean whites showing around the marbles.

Gana was not a big man but his shoulders were wide and his hands were big enough to make the folding fighting knife look smaller than Hannibal knew it was. When he spoke, he surprised Hannibal again. His voice dipped to an unexpected register, below baritone but not quite bass.

"Is it worth dying for?"

Cochran looked perplexed until Gana nodded at the camera. Cochran looked from the camera to the wide blade and back again. Cochran held the camera out away from his body. Gana snatched it with his left hand, held it high over his head, and slammed it down to the street. The snapping of plastic and the crackle of glass breaking dominated the street for a moment. Gana nudged the remains of the camera over behind his front tire. Then he took two purposeful steps toward Cochran. Hannibal touched his automatic and prepared to stop the action from going any further.

The passenger side window lowered, and a warm, accented voice said, "Darling, it is not worth it."

The rage flew from Gana's face as he turned to the car. All Hannibal could see inside was hair, black and shiny as a raven's wings, flowing in a cascade of curls halfway down a woman's back. This would be Viktoriya Petrova, Hannibal assumed. Her voice had been enough to break Gana's rage. In a moment he would become more aware of his surroundings.

Hannibal turned and walked away at a casual pace. Behind him, he heard low conversation between Gana and Viktoriya, then Gana's door opened and closed. He heard the Mercedes pull away in the opposite direction. He heard the finality of the camera being crushed under the tires. And he heard Cochran mutter a single profane epithet before he too drove away.

Hannibal continued without a backward glance. When he reached the corner, he crossed to the side on which Gana lived. Only then did he look up the block, but both the Saturn and the Mercedes were gone. He continued to the next corner, turned again, and found himself in front of a long winding flight of stone steps. He started up them, between waves of purple, blue, and white flowers growing out of an evergreen plant. Daffodils scattered among the ground cover nodded their yellow heads at him as he passed.

A broad patio ahead held a wrought iron table and chairs where two people sat separated by a large French press coffee maker and a pair of cups. The woman was in her forties, with hair cut in a trim bob that left a thick slice of hair to hang at an angle between her eyes. It was the same ink black as the woman in the Mercedes. This would be Raisa Petrova.

The man facing her had come to breakfast in a gray wool suit. Hannibal picked up his musky fragrance from three feet away. He was wearing too much cologne and too much eyebrow, and he looked at Hannibal the way a deer watches a wolf trot into view. Hannibal tried to defuse his discomfort with a smile, but the woman turned a dazzler on him that put his own smile to shame.

"Can I help you, young man?"

Those were the woman's words, but they sounded just like "would you like to come to bed with me?" Hannibal stopped ten feet away and tried to take them both in with his greeting.

"Good morning, Mrs. Petrova. Good morning, sir. I'm sorry to bother you. My name is Hannibal Jones and I was hoping to have a few words with you about Mr. Dani Gana."

"Please, come sit," Raisa said without even a beat of hesitation. "Yakov was just leaving."

Judging by his face, Yakov was unaware of his plans to depart until that moment, but he was a gentleman. He stood. Raisa offered her hand and he kissed it. Then he nodded toward Hannibal and stepped past him down the winding stairs toward the street. It was too late to apologize to him so Hannibal again turned to Raisa.

"I really didn't intend to interrupt your morning, ma'am."

She waved his words away. "Relax, young man. Yakov Sidorov is my physician, not my lover, although I'm sure he would want it otherwise. Besides, I think Aleksandr Ivanovich sent him to spy on me. Now come, sit, and tell me what you want to know about Dani."

Hannibal continued to stand. "You know Ivanovich?"

"I will not discuss it further unless you sit." She poured from the press into her cup, picked up Sidorov's cup and stepped into the house. When she rose, Hannibal could see that she had a reasonable shape hidden inside her flower print dress. She returned in seconds with a clean cup which she also filled from the press. Hannibal understood the law of house rules. He sat opposite her, in the chair still warm from Sidorov's expectations. He sipped the black liquid in his cup, realizing too late that it was tea.

"You are good," Raisa said in what Hannibal identifed only as an Old World accent. "You didn't flinch. Tea is better for you than that coffee you Americans drink all day."

"It's good and strong," Hanibal said, "but tea doesn't give you the aroma like coffee does. Now, you know Ivanovich?"

Raisa smiled and made a show of pulling a cigarette from a silver case. "Of course, dear boy. He has been sniffing around my Viktoriya for years. Ever since my dear husband, God rest his soul, brought him into that ugly business he was in."

She paused, holding the cigarette out, until Hannibal noticed the small box of matches on the table. He struck one, freeing the sharp scent of sulfur. She ignored it as she leaned in, drew a lungful of smoke, and let it carry her words out.

"He is a violent boy who does the dirtiest work for gangsters. But when Vitoriya saw Dani, she realized what a good man looks like."

Hannibal blinked away the smoke. Raisa was starting to sound like a bad imitation of Shirley MacLaine. Was it the accent the actress had used in *Madame Sousatzka* or the attitude from *Steel Magnolias* that gave him that impression? He turned his gaze back down the path while he gathered his thoughts.

"You like the flowers, young man? Those are periwinkles."

"Periwinkle was a color in my crayon box when I was a kid," Hannibal said, "but that color didn't match any of these. And just how much do you know about this good man Dani Gana? How did he come to be so wealthy?"

"Why do you care? Are you here working for Aleksandr Ivanovich too?"

"Are you paranoid, Mrs. Petrova?"

He had guessed correctly. She did not want her sanity questioned, and if she insisted that everyone was sent by Invanovich that would be evidence that she was becoming paranoid. Blinking back those thoughts, she leaned in, as if to share a confidence. Hannibal moved forward too, looking around as if to make sure no one was listening.

"Dani Gana is a very important man. He is no simple financier. He is Algerian, you know."

"Yes," Hannibal said. "I know." *What else you got?*

Raisa set her jaw and raised the stakes. "He is living in exile from his own country. Gana is not his real name."

Inside the house, a cockatiel screamed. Hannibal looked into Raisa's eyes from behind his sunglasses. "How do you know he's telling you the truth?"

Raisa almost leapt to her feet, snugged her floral gown around herself, and moved off into the house. Hannibal sipped his tea and examined the irregular flagstones underfoot. The house must have dated from the 1920s or before. With four levels, an attached garage and maybe a fireplace it would go for a million six or seven if she put it on the market.

Mrs. Petrova returned with a flourish, leaving her front door open. She slapped a letter down on the table and glared at Hannibal as if daring him to pick it up. He did.

-4-

As soon as he saw it, Hannibal understood why Raisa thought this letter was so important. It was typed on heavy, crème-colored stationery with a classic watermark and it carried the letterhead of Leon Martin, a vice president of the Chemical Banking Corporation in New York City. It was a formal letter of introduction addressed to Raisa Petrova.

This is to introduce you to Dani Gana, who has been a substantial depositor at our institution for five years. He has asked our bank to formally introduce him to you because of your position as a pillar of the community in Washington.

Mr. Gana is a man of influence in both business and government circles in his native Algeria. He now wishes to establish financial ties in the United States and has asked us to help him establish valuable contacts.

Mr. Gana will be in your area in the next few days and he shall be contacting you soon to arrange a meeting.
I am sure you will benefit if you agree to see him.

Sincerely

If Gana wanted to establish his legitimacy, this was a powerful bit of evidence. Assuming, Hannibal thought, that the letter itself was legitimate.

"I take it you know Mr. Martin?" Hannibal asked.

"He has handled my personal finances for more than a decade."

"I see. Well, thank you. This helps a lot. May I borrow this? I'd like to contact Mr. Martin to confirm his relationship with Mr. Gana."

"Perhaps," Raisa said, lowering herself into her seat. "On one condition."

"And that would be?"

Raisa leaned in again, pulling out her seductive voice. "You are a professional investigator, yes? Someone has hired you to investigate Dani. What I want you to do is to drop the case. Give these two a chance to succeed. Give my Viktoriya a chance to find her happiness."

Hannibal wondered if it would make any difference to Raisa if she knew that the life of the woman he loved hung in the balance. No, he decided, it would not. Like any mother, the happiness of her child was her highest priority. But did Ivanovich want to destroy Viktoriya's life? All he had asked for was the truth.

"I promise that I won't do anything that hurts either of them if Gana turns out to be all you say he is. But before I make that determination, I have to meet the man himself."

"By all means, go and meet him," Raisa said, sitting back and swallowing half her cup of tea in one long drink. "I expect him to be back from his morning business by eleven. I'll call and tell him to expect you."

* * * * *

Before speaking with Dani Gana, Hannibal had a previous appointment. The time in his car gave him a chance to think through his conversation with Mrs. Petrova. He considered why the letter from a banker might mean so much to her. She did have a fine home, but its value had nothing to do with the cost of maintaining it. His read of the woman was that she would never part with it, even if she couldn't afford to keep it up. It was symbolic of the fortune her husband had made for her and her daughter. A wealthy man in her daughter's life could be insurance of a sort.

But if she wanted the man to stay in his daughter's life, that raised its own questions. Knowing that Hannibal was investigating her prospective son-in-law, why had she dealt with Hannibal so kindly?

It didn't take Hannibal long to reach the meeting place for his appointment. The drive to one of the southwest entrances to Rock Creek Park was brief, and it took Hannibal only five minutes to find the man he had arranged to meet.

On a map, the District is an almost perfect square balanced on one corner. Rock Creek Park is a long swath of green shoved up into the upper corner, with the Maryland towns of Chevy Chase on its left and Silver Spring on its right. At the worst of times it has been an island of tranquility in the tumultuous city, a place where ash, beech, birch and butternut, hickory, elm, and cedar trees can all live together. It is also a place where bikers and hippies, hikers and joggers, Republicans and Democrats, and even law-abiding citizens and retired professional criminals can find peaceful coexistence.

Before he made eye contact with Anthony Ronzini, Hannibal spotted his two-man protective detail. These were big, beefy men who wanted the world to know they were there. Ronzini had few living enemies, but his boys didn't want any muggers or pickpockets to think he was an easy target. They both recognized Hannibal as he approached and one tapped his boss on the shoulder. Ronzini stood back, letting an elder jogger pass him on the gravel path he had chosen for his morning constitutional.

Ronzini was a big man who appeared physically soft, but if you looked into his eyes you could still see the hardness of his youth. As a young man, Ronzini made his fortune as a pimp, a gambler, and a fixer. Now he was simply a man who knew people, knew things, and took a slice of other people's activities in exchange for his permission to do business unmolested in certain parts of town. Hannibal had never imagined this man wearing a blue sweat suit and running shoes, but even in that outfit he exuded a quiet menace.

"Good morning, Mr. Ronzini," Hannibal said in the soft voice he used for those he wished to show respect. "How is your son these days?"

"Salvatore is doing well up in New Jersey," Ronzini said, walking at an easy pace. "I must grudgingly thank you for showing him the error of his ways when he was dealing drugs. He is really doing much better in gambling operations."

Gravel crunched under their feet. The air was crisp and sweet from the mingled scents of a bewildering variety of trees and flowering plants that formed an endless green tunnel for them to walk down. Yet Hannibal carried a sour taste in his mouth as he considered asking Ronzini for assistance.

"Go ahead," Ronzini said, as if reading Hannibal's mind. "It gets easier each time you admit you need someone else's help."

"It's not someone, it's you," Hannibal said. "I shouldn't have to go to a criminal to get my job done."

"But I seem to be the person who knows what you need to know," Ronzini said, taking a deep breath and letting it leak out. He seemed to enjoy his life more than a retired professional criminal should. "What do you need to know?"

Hannibal walked with his hands in his pockets, eyes to the ground. "What do you know about the Russian mob?"

"Could you be a bit more specific?"

"Aleksandr Ivanovich."

Ronzini stopped in his tracks. His two escorts looked around as if they sensed ghosts in the woods. Ronzini turned to face Hannibal.

"You know, I respect you," he said. Hannibal felt a blush begin, and then hated himself for being flattered by this man's respect.

"Thanks, I guess."

"No, seriously, I do," Ronzini said. "In a lifetime of dealing with dangerous men, you are one of the most

29

dangerous men I've ever met, and one of the most determined. You are smart and tough and you have character. There are few I would bet on against you. So when I say this Ivanovich is a man that you don't want to mess with, you should understand what that means."

"Don't always have the choice."

"Unless what you are really asking for is some help from a few of my boys. Is that it?" Ronzini resumed his walk. He seemed to enjoy the fresh air and verdant view. A step behind, Hannibal considered this veiled offer. He probably could get a team of professional muscle to go after Ivanovich. But that would mean they'd have to go crashing into his office. But if Ivaonvich was telling the truth, that would also mean that his agents would hurt or maybe kill Cindy. He could not put her at risk, and besides, that simply wasn't the way he worked.

"No, forget that. The guy I really want to know about is named Dani Gana."

"Oh yes, the recently arrived Algerian," Ronzini said with a nod. "He's quite a hit in some parts of the city's high society."

"Yeah. Do you happen to know if he's who he says he is?"

"I haven't had any reason to doubt it," Ronzini said. "The right people seem to know him."

Hannibal saw a rabbit near the edge of the trail. It wriggled its nose and watched the men pass as if they represented no danger. If that bunny only knew, Hannibal thought.

"I've heard that Gana is a legitimate businessman. I've also been told he has ties to the Russian mob. The one thing everyone seems to agree on is that he has money. Know anything about that?"

"I know he opened an account in the Provident Bank two weeks ago. Opened it with a couple hundred thousand dollars."

How does he know this stuff? Hannibal wondered. Aloud he asked, "Is it mob money?"

"Who do I look like, Tony Soprano?" Ronzini asked.

Well, yes, you kind of do, Hannibal thought.

"I need to find out where that cash came from," Hannibal said. "If he stole it, things go one way. If he earned it, things go another way. If he borrowed it to impress his prospective mother-in-law, well, then he's busted."

Ronzini stopped at a wooden bench on the side of the trail and smiled at Hannibal. "This is about vetting a groom? You never cease to surprise me. Who is the lucky girl?"

Hannibal moved to the opposite edge of the trail. "Her name is Viktoriya Petrova. The reason I asked about the Russians is that she has mob connections."

Ronzini laughed one loud, harsh laugh. "Viktoriya? Is this Raisa's little girl?"

This time Hannibal said it out loud. "How do you know this stuff?"

"I got history with the Petrovas," Ronzini said, his smile fading off into the past. "Pleasant history, as it happens. I knew the girl's father, Nikita. For his little girl, I'll check into this Gana for you. If he's not legit, you can run him off her, right?"

"That's the job," Hannibal said. "I take it you liked her old man."

"Respected him," Ronzini said. "He was a fixer, helped the Russians get established in this town, but he was also kind of like you. Smart guy, tough guy, lived by his own code. Nobody to mess with. Cops said he threw himself off a roof."

"What do you say?"

"I say guys like you don't throw themselves off roofs. I know how things were back then. I'd put my money on Ivanovich."

Hannibal nodded and stepped closer so that Ronzini's bodyguards would not hear his words. "I really appreciate the information, Tony. And thank you for checking into Gana. I promise you I'm going to look out for the girl's best interest."

Ronzini nodded. They both knew that his boys didn't like to hear people using Ronzini's first name. They took it as disrespect. But as Hannibal turned away, Ronzini pulled his jacket lapel.

"One more thing. The Santiago girl. She's got a mouth on her, but she's a righteous innocent."

"Yeah? What about her?" Hannibal ignored the hand, watching Ronzini's eyes.

"Those boys watching her. Maybe it would be good to have some boys watching them? You know, just in case something happened."

How does he know this stuff? Hannibal considered Ronzini. He was no longer a crime leader, but he was a player, and not without influence. He didn't have to bother with these things. There could be only one reason for such an offer.

"That would be... thank you, Tony. I owe you a big one."

"You already owe me big, Jones. Now go find out what you can about this Gana, and I'll do the same."

* * * * *

In his car Hannibal decided to try again to play with one of his new toys. The Volvo S60 was a gift from a wealthy client as compensation for Hannibal's previous car that was totaled while working that client's case. Cindy had given him an iPod, loaded it with his music, and showed him the basics of how to make it work. Monte, the teenager he mentored, had installed a device that allowed him to plug the iPod into the Black Beauty's stereo system, directing his chosen tunes through an impressive bank of Bang and Olufsen speakers. He could control it all from the steering wheel. If he pushed the right buttons in the right order, he could get the telephone to work, hands free, through those same speakers.

He knew it was childish, but that in no way reduced his joy when he managed to call Cindy without taking his hands off the wheel.

"Hey, baby. You messing around with the car phone again?"

"Yeah, but this time I did it on purpose," Hannibal said. "I just wanted to tell you..."

"That you're taking me to dinner at a place I've never been before?"

"Sorry, Cindy," Hannibal said, trying to keep his tone light. "I'm afraid I'm stuck on a case and won't be able to see you tonight. I also won't be able to get away to look at that house with you today." Not quite a lie, he thought, but close enough for him to hate it.

"No problem," she said. "I was busy too, so I moved the appointment to tomorrow."

Hannibal gritted his teeth. "Well, I expect this case to keep me busy tomorrow too."

"Yeah, well I know you didn't really want to go anyway, lover, but it's OK. I'll give you a full report. What's the case about?"

His relief that she didn't push about his absence was crowded out of his head by unexpected disappointment. A part of him wanted it to be a big deal to her. He stopped at a red light, took a deep breath, and put his smile back into place. He knew she would hear it on the other end of the phone.

"I've been asked to check a guy out before he marries into a certain family. You know, make sure he's legit and who he says he is, and so forth."

"Anything a lawyer could help with?" Cindy asked.

"I don't know. He claims to be Algerian. Know any way I could prove that?"

Hannibal thought she might have insight into the customs process or some similar legal check, but she surprised him. "Well, I do know this professor at Howard. Krada's his name, Jamal Krada. I think he teaches history. Anyhow, he's from Algeria. I bet he could tell you if this other guy's really from there."

"Hey that is a really good lead, babe. Thanks."

"You're welcome, lover. But listen, I need to get into court now. Talk to you later?"

They said their hurried good-byes and Hannibal used operator assistance to find his way through the Howard University telephone tree to Jamal Krada's office. As it turned out, Krada had no morning classes. When Hannibal dropped Cindy's name, Krada invited him to lunch at his home. He was just completing the arrangements as he pulled into a parking space in front of Gana's house. Black Beauty was now in the space the brown Saturn had occupied earlier. As he looked up the driveway to the front door, he hoped his visit would have a happier ending than Ben Cochran's had. He walked up the winding asphalt path and rang the bell. He was startled at how quickly it swung open, as if the resident had been waiting for someone.

Gana stood in a sky blue suit and wingtips polished until they glistened. He scanned Hannibal up and down, staring into his sunglasses for a second before saying, "You must be Hannibal Jones, the private detective that Mrs. Petrova told me about. It is an honor to be investigated."

-5-

Dani Gana turned his back to Hannibal and led him into the house without looking back. It was an unexpected expression of trust. Hannibal followed Gana through the house, which looked bigger on the inside than it had from outside. Gana paused in the living room and stared into the fireplace as if trying to decide something. This gave Hannibal a chance to look around. He was admiring the shoji screens in the dining room when he noticed what looked like a packing box beside a large oak desk. One side of the desk was covered with papers, but the pigeonholes on one side were all empty.

"Yes," Gana declared, indicating that he had made a decision. He moved quickly into the kitchen and returned with a large coffee mug. Then he led Hannibal through the living room to the patio beyond.

The patio overlooked a modest swimming pool. Beyond that, a long terraced garden separated them from the back of the Petrova house. Gana opened the insulated carafe on the table and filled a mug for Hannibal, then filled his own that was already there.

"Yes, this is better than being cooped up in the house," Gana said. "Now have a seat and tell me how I can help you."

"Actually, I thought I might be able to help you," Hannibal said. "I was in the area this morning to speak to Mrs. Petrova. When I was walking past this house it looked like you were having a bit of trouble with somebody."

"That was minor," Gana said, flashing a broad smile. Up close, his smile dazzled and his eyes twinkled with energy. "A little fender bender, actually. I did have to take my car in for repair after the incident." He sipped his coffee, watching Hannibal over the edge of his cup.

"That I might be able to help you with," Hannibal said. He pulled a card from his pocket and slid it across the table. "Here's a very good limousine service I often use when my car is in the shop. So, you don't mind talking to me? I'd just like to know a little about your background."

"I have nothing to hide from Hannibal Jones, the famous Washington troubleshooter. Ask me anything."

"All right," Hannibal said. "I'd like to know how you met the Petrovas but I'd also like to know how you know me."

"I've known Viktoriya Petrova for years. She knows that I will give her love and a good life. And you are a professional, I know that much. So someone must have hired you. Who would want to investigate me?"

Hannibal sipped his coffee, then sipped again and smiled. "Very nice."

"Isn't that good?" Gana asked, crossing his legs. "I have it imported from Algeria. Did you know the Sufis made this drink so popular? Members of the Shadhiliyya order spread coffee drinking throughout the Islamic world back in the thirteenth century. A Shadhiliyya shaikh was introduced to coffee drinking in Ethiopia. To this day the shaikh is regarded as the patron saint of coffee-growers back home. In fact, in Algeria coffee is sometimes called shadhiliyye in his honor."

"I am familiar with the coffee of the region," Hannibal said. "How do you know me?"

Gana watched the sun glint off the surface of the pool for a second before answering. "I will admit that when Mother Petrova told me that you planned to visit me I went to the computer and Googled you. Does this trouble you?"

"It's all public knowledge," Hannibal said, although it did make him a little uneasy. Had this man read the web log Cindy talked him into starting? He couldn't say why that bothered him a bit, but now that he thought about it, it seemed odd that no one had done it before.

"And now to my question," Gana said. "Who has hired you to check up on me? It is Ivanovich, isn't it? Mother Petrova believes it is. You know, he is simply a jealous suitor who is a poor loser."

The coffee was dark and rich. As he drank, Hannibal could see all that everyone else saw in Dani Gana. He saw the hypnotic lover who must have swept Viktoriya off her feet. He saw the suave gentleman who would impress any mother with a daughter of marrying age. And he could also see the dangerous risk taker and potential killer Ivanovich knew. The man was smooth as polished marble, but Hannibal would bet he could be just as hard. He returned Gana's smile, still not sure which of them was the mongoose and which the snake.

"Sorry, I really can't go around revealing the names of my clients. But surely this Ivanovich guy can't be the only person on earth interested in you. Who else would want you investigated?"

Gana returned one loud, harsh laugh. "Very good, Mister Jones. But no, I don't think it is in my best interests to offer you a list of my enemies." Gana emptied his mug and set it down with a decisive thump. "In fact, I'm not so sure I should help you at all."

Gana had uncrossed his legs and crossed them the opposite way, and was shaking one foot as he talked. Hannibal reflected that he had the makings of a charismatic leader and might well be a master of the boardroom and wonder in the financial business. He also considered that only a very thin line separated the charismatic leader from the expert confidence man.

"Surely, you'll give me a chance to relieve any doubt Mrs. Petrova may have before you leave town, which I've noticed is likely to be soon."

Gana rested his palms on the patio table and stood. "Mrs. Petrova has no doubts about me. She has already accepted me as her future son-in-law. And Viktoriya has no doubt of my love and dedication. I owe you and your mysterious client nothing. Yes, it is almost time for me and my Viktoriya to start our new life. I have some business in this city to clean up, but I can take care of it in a couple of days. That means that you have forty-eight hours to learn whatever you can learn, Mr. Jones. Perhaps you should get started now."

-6-

Jamal Krada lived fifteen miles almost due north of Dani Gana's house. Late morning traffic was surprisingly light for Hannibal. Driving up Wisconsin Avenue got him into Maryland. A short jog over to Connecticut Avenue let him cruise on up to Rockville, one of the District's bedroom communities. Where else, Hannibal wondered, could a city be the county seat and third largest city in its state and still be considered a suburb?

After making great time up Connecticut, Hannibal lost it all wandering around Thistlebridge Road, Thistlebridge Drive, and Thistlebridge Way until he found the right address. Rolling into the driveway in front of the two-car garage on a quiet suburban street, Hannibal found himself reevaluating the worth of a degree in education. He wasn't sure what kind of home he thought a college professor could afford, but he certainly didn't think this two-story brick colonial would be on the list. Hannibal knew that the student body at Howard University was only about ten thousand strong. Almost all of them were African American and not at the top of the economic ladder. If this was typical of a Howard University professor's home, he figured the faculty at Yale must drive Bentleys.

Hannibal pressed the button. Thirty seconds after he heard the chimes the door swept open and a hand thrust at him.

"You must be Hannibal Jones. Ms. Santiago has mentioned you from time to time. Jamal Krada. Very pleased to meet you, sir. Do come in."

Krada drew Hannibal in and launched across the two-story foyer, past the center staircase and gourmet kitchen where a young woman busied herself gathering food. They settled in a separate breakfast room at a small table.

Krada was the kind of professor who could have held Hannibal's attention. Energetic and enthusiastic, he seemed excited to have someone to talk to. His coloring matched Gana's, although his eyes were softer and he wore a fan of wrinkles at their corners. His full head of hair was proudly white and cut in a conservative Western style.

"Professor Krada, thank you for talking to me," Hannibal said. "I just wanted to ask you…"

Krada help up both index fingers like tiny stop signs. "Please. Food first. Nina!"

The woman in the kitchen moved forward, carrying a tray. She was average height but the kind of thin that made Hannibal think that if she had not been wearing that simple, natural colored shift, he could have counted her ribs. Her skin almost matched the natural cotton garment, and her hair was a darker shade of the same neutral color. She was pretty, but not in a way that jumped out at you. Her eyes were like those in some paintings that seem to follow you as you move around the room.

"Mr. Jones, this is my wife, Nina," Krada said as she settled the tray on the table. Without a word she placed a bowl of soup, and a plate holding a sandwich in front of each of them.

"This looks great," Hannibal said, pulling off his black driving gloves. "But you really didn't need to go to all this trouble."

"Nonsense," Krada said, patting his woman on the backside. "You are a guest in my home. Still, it is nice to be appreciated, eh, Nina?"

"Yes. It is." She locked eyes with Hannibal, just for a moment, and he thought her few words carried far more meaning than her husband noticed. Then she tipped her head toward him and moved away. Krada picked up his spoon and sipped.

"Nina has learned to make the best lentil soup. Now, what can I do for you, Mr. Jones?"

"Hannibal, please. And Cindy thought that you could help me with a case I'm working on. I'm doing a background check on a man who claims to be a native of Algeria, and I need to establish if he really is. Any ideas?" Hannibal sipped from his spoon and smiled. It really was good. He thought there was as much beef as lentils in the tomato-based soup. In fact, it was more like a stew, with potato, carrots, celery, garlic, onion, and lots of spices.

"You know, I do have an idea or two," Krada said, shaking his spoon at Hannibal. "As a professor of history I am always amused at what is or isn't common knowledge in different locations. Is this man educated?"

"I believe so," Hannibal said, picking up half of his ham sandwich.

"People in other countries know a lot more about America than Americans know about them. They understand your political system, they know why Nixon was impeached and how you became involved in the Vietnamese civil war. However, few of them know that George Washington told the truth about chopping down a cherry tree or that Columbus sailed the ocean blue in fourteen hundred ninety-two."

"The useless stuff we learn in grade school," Hannibal said.

"Just so," Krada said, warming to his subject. "These are things that only American school children are taught. There are similar things taught to schoolchildren all over the world. I believe I could come up with a list of questions that only an Algerian child, or someone who had been one, might know."

"That sounds great," Hannibal said, this apparent solution warming his heart the way the spicy soup warmed his belly. "If you could put together a few questions this afternoon, maybe after your classes, it would really help me."

41

Krada wiped his hands on his napkin before extending one to Hannibal. "I will do my best. Please thank Miss Santiago for sending you my way. And now, I really must prepare for my classes."

Hannibal rose and walked with Krada to the threshold. Nina appeared just as her husband was opening the door. On an impulse, Hannibal stepped around his host to shake her hand as well.

"I just wanted to say it was a pleasure to meet you, ma'am, and to thank you for a very nice lunch."

"My pleasure," she said, but only offered a half smile. As Hannibal was saying good-bye to Krada, she looked over his shoulder and the look she gave Hannibal seemed to have meaning.

On his way to his car, Hannibal's mind returned to the wonderful stew Krada's wife had made. It must have required a great deal of time and effort. A woman who would do that deserved more respect in his estimation. He would not question how things were done in another man's house, but he regretted that Mrs. Krada didn't join them for lunch.

It was the kind of minor detail he would sometimes dwell on, but once behind the wheel of the Volvo, Hannibal pushed the Kradas to the back of his mind. Time was very short and he wanted Ivanovich out of his life as quickly as possible. He began assembling what would be his report, just as he would for any client. He had to be able to account for his time and explain why he thought he was closer to knowing what the client wanted to know. As long as he thought of Invanovich in those terms, as the client, he figured he could keep his rage under control.

Still, by the time he parked across the street from his home he had a hard time pulling his black leather driving gloves away from the black-leather-covered steering wheel. He stood and leaned against his closed car door, centering himself by watching the recently planted tree on the sidewalk just up the block.

The poor little guy was just beginning to lose its first set of leaves. If Hannibal had a least favorite season it was this one, autumn. Winter and summer were sure of their identity, and spring was the time of renewal. Fall was not the time of death. That was winter. Fall was the time of dying, which Hannibal found much more tragic. Fall was watching the life seep out of living things that were fighting and struggling to hold on to it. And even though Hannibal knew that the tree would be back in full bloom by March, he was sure the tree didn't know it. All it knew was that the life it gained in the last eight months was being stolen and it was sinking into a deep sleep.

Filling his lungs with the crisp air, he pushed off of Black Beauty's lacquered hide and crossed the street. When he opened the building door he intended to steer left into his apartment for fresh coffee and a small, quiet dinner. The sound of his office doorknob being rattled snapped his head around to the right. The man at the door, Cindy's father, was short and bulky, and his hair was gathered on the sides and back of his head. Ray Santiago turned from the door, smiling at his downstairs neighbor.

"Hannibal, where you been? I'm not used to finding your office locked in the middle of the afternoon unless you're on a hot case. Open her up, Paco. From the look of you, we could both use a beer."

-7-

Hannibal returned his friend's smile but kept his feet rooted in place. "Ray. What's up, buddy? Bad day? I'm not used to seeing you around this early."

"Yeah, running the limo company been taking up way too much of my life," Ray said, pulling the stub of a cigar from his mouth. "Figured I'd just visit with you for a while before I went to have dinner with Cintia. Now come on, open this door that's standing between me and my beer."

"You deserve a break," Hannibal said, wondering if his visitor was on the other side of that door aiming a pistol at it. "Unfortunately, the fridge on that side is tapped out. But I got a beer or two in the apartment. Come on."

Hannibal turned and headed for his apartment door, fighting the urge to scream a warning at Ray. He anticipated the sound of gunfire any second but instead he heard a brief pause, then Ray's footsteps behind him.

"Yeah, I guess you've had enough of the office for one day," Ray said, following Hannibal into his kitchen and right to the refrigerator. He kept an assortment of beer for visitors, but he knew that Ray's tastes mirrored his so he pulled out a pair of Sam Adams black lagers. They carried the bottles into the living room before twisting off the caps. Hannibal dropped into his recliner while Ray settled into the center of the sofa.

"So, rough day, eh?" Hannibal asked, chasing the question down with a long swallow from his bottle. The thick, smooth liquid rolled down his throat, relaxing him on its way down.

"Yeah, man, it's a lot easier to deal with people you're driving than to deal with drivers who work for you. It's harder than hell to keep them all busy but if you don't have enough you can't grow, you know. Life was easier when I was just a cabby."

"You wanted to own your own business," Hannibal said. Then a memory floated to the surface. He pulled a pad from his jacket pocket and quickly wrote down a name and address.

"What's this?" Ray asked. "You need help on your case?"

"Yeah, but it's also me throwing some business your way." Hannibal handed the note to Ray. "I gave this guy your card today. His car got crunched and he'll need a ride for a couple of days. I gave him a recommendation but it wouldn't hurt for you to make contact and let him know how much you want the work."

Ray leaned back, took another swallow of beer, and looked at Hannibal "This guy's part of the case you're working?"

"Uh huh. It would be nice to know where he goes. He's not local. He's from Algeria, just renting a place in Woodley Park."

"Really?" Ray said, slipping the paper into his shirt pocket. "One of my drivers is from Algeria. I got a lot of guys from Africa and the Middle East, and a good handful of West Indians too. And there's that Panamanian guy."

"Sounds like you got a regular rainbow coalition going on there, buddy," Hannibal said.

"Not quite," Ray said. "I only got one white guy driving, and I'm pretty sure he's gay."

* * * * *

Less than an hour later, Hannibal was walking Ray to the building door.

"You sure you won't come with?" Ray asked as he stepped out onto the stoop. "You know Cindy's always glad to see you."

"No, man, you need your father-daughter time. Besides, I think I'll make it an early night. Later."

Hannibal closed the door and counted to ten to make sure Ray wasn't going to double back for something he forgot. Then he marched to his office door, unlocked it, and stepped through. It locked behind him when he closed it.

Ivanovich was staring at the computer monitor, apparently surfing the Web. His left hand was lying beside his pistol. He glanced up when Hannibal entered, then turned back to whatever he was looking at. Hannibal's headphones hugged Ivanovich's head. Hannibal's eyes traced the cord back to his bookshelf stereo. A compact disc was spinning in the player.

"You went in my tunes," Hannibal said through clenched teeth. Ivanovich cocked an eyebrow at him and uncovered his left ear.

"You went in my tunes," Hannibal repeated.

"You make it sound as if I had violated you," Ivanovich said. He was smiling, but Hannibal was not. Ivanovich eased his hand onto the butt of his gun. "You have an interesting and surprising collection."

"You were expecting the collected works of Barry White and George Clinton?"

"I wasn't expecting this." Ivanovich unplugged the headphones and the industrial thump of Nine Inch Nails filled the room.

> *Broken, bruised, forgotten, sore,*
> *Too fucked up to care anymore,*
> *Poisoned to the rotten core,*
> *Too fucked up to care anymore!*

"That figures," Hannibal said. "Trent Reznor's nihilistic lyrics are just perfect for a heartless assassin."

"Nihilistic?" Ivanovich grinned again, tapping the tip of his silencer against the desk. "Not a word, or even a concept I would have expected from you. But then, you couldn't be stupid and do what you do. In fact, you must understand human motivations better than most."

"Yeah, I'm a regular Dr. Phil," Hannibal said, dropping into his visitor's chair. "You want a report of today's progress?"

"That would be good. I was about to order Chinese. What do you like?"

"It ain't bad enough you bogart my office? I got to eat with you now?"

Ivanovich's eyes moved down and his smile faded. For a moment, Hannibal thought he had touched something tender.

"No," he said, his eyes returning to Hannibal. "It is not required that you eat with me. I simply ask you to. Heartless assassin is a lonely life. Even more so for the assassin who has a heart and cannot be with the one he wants to protect. This feeling you now know. In any case, I would have enjoyed a conversation about nihilism, and Kierkegaard's view of self-actualization. I know you think of such things. Who do you have to discuss them with?"

"I..." Hannibal lowered his eyes and his voice. "I, um... I like General Tso's chicken."

- 8 -
Thursday

The next morning found Hannibal parking in Dani Gana's driveway. His day had begun with a long run, a hot shower, and a modest breakfast. Then he spent the better part of an hour on the telephone with Jamal Krada. The history professor was excited to have come up with a short quiz that he was certain would catch up anyone who was just pretending to be Algerian. Hannibal copied down the questions and answers, then discussed them with Krada. It seemed important to make sure he understood enough background to catch someone who had a surface knowledge of the subjects he would bring up.

As he approached the door, Hannibal mentally rehearsed the conversation he expected to take place inside. But as he reached for the doorbell he heard a scream. It was short, but it was definitely a scream. His right hand dropped to the doorknob while his left reached under his arm. The doorknob turned. Unusual in this city, but not unexpected in this neighborhood.

Hannibal slid his Sig Sauer P229 free of its shoulder holster as he stepped inside, wondering if Gana was finally showing his true colors to the girl. His visit to Krada's house had shown Hannibal the level of respect Algerians show their women. The front room was dark, all light coming from the kitchen. Fearing for Viktoriya's safety, Hannibal moved along the wall in silence. As he approached the kitchen, the smell of fried potatoes hung in the air. Had she burned his hash browns? Would that spark a slap in their culture?

He saw them before they saw him. Gana was running water on his hand in the sink. The woman across the room looked frightened but unhurt. Viktoriya Petrova was a couple of inches taller than her mother but otherwise she was what Raisa Petrova's graduation photo would have looked like. Her skin was very fair with a hint of rose coloring, and the curls of her shiny black hair rolled down to her shoulder blades. When she saw Hannibal step out of the shadows, gun first, her hands shot out toward him as if she could stop him with her palms from across the room.

"No, please, don't shoot my husband."

"What the hell are you doing here?" Gana asked, his voice rumbling.

Hannibal holstered his weapon. "Sorry. I heard a scream and I guess I just reacted by reflex. Husband?"

"A civil ceremony this morning," Gana said, turning off the water and picking up a dish towel. "Not that it is any of your concern. In fact, there is nothing happening in my home that concerns you."

"Really?" Hannibal asked, walking across the room toward the sliding doors. "Is that blood on the doorsill there? Sure looks like blood."

Viktoriya looked at Gana while Hannibal touched his finger to a small red stain just above the door handle. There was not enough to indicate a stab or gunshot wound, unless a lot of cleanup had taken place before the scream.

"Oh, Dani was over there after he cut himself," Viktoriya said.

"Yes, I was trying to help in the kitchen. I guess I shouldn't try," Gana said, wrapping the towel around his hand.

"Really?"

"I must have leaned against the door there for a minute while I was shaking my hand, trying to control the pain. I realize now that Viktoriya did scream when she saw me bleeding, but, really, it's minor."

It sounded like a hasty attempt at damage control to Hannibal, but he could hardly justify asking Gana to unwrap

49

his hand to prove there was an injury. He had no idea what might have actually happened in that kitchen, but he could see that the girl was unharmed. Besides, he wanted to preserve his status as invited guest long enough to gather more information.

"I guess that's none of my business," he said. "You know the reason for my visit."

"Yes," Gana said, leaning on the sink. "There are people who question my identity."

"People?" Viktoriya asked.

Gana waved the question away. "Your mother has already told Mr. Jones here that I am living in exile from my native Algeria. He does not realize how far reaching a jihad can be in the Moslem world." He turned to Hannibal. "You must see that I cannot give you my real name. In fact, I am hoping to convince you not to share what you have already discovered."

"I won't tell anyone anything if you convince me that you're not a fraud."

"But how can he do that without revealing his family name?" Viktoriya asked.

Hannibal pulled a chair out from the table, spun it around backward, and sat. "I think I've come up with a solution. I don't have to know your name to do my job, just be sure that you're really from Algeria. I consulted with a subject matter expert. He gave me three questions that, if answered correctly, would make him pretty sure that a person was a native of Algeria. Are you game?"

"You Americans have a word for this kind of thing," Gana said. "This is bullshit." He stalked toward the back door where Viktoriya met him.

"Dani," she said, "you don't want to do anything that will make Mother doubt you. Why not just answer his stupid questions?"

"You mother will not doubt me," Gana replied, his smile slowly returning.

"All right then," Viktoriya said, sliding her fingers down the buttons of his shirt. "Then consider whoever this is that

Jones is working for. Would it not be better, safer, to get that person out of our lives?"

Gana closed his eyes. Viktoriya traced his jawline with her first two fingers. Gana's shoulders dropped and he returned to the table.

"All right, Jones, if it will put this inquisition to rest." Gana dropped into a chair on the opposite side of the table. "What kind of questions do you have?"

"Well, for example: what happened in fourteen hundred ninety-two?"

Viktoriya's brows furrowed. "Columbus?" Hannibal showed her his palm, indicating that she needed to be quiet.

"That is the year my people immigrated," Gana said. Viktoriya's face showed her confusion, so he continued. "Algeria's original people were the Berbers. She was occupied by the Phoenicians, by the Romans, and then the Arabs, of course. But in 1492, Spain expelled their Jews and my people, the Moors. They moved en masse into Algeria and settled there."

Hannibal nodded. "Thanks for the history lesson. Now, can you tell me what Hoca looks like?"

Gana looked puzzled for a moment, but then smiled. "I see. You probably mean Hoja. Hoca means teacher in Turkish, and the character is Turkish, but his name is Hoja. I can see that the difference in pronunciation would be difficult for your Western tongue."

"Yeah, curse my Western tongue. What did he look like?"

"This was a good choice," Gana said, smiling again and nodding. "Only Americans would describe your Santa Claus correctly. Hoja is also a character of myth, sort of a roly-poly man in a turban who always rides in on a donkey. In the stories he is a crafty fellow, who punctures the pompous by pretending to be naïve. Sort of a wise fool. There are dozens of stories. Would you like to hear one?"

"That's all right," Hannibal said.

"I'm glad you paid attention in school," Viktoriya said, pulling one of Gana's legs out and settling her petite behind on his lap.

"These are things you learn in your home or in the streets." Gana said.

"Yes, like how to enjoy your tea at the right hour," Hannibal said. "What was your favorite tea for the tea hour back home, Mr. Gana?"

"Ahh, the tea hour," Gana said, and his eyes seemed to drift back into the past. "In my home there were three of them, always in the same order. My favorite was the first, the strong tea. Strong like life. The second was bitter, like death." He turned to Viktoriya and his voice softened. "The third tea was sweet and symbolized love."

"So if you only wanted one, you would take the first?" Hannibal asked.

"That would be rude. If you only want to take one, you should wait for the last, which is the worst. Now, anything else you'd like to ask me?"

Gana seemed to have warmed to this game. He sat with his bride's hand in his, looking eager to prove himself again.

"Just one more thing," Hannibal said. "When you wandered into your local café, what was your favorite local beer?"

Gana chuckled and wagged a finger at him. "A trick question. You know full well that local cafes don't serve beer in my country. I used to get mine at international hotels or the embassy. And my favorite was Stella Artois."

"I grew up in Germany," Hannibal said. "I know that's a Belgian beer."

"Yes, but it is brewed in Algeria as well, under Belgian control. If you insist on a truly local beer, then I would choose Tango, which is OK but little sweet for my taste."

It was enough for Hannibal. The replies had rolled off Gana's tongue, in the smooth way all words seemed to roll off his tongue. But, they did feel like answers from the gut to Hannibal. Gana might or might not be a political exile in hiding, but he appeared to be a native Algerian. And maybe he wasn't putting anything over on his new bride after all. Hannibal stood, almost ready to let this couple go on with their lives.

"One last thing I'd like to know. Why are you so concerned with being photographed? I saw you exchange words with that fellow yesterday morning. Of course, it was at a distance, but…"

"That bastard." Gana's face turned from bright to threatening as if someone had flipped a switch. "You must understand that the enemies of my family have sent this man to find me. If the local ayatollah receives a clear photo that proves my location, he will send his zealots to kill me. I must defend myself against these jackals."

* * * * *

Hannibal went to his car wondering if he was adding to the pressure on a man who was already being persecuted. The parking space he had found faced away from his next destination, so once he started his Volvo up he had to drive a block the wrong way, turn left and go over a block, then turn left again. Now he was aimed the right way, but moving slowly on a side street that was too narrow to have cars parked on both sides. This didn't discourage any of the local residents from parking there, daring any passers-by to ding their vehicles on the way through.

Had he been able to drive any faster he might have missed it. As it was, he had to ride the brake to ease past Ben Cochran's brown Saturn, distinctive in its inconspicuousness. It seemed that at least one person was still pursuing Gana. Cochran must still have been trying to get a good photo.

Thumbing his steering wheel controls to bring up Led Zepplin, Hannibal considered the possible significance of this otherwise insignificant man. Gana had given a very convincing performance in his kitchen, but something still didn't feel right. If the Algerian religious establishment had the resources to send spies all the way to America in pursuit of their infidel, would they hire someone as amateurish as Cochran appeared to be? That aside, wouldn't they find a Muslim to do their spying? Would they hire a man who was so white? Hannibal knew it was dangerous to judge a person by his appearance, but he could not imagine Cochran turning out to be a disciple of Allah. It just did not seemed likely that an angry ayatollah would trust followers who were not of the same faith.

If Gana was who he said he was, who was really after him and why? Hannibal pulled his little notebook from his inside jacket pocket. Gana had come to Washington upper society with an official endorsement. Muting his music to dial his telephone, Hannibal decided to find out just how valuable that endorsement was.

"Good morning. Leon Martin, please."

- 9 -

Irritations seemed to come to Hannibal in clumps. Trying to reach Leon Martin, vice president of the Chemical Banking Corporation, was getting on his nerves. He lost track of how many times he was transferred and put on hold. When his frustration level reached "slap somebody," he hung up and called Raisa Petrova.

"Mrs. Petrova, it's important that I speak with your banker. Would he recognized your name.?"

"I should say so," she said. "We have spoken several times. I handled much of the family financial matters while Nikita was out handling business."

"Then I need you to get me on the phone with him."

"And why should I want to do that?" Mrs. Petrova asked. "You are only looking for evidence that will hurt my Viktoriya and her man. You think he's some sort of fake."

"Yes, ma'am. And don't you want to prove me wrong?"

This was the kind of twisted reasoning that Raisa understood. In conference call mode, Hannibal used her as a battering ram against the bastions of New York capitalism.

This verbal battle had taken place mostly while Hannibal was parked under a towering ash on a quiet and shady street about ten minutes west of Gana's house in the equally upper class Crestwood area. Hannibal had tucked his car in behind a Lexus parked down the block but within sight of the elegant blue-and-white home Cindy would view soon. Hedges fronted the house, and a large dogwood with its arms akimbo rose up out of the front lawn, waving off unwanted visitors. The Realtor's sheet lying on his passenger seat called it a "spacious, immaculate 5BR/3.5BA home" with a modern kitchen, huge den and family room, beautiful secluded garden, patio, screened porch, and two-car garage. It was huge and beautiful and forty-five years old with "character" and pegged oak floors. It was, in short, Cindy Santiago's dream house.

A two-car garage, when the girl didn't even have a driver's license. What could a single woman possibly do with all that space? He might never know. But even if he could not be seen with Cindy or have a conversation with her, he could observer her reaction to the house. It was as close as he could get to spending time with her until he had satisfied Ivanovich that the case was over. Under normal circumstances he might feel funny spying on his woman this way, but he knew that three or four other observers were out there. In this situation, one more person watching her made little difference.

"Leon Martin. How can I help you?"

The voice prompted Hannibal to pull himself back into business mode. Martin needed to believe he was sitting in his office, not out in his car. He explained that he was a professional investigator vetting a new potential investor for some major corporation.

"Sir, we are in possession of a letter of introduction written by you to a Mrs. Raisa Petrova, confirming the credentials of one Dani Gana of Algeria."

"Yes, well, as I told Mrs. Petrova a few minutes ago, the letter is from our bank. I was simply the officer authorized to sign it."

"I see," Hannibal said, holding a pen over a pad while one eye monitored the driveway down the block. "Now sir, do you have personal knowledge of Mr. Gana? Have you met and spoken with this gentleman?"

"This is highly irregular. If Mrs. Petrova hadn't personally asked me to speak with you…"

"Yes, but she did," Hannibal said, adding a little edge to his voice. "I'm sure you understand that with these kinds of sums involved, my clients want to be very certain of the people they do business with." No need to specify what kinds of sums. The banker would mentally fill in whatever he thought was a lot of money. "Did you handle Mr. Gana's accounts personally?"

"Yes, I handled his accounts, but no, we haven't met. However, understand that Mr. Gana is one of our more substantial foreign customers. He was recommended to us personally by a United States senator whom I'm afraid I cannot name."

Hannibal watched a midnight blue Lincoln Towne Car ease down the street from the opposite direction and slide into the target house's driveway. "I quite understand, sir. Did you have the opportunity to speak to the senator yourself?"

"No, but I have his letter here. It is a glowing testimonial."

Hannibal's mind was elsewhere before he politely ended the conversation. Gana had come to Washington with a recommendation from a New York banker, but that letter was written based on a letter of recommendation from a Beltway insider. Why not cut out the middleman? Why was it so important for him to be accepted by the Washington inner circle? That certainly wouldn't protect him from a fanatical jihad.

Up the block, the passenger side door opened. Hannibal assumed there was a lot of conversation in the car while the real estate agent explained how much Cindy was going to love this house. But now the showing would begin. To Hannibal's surprise, the showing started as the Realtor stood up outside the car.

Hannibal thought of real estate agents as retired schoolteachers or bored housewives. This one was very male, black, and built like a running back. Hannibal judged him at that distance to be about six feet three but the black pinstriped suit made him look even taller. This was the guy she had been following around for several weeks, walking in and out of vacant houses. He walked around the car and opened the passenger door. Cindy swung her legs out onto the asphalt and stood quite close to him. She looked up into his eyes while they exchanged a few more words and shared the smile that Hannibal thought of as his.

A tap on his window spun Hannibal's face to his left. The man standing beside the car recoiled and raised his hands on either side of his chest.

"I'm not the enemy," the man said. Hannibal could only guess how much anger his face was reflecting when he turned. He powered his window down, forced a smile, and let his eyebrows rise to their normal position.

"Sorry, didn't mean to... I was thinking of something else. Something I can do for you?"

"I think it's the other way around," the man said. "I'm here at Mr. Ronzini's request." He was a medium-sized man with a neutral face, but Hannibal noticed the bulge at his waist under his gray sweatshirt.

"I see. So what brings you here?"

The man rested his elbow on the roof of Hannibal's car, facing forward. "I'm watching him watching her."

Another man was walking toward them across the street, on the side Cindy's dream house was on. He was also a neutral looking man with vaguely Eastern features. He would pass the house in a moment.

"I appreciate that. Really. But maybe I should be gone before this guy spots me."

"OK, but take this," the man said, passing an envelope through Hannibal's window. "Mr. Ronzini figured you'd turn up here sooner or later. He said when you did to give you this letter."

Hannibal thanked the man, who then stood away from the car, about to turn and walk away.

"Hey, hang on a second, friend. You got a name?"

The man looked at Hannibal with no expression at all on his face.

"No."

And then he was gone, another faceless soldier in an underground army. Pulling away from the curb, Hannibal wondered what the job description looked like for the position of thug. Did they have a union, have to update their resumes, hassle about their benefits?

Another part of his mind wondered how long Cindy and the broad-shouldered Realtor would be in that house.

Four blocks later, Hannibal stopped at a red light and used the pause to open Ronzini's envelope. He resented Ronzini knowing that he would try to see Cindy even if he couldn't talk to her. He hated knowing he was in this man's debt. But it gave him some small measure of peace to know that Ronzini's men would give their lives to defend anyone under Ronzini's protection.

Inside the envelope he found a single sheet of expensive stationery folded in thirds. The note was handwritten, in a firm, aggressive hand that had to be Anthony Ronzini's. Under a large letter H it read:

Thought you might want to know that Nikita Petrova didn't leave behind the fortune most of the Russians assume he had. A quick look at Raisa P's finances showed that she's running out of money.

There was no signature, but none was needed.

A horn blaring behind him prompted him to surge forward and catch up with traffic. This news offered a good reason for Raisa to fool herself about a wealthy young suitor asking for her daughter's hand. He drove home on automatic pilot, pushing this new puzzle piece around with the other bits of information he had gathered.

By the time he got home, he had to admit that he himself should have been the target of much of the rage he was feeling. His anger at Ronzini was based on his own inner belief that people were either good or bad. Bad people doing good things made him almost as uncomfortable as good people going bad.

He parked in his usual place and hurried into his own apartment without encountering another soul. He hung up his jacket, pulled off his tie, and poured Kenyan coffee beans into his grinder. Strong, fresh, hot coffee was Hannibal's drug of choice for dealing with his emotions. In this case, that meant his anger.

Listening to the whirring gnash of the grinder's teeth, he also had to admit that part of his anger toward Ivanovich was misplaced. It was not his fault that Hannibal had gotten so deeply involved with this case. Coffee aside, the real drug that Hannibal was hooked on was mystery and although he didn't expect it, he had stepped into one here. While filling a carafe with water he considered the disturbing fact that, had he known what he now did about the situation, he would have been willing to investigate it anyway. Regardless of his feelings about Ivanovich, he couldn't ignore the very real danger Viktoriya's mob-connected mother might be putting her in, especially if Gana was on the run from the law or his country's legal government.

Aside from the case, Hannibal's mind was clogged with thoughts about his own isolation. Ivanovich had found it quite simple to create a situation in which Hannibal was not able to discuss the case with any of his closest confidantes. Just as he had to keep an eye on his top priority, keeping Cindy safe, he had to keep his neighbors out of the case to shield them. He trusted Ronzini on the subject of who not to mess with and knew that if Ivanovich had nothing to lose he would be a danger to all those around him.

But in the meantime, Hannibal couldn't think of anything else he could do to finish his assignment. Like most days, when the work was done, Hannibal changed into a pair of jeans and a t-shirt. Hours passed in solitude, filled by frozen egg rolls and a marathon of television episodes. Cindy had given him a DVD of the short-lived *Blade* television series. He had enjoyed it more than he had expected to, and couldn't wait to tell Cindy. He tried hard not to notice that she hadn't called him to talk about her day or the house she looked at. She was probably working late again, as lawyers so often do.

When the phone did ring, Hannibal checked his watch before answering. She really had worked late.

"Hello," he said, eager to hear her voice again, even if he had to tell her he couldn't talk.

"Come over for a drink." It was Ivanovich's hard, accented voice. The anger Hannibal had put away earlier in the day popped out of its box.

"Bitch, I'm done working for the day. I'll get more answers tomorrow."

Pause. "I thought a bitch was a woman only. Come over for a drink." This time Hannibal noticed a slight slurring. He must have started drinking alone.

"Look, Alex, it's after eleven. I need my sleep."

"Aleksandr," Ivanovich said. "Never Xander. Never Lex. Never Al. Never Alex. You are not asleep. You are alone. Like me. Come over for a drink."

Hannibal thought about his own isolation, and about the fact that Ivanovich had not left that office for more than forty-eight hours and in that time had seen no one except Hannibal and, he assumed, a delivery boy from the liquor store. Well, he did it to himself, Hannibal thought. Screw him. He was about to say it aloud when Ivanovich appeared to remember something from their very first conversation.

"Please."

* * * * *

When Hannibal walked into his office, he bypassed the wall switch for the ceiling light. His desk lamp shed the only light in the room. Ivanovich seemed more at home in the relative gloom. He was still in Hannibal's desk chair. His pistol still lay on the desk pointed toward the door. The black photo album still lay open in front of him. But Ivanovich had changed into a t-shirt, one of those you see so often in Washington gift shops, that said "You Don't Know Me," and in smaller lettering, "Witness Protection Program." He held a tumbler of clear liquid in his right hand. He put it down to pour vodka into a similar glass on the desk.

"So, you can call a man a bitch?"

"Anything can be a bitch," Hannibal said, picking up his glass. "A man you don't like. A woman you do like. An object like, oh, I don't know. You poured some nasty vodka into this bitch and I picked it up. Hell, life's a bitch." He took a swallow from his glass, finding the drink surprisingly smooth but just as fiery as he expected.

"So sit," Ivanovich said, reaching behind his head to start another Nine Inch Nails CD. "Tell me of your progress, Mister Detective."

Hannibal dropped into his visitor's chair as the warmth from the drink spread through his body. He noticed that his office smelled just a bit like fried food, and the cartons in his trashcan confirmed the reason. Did this guy live on Chinese takeout?

"The way I see it, you gave me four jobs," Hannibal said. "I've got a banker who confirms in writing that Gana is who he says he is. I got an expert to help me test him for background knowledge and I'm convinced he's from where he says he's from. In conversation with him and the Petrovas, it became pretty clear that he's primarily here for the girl."

"Viktoriya," Ivanovich said, raising his glass and emptying it, almost as if he was toasting the woman's name.

"Yes. That leaves the money. Normally, Ms. Santiago could help me with that part, but I have another friend with connections who will be able to tell me in a day or two where Gana got his money. That's all you need to know, right? Then you disappear from my life—and Cindy's."

"You miss her, don't you?" Ivanovich asked, signaling to Hannibal to return his glass. When Hannibal didn't answer he said, "Yes, that is the deal."

"You want details?" Hannibal asked, setting his glass back on the desk.

"Please," Ivanovich said, refilling the glass. "As much detail as possible. I want to know everything you've learned about this man Gana, and how you came to these conclusions."

While listening to heavy industrial rock and sharing three more rounds of drinks, Hannibal recounted his day, omitting his detour to see Cindy. Ivanovich was not pleased but he was satisfied, which meant that once Ronzini put Hannibal on the money trail he would be free. He didn't say so, but with Ivanovich gone he would also feel free to pursue the real mysteries raised by his investigation without worrying about Cindy. God, he missed her. More than this Russian killer could know. What could a murderer for hire know about human feelings anyway?

"You are thinking too hard," Ivanovich said. "What is on your mind? Your woman? She is safe."

Hannibal stared at his glass instead of his client. "Actually, I was thinking about you. I know who Dani Gana is now. I know who Viktoriya Petrova is. Just who the fuck is Aleksandr Ivanovich?"

- 10-

Ivanovich stood up, maybe just to stretch his legs, maybe to see himself more clearly. Hannibal watched him, trying to center his mind. He knew that the casual profanity was a sign that the alcohol was loosening him. He seldom drank and for that reason his tolerance for liquor was low.

"Your real question is, how do you get the job of assassin in the Russian Mafiya? Is that not so?"

Hannibal emptied his glass anyway. "No. Let me ask you the same shit you want to know about your rival. Who are you? Where are you from? Why are you here?"

"I am a man born to dirt-poor farmers in Georgia," Ivanovich said, staring at the wall like a student giving a dissertation. "Too poor to seek a proper education. So poor that I sought refuge in military service. So I signed up to fight for my country, much as your father did."

Ivanovich paused while he refilled his glass, as if he could not talk and pour at the same time. When the bottle was empty he reached under the desk and produced another, opened it, and filled his glass to its rim.

"Little did I guess that I would be fighting my own countrymen in Chechnya."

"That must have sucked," Hannibal said, wondering how much alcohol Ivanovich had had delivered to his office.

"I was a teenager. A boy. But I grew up a lot in those three years. My father had taught me to hunt and I stood out on the firing range. Then my colonel said he saw something in me. Whether it was the strong hands of a farmer or the cold impatience of a boy who had nothing to lose I don't know.

Anyway, he selected me for sniper training. There was a bonus involved, so of course I excelled."

"So you had a talent for hitting the target. How'd they know you had the nerve for killing?"

Ivanovich paced to the window and looked out for a moment. "They knew after that riot in Chechnya when I gunned down half a dozen citizens." He quickly returned to the desk and raised his glass. Hannibal thought he was trying to rinse the taste of that memory out of his mouth.

"Sounds like you had a future in the army."

"Yes, but the world moves and we move with it." Ivanovich glanced at the photo album, then quickly away. "The colonel was my benefactor then. At the time, military officers often raised funds in unauthorized ways. He left the army and asked me to go with him. He had plans. He was going to America to turn his black market business into an empire. He needed a good gun at his side. He offered me more money than I had ever seen. I followed him here. How could I know I would find the girl I left behind?"

Hannibal stood to sit his glass on the desk. "Excuse me?"

"The Petrovas were neighbors back home. Nikita Petrova was also a soldier. He served in Afghanistan under fire, and in Algeria undercover. But when I was in secondary school, I knew him as the man who would only let me visit his daughter in his presence or his wife's. I knew I loved Viktoriya even then. You see? I've carried this picture for so many years."

Hannibal looked down to see a photo of Viktoriya, the girl he had only met that day. In the photo she was just a child of perhaps fourteen. "Your childhood sweetheart. Touching. And you come to the U.S. to help launch a crime family and learn that her father is in fact a godfather."

Ivanovich turned, spilling his drink as he moved closer to stare into Hannibal's eyes. "You asked a question. I open my heart and you greet this with sarcasm?"

Hannibal stared back, leaning even closer. "Save that shit for somebody who's scared of you. Which maybe isn't as many people as I thought. I know you're here because you're hiding out from the mob, and now I know why. Daddy wouldn't let you have his little girl, so you got him out of the way."

Ivanovich's eyes blazed and for a moment Hannibal thought he would get a chance to kick this arrogant Russian's ass. Instead, Ivanovich looked down at the bottle and refilled his glass.

"Nikita Petrova was a great man," he said in a low voice. "He was my mentor when I arrived here and explained to me that I did not need to live in thrall to the colonel. I could be my own man and do my work for anyone in the mob. I did not kill him."

"Well, your fellow mobsters sure think you did."

Ivanovich strode to the window again, staring out at the darkness. "Nikita Petrova killed himself. He stepped off the roof of an apartment building he had bought over in Virginia as an investment for Raisa. Ask the police if you don't believe me."

"From what I've heard, he was respected by the underground. He was wealthy and had a great family. Now why on earth would he commit suicide?"

Just as Ivanovich turned to return to the desk, Hannibal noticed the pistol. In the second it took him to fully realize its significance Ivanovich was back beside it. "Not everyone knew his pain."

"Pain?"

"Nikita was in constant pain," Invanovich said, leaning against the wall behind the desk. "Shrapnel had sliced into him in Afghanistan. Doctors said that he would not survive an attempt to remove it. He had a terrible limp from it. It must have become too much for him."

Hannibal stood at the front of the desk and casually leaned his hand on it. "But the entire Russian mob thinks you did him, as you have so many men who were in somebody else's way. Because he was so popular, I guess you aren't so popular. You'll never get her back, you know. So why am I working so hard to dig up dirt on this Dani Gana guy?"

"It is as Trent Reznor says. Sometimes, just as nothing seems worth saving." Then Ivanovich focused his eyes on Hannibal's again. "I can't watch her slip away."

"So, what if Gana really is bad for her, which I doubt," Hannibal said. "After all, he's rich, handsome, smooth, apparently legitimate, and, by the way, he sure looks like he loves her." He wondered if Ivanovich was drunk enough, and emotional enough, to get careless.

"You are wrong." Ivanovich crossed his arms, his jaw jutting out. It was less the picture of a deadly killer and more a study in stubbornness.

"What if I am?" Hannibal asked, wrapping his right hand around the bottle. "She's a farmer's daughter turned Washington socialite. She's got nothing to do with the way her father made his fortune here. Do you really think she'd give the time of day to a hired killer like you?" With the location of the pistol locked in his mind, he watched Ivanovich's eyes.

"You can say this? You?" Ivanovich emptied his glass again and crossed his arms. "We are the same, you and I. Don't you realize that?"

"I don't go around killing innocent people," Hannibal said, lifting the bottle to refill his glass.

"Nor do I," Ivanovich said, his words carrying a slight slur. "I remove only those who are already preying on the innocent. Most people, they are like sheep. You know this. The people I work for are wolves, preying on those sheep. The people who hire me send me to cull the herd of the wolves that can't follow the rules of the pack leaders."

"Right. You're trying to tell me that you're just there to maintain order."

"Yes," Ivanovich said with a grim smile, pointing at Hannibal. "Just like you. That is why I came to you for help. Because we are alike."

"Don't you dare compare yourself to me," Hannibal said. "I am not like you."

"You don't see yourself as a wolf?" Ivanovich crossed his arms again, leaning back against the wall, his eyes again hooded, his mouth set in a derisive smirk. "Are you then one of the sheep?"

"Nope. I'm one of the sheepdogs. I keep the wolves at bay. And you…" In midsentence, Hannibal's left hand released his glass and darted toward the spot on the desk where the silenced automatic lay.

But it was already gone.

Hannibal leaned on his hand in an awkward position, frozen, staring at the muzzle of the silencer aim at the spot between his eyes. A few tense seconds passed in silence.

"And I?" Ivanovich said, his words no longer slurred. "I am a little faster than you. A little faster, and a little smarter than you think I am."

Hannibal righted himself, backing off two steps. His eyes never wavered from Ivanovich's eyes. The odor of spilled alcohol was sharp in his nose, and he thought he could feel more alcohol popping out of the pores of his forehead, but he would not let his voice waver.

"I had to try."

"Of course," Ivanovich said, smiling. "I would have. In a way, I would have been disappointed if you didn't try. But now, how can I trust you? And if all you say is true, then maybe my efforts here have no purpose. In which case, you no longer serve any purpose for me."

Hannibal clenched his teeth, prepared to pay the price for his gamble. Watching Ivanovich's finger tighten on the trigger, Hannibal regretted that there was no one else to protect Cindy.

-11-

The knock at the door made Hannibal's breath catch in his throat. Ray's voice tripled his pulse rate.

"Hey, Hannibal. You in there, Paco?"

Ivanovich moved the pistol's barrel two degrees to the left. Now the bullet would brush past Hannibal and poke a tiny hole in the office door and Ray Santiago's chest. A quick follow-up shot could still take Hannibal down before he had time to move. He couldn't stop the Russian from killing them both, but he had to try. Ray didn't deserve to die. He was an innocent in this case.

"One of the sheep," Hannibal said under his breath. Ivanovich heard and shifted his focus from the wooden door back to Hannibal's face.

"Come on, man," Ray said. "I wanted to let you know. That guy you're investigating? He ain't for real."

Ivanovich looked at Hannibal with an open-mouthed half smile. Hannibal interpreted the expression as a look of relief. Relief to hear he might be proven right, and maybe relief at having a good reason not to kill Ray. Keeping his gun on Hannibal, he went to the next room and pulled the pocket doors together, leaving just enough of a gap to see through. Or shoot through.

Hannibal released his breath, feeling some relief himself. He knew that Ivanovich shared his curiosity and would not kill anyone now. He wanted to know what Ray had to say. Hannibal unlocked the door and Ray started in past him, but stopped as he recognized the look on Hannibal's face.

"Hey, Paco." Ray grasped Hannibal's shoulders. "You're not looking too good. And whew, what is that? You been in there drinking alone all night?"

"Not yet," Hannibal said. "And the smell is so strong because I dropped a glass and spilled a while ago. But never mind that. What did you mean about Dani Gana not being for real?"

"He ain't," Ray said. He brushed past Hannibal to drop heavily into the chair Hannibal had vacated a few seconds earlier. "You remember you said he needed a driver for a couple days? Well, I called him and set it up. Thanks, by the way, for the lead. Bachir says he's one hell of a tipper."

"Bachir?" Hannibal asked, still standing in the doorway.

"Yeah. He's Algerian. I figured your man would like having a driver from the same country, you know?"

"Makes sense."

"Right, only Bachir says he ain't. While they were driving today he started talking to him in that crazy stuff they speak."

"Arabic," Hannibal said. "You saying Gana don't speak Arabic?"

Ray pulled a thin cigar out of his pocket. "No, Bachir says he speaks it fine. Just got the wrong accent. Now, Bachir says they speak the same language in all the Arab countries, but it's all different. You know, like guys from Texas speak English, but they don't sound like guys from here."

"So your man says Gana isn't Algerian."

"Says this guy's probably never been in Algeria," Ray said, pulling out an ancient Zippo lighter and puffing his cigar into life.

"OK, then where's he from?"

"He don't know," Ray said. "Says there are like twenty other countries he might be from. Bachir just says that for sure he ain't Algerian. Say, you going to offer me some of that?" Ray hooked his thumb toward the half-empty second bottle of vodka.

"Why don't you grab it and let's go," Hannibal said, taking one step into the hallway. I was about to turn in anyway. You can take the bottle on up to your room and finish it. I really don't need to drink any more."

"Yeah," Ray said, standing and grabbing the bottle by its neck. "I can see that for sure."

- 12 -
Friday

Morning brought shifting clouds and the first truly cool breeze of the season. Driving into the city of Fairfax, Virginia, Hannibal's thoughts were also gray and shifting. If Ray's driver was right, Gana wasn't really a native Algerian but he very much wanted people to believe he was. He must have been a world-class confidence man to have done the kind of deep background research necessary to answer Hannibal's questions. In Hannibal's experience, the only people who knew their legends that well were in the espionage business. If his enemies were actually hunting a spy, Viktoriya might really be in danger just standing too close to him.

But Hannibal's houseguest was much more confounding. Was he capable of killing the father of the woman he loved? Hannibal wasn't sure, so he decided to take him up on his suggestion and talk to the police.

A quick Internet search brought up old newspaper reports and gave him the few sketchy facts made public about Nikita Petrova's death. One of those facts was the name of the primary investigating detective and that fact made Hannibal smile. He knew that name.

He parked in the large lot attached to the county building complex because an earlier call had told him that the man he needed to talk to was testifying in court that morning. He loaded his cell phone, loose change, and automatic into his glove compartment. He wouldn't need them, and he wanted to avoid as much drama as possible at the metal detectors.

Once inside, he sat at the back of a courtroom, waiting for the detective's turn to testify. He did so in concise terms, with the kind of fanatic accuracy that makes it almost impossible for opposing council to reinterpret the facts. When he was finished, he nodded to the judge and left the stand with little fanfare. At the same time, Hannibal left his seat for the nearest exit.

He was beside the door for less than a minute before saw the detective approaching him. As usual, he wore a tan suit and a bulldog's expression. His straw-colored hair was still cut in a severe, military style, and his blue eyes still spoke of how dangerous he could be. He stopped in front of Hannibal, his hands going to his hips.

"Well, if it isn't Hannibal Jones, defender of the innocent."

"Orson Rissik," Hannibal said with a smile. "Prosecutor of the guilty. I see you're still bringing them in and locking them up."

"That's what they pay me to do," Rissik said. "But what brings you to the courthouse today? One of your clients in trouble?"

"Actually, I'm here to see you," Hannibal said. "Can I buy you lunch?"

Rissik shrugged. "Sure. I've got a pretty short break and I was about to walk down the hill to get a sandwich. Come on."

The two men crossed the street and continued down the sidewalk. Hannibal didn't usually like to work with the police because so many of them had their own agenda. Orson Rissik had only one agenda that Hannibal knew of. He wanted to put criminals in jail.

"So, you said you were looking for me but you didn't say why."

"I wanted to get some information related to a case I'm working on right now," Hannibal said. "I need details on the Petrova murder."

"That was three or four years ago," Rissik said, his brows pulling together. "A real tragedy. He left a wife and daughter, I think."

"That's the one. I'm just trying to find out if it was officially declared a murder."

"That was three years ago," Rissik said. "You expect me to have the details of the case off the top of my head?"

"I know you, Orson," Hannibal said. "There's a reason you made chief of detectives. You never let go of the important stuff, because you know that a lot of times these cases circle back on you."

Rissik nodded, acknowledging the compliment. "Okay, that case sticks in my mind for a couple reasons. At first, I wasn't even sure it was him. The ID was kind of difficult."

"I can imagine. I hear he did a face plant off a roof."

Rissik stopped to pull the restaurant door open. "The roof of a six-story office building. Splat. Like a bag of beef stew."

Hannibal shuddered. "Colorful metaphor, Chief. Hey, is this where you want to eat? I thought we'd go to a restaurant."

"Subway is a restaurant," Rissik said. "It's close and quick. And like I said, you can buy me a sandwich." Turning away from Hannibal, he ordered roast beef and mayo on whole wheat. The counter girl was making it before he spoke. Hannibal figured he ate the same thing every time he walked in, which must have been often.

"OK, so he was hard to identify. How'd you know it was him?" Hannibal glanced at the menu and ordered the lunch special without really noticing what it was.

"His wallet was lying on the roof, next to a Tag Heuer Kirium Quartz that his wife identified as his." They sat in a booth and both men glanced at the Porsche titanium watch on Hannibal's wrist that was a Christmas gift from Cindy and at the more modest Esquire watch Rissik wore that was surely a present from his wife. Hannibal was the only one who was a little embarrassed.

"Leaving things like a watch and wallet behind is typical of suicides, isn't it?"

"Yep," Rissik said. "Or of a killer wanting to make his work look like a suicide."

"So you traced him from ID in his wallet, and his wife ID'd the body," Hannibal said, unwrapping his lunch. He thought it would be an extraordinary killer indeed who would leave a two-thousand-dollar watch behind.

"Right. His clothes and other effects allowed her to be pretty darned sure it was her husband. Besides, she said he had been threatening suicide for a while."

"Really?" Hannibal took the first bite of his sandwich. He savored the flavor of the variety of meats and cheeses that together formed the taste he associated with "sub sandwich." As soon as his mouth was empty, he asked,. "Was he depressed? I thought his life was pretty good."

"She said he was worried about all the debt he was in," Rissik said, almost finished with his food. "And I guess he had some war injuries that bothered him."

"So he talked about suicide, prepared like a suicide, and you haven't mentioned any real evidence of foul play. Why a murder investigation?"

"You know how these things work, Jones," Rissik said. He finished his food, folded the paper into a neat bundle, and shoved it into the bag. "If we rule suicide right away, that stops the investigation. And I'm sure you know that he had mob connections. Otherwise, we wouldn't be having this conversation."

"You think maybe he owed money to some gangster who had him taken out?"

Rissik raised a finger, signaling caution. "Now don't put words in my mouth. There was absolutely no evidence of foul play in that death. And believe me, I looked. Of course, Raisa insisted that she had no idea who was holding the marker on this big debt she kept hearing about. But who knows. If I wasn't a cop, maybe she'd have told me more. If I wasn't a cop, I'd sure ask her."

"Subtle, Chief, real subtle. But you know, I might just take the hint."

* * * * *

The people who live in Fairfax County, Virginia, think they deal with hateful traffic. Because he did most of his driving in the District, Hannibal knew better. The highway out of Fairfax, I-66, was well populated, but at least traffic was moving. It wasn't until he hit the Key Bridge that driving turned to crawling. The last couple of miles were horrific, thanks to some very narrow streets that people still parked on. He had to fight his way through the rabbit's warren of Georgetown to reach Mrs. Petrova's house. He hoped that when he got there she would give him some of the answers he needed.

Navigating this way through a side street, Hannibal again spotted the brown Saturn. He figured Cochran must be on the job, spying on Gana just a couple of blocks away. Maybe he was on the side of the good guys after all. He was certainly dedicated if he was leaving his car on a Washington side street again and again.

"Parked in the exact same place," Hannibal muttered to himself. "What are the odds?"

Then he thought about his own words. What were the odds? It seemed more likely that the car had not moved since the day before. Why would Cochran leave his car there?

Curiosity made Hannibal pull over and park in the nearest spot, almost a block away. As he walked toward Cochran's car, a vague sense of unease grew inside him, matching the dark clouds above. When he reached the car, his feelings seemed to be confirmed. It was parked a couple of feet too close to the fire hydrant. Tickets slipped under the windshield wiper indicated that the car had been in the same place since the morning before. Hannibal tugged on the door handle and was surprised when it opened. No one would leave a car illegally parked for so long, not on purpose, and certainly not unlocked. Maybe something had happened to the snoop, something more than having his camera smashed.

Hannibal went back to his car. He still didn't know who Cochran was, but he had his doubts that the man could be in the employ of Muslim terrorists. And if Gana was lying about that, then Cochran's story might be true. He could be an inept private eye, in over his head. And that meant that he might actually know something useful. He might also be in serious danger, or even lying somewhere hurt.

But before searching the hospitals and morgues, Hannibal figured he'd see if Cochran was just nursing a minor injury in his hotel room. And since Cochran had commented that he was "stuck in the Ramada," Hannibal figured he wouldn't be too hard to find. He turned out to be registered at the second hotel Hannibal called, just outside the District in Silver Spring, Maryland.

Whatever information Raisa Petrova was holding, it would keep. Right then Hannibal thought that finding Ben Cochran might tell him more about Gana. He took the short drive up Georgia Avenue to the chosen Ramada Inn. A bored desk clerk with a serious acne problem gave him the room number. He knocked on the door, then stepped back to make sure he was visible through the little peephole. Feet tapped to the door on the other side, followed by a few seconds of silence. He heard the deadbolt turn, and the door opened in. He was surprised to find himself facing a buxom redhead.

"What can I do for you, handsome?"

-13-

"I'm sorry," Hannibal said. "I was looking for Ben Cochran."

"And you got his wife instead," she replied, presenting her hand.

"Hannibal Jones," he said, taking her hand. She shook firmly, like a man, and looked him in the eye as she did.

"You can call me Queenie. Come on in. How do you know Ben?"

The woman's red hair went down to the roots, but it was up in the big-hair style that Hannibal hoped would some day go out of style even in the Deep South. Walking behind her, he could not help but notice her figure. The woman was heavy-chested and broad-hipped, but everything was in the right proportions. Her American flag t-shirt and jeans were just a tiny bit too tight, but that only accented her shape, which Hannibal would have described as robust. He thought that perhaps this was what happened to a woman if she quit pole-dancing cold turkey.

"I bumped into Ben because we were watching the same guy."

"You're shitting me," Queenie said, slapping a pack of Camels against her index finger to make one of the cigarettes pop out. She captured it with her lips and slid it free of the pack.

"Nope. Same mark," Hannibal said. "I was kind of hoping to put our heads together on this. You know, team up."

"Well as you can see, Benny ain't here." Queenie never looked toward Hannibal for a light, just pulled out a pack of matches and lit her own cigarette.

"Maybe you can help. I just want to know why he'd want pictures of the man."

"He's just got this crazy idea he can blackmail Gana with some pictures," she said, putting one red high heel up on the chair she was standing beside. "Like, do what I say or I'll let the whole gang know where you are."

"So he is on the run."

"Better believe it," Queenie said, shooting a narrow stream of smoke his way. "That's what happens when you steal from your betters. The boss is pretty pissed."

"Your boss?" Hannibal asked. He regretted the question as soon as he voiced it. Asking too many can make some people suspicious.

"Who did you say you were again?"

"Hannibal Jones." He gave her a card as a sign of his legitimacy. "I'm a local private investigator. I don't want to mess up Ben's action, but it's hard when I don't know what the action is."

"Ben didn't tell you why he was there?"

"We didn't have much of a chance to talk before Gana came out of the house after us," Hannibal said.

"You kidding?" Queenie said, flicking her cigarette's ash into a tray. "What did he do?"

"I took off before Gana caught up to Ben. I think he broke the camera though."

"Damn," she said, breathing smoke as she spoke. "That thing was expensive."

"How does he know Gana anyway?"

"He don't know him. I do." Queenie took a long drag on her cigarette and started marching her spiked heels around the room. "This Dani Gana character and I worked together once. He had a sweet deal. Then one day he disappeared with some of the boss' money. Very uncool. The boss wanted us to hunt him down but I figure there's no percentage in turning him over to the boss. My thinking is he'll be willing to trade the money for his freedom."

"Ben didn't seem to me the kind of guy who'd be up to blackmailing somebody like that," Hannibal said, leaning on the back of the chair that still held the imprint of Queenie's heel.

Queenie stopped pacing and looked at Hannibal over her shoulder. "You look like you're up the challenge," she said in a way that made Hannibal doubt she was talking about blackmail. "Maybe you could help us out."

"Help you out how?"

"You're a detective," she said, as if that made everything obvious. "You just help us find the money and get it back, and we'll give you a nice cut."

Hannibal eased down onto the chair. "You're all about the money, ain't you? If I was you, I'd be more worried about Ben."

"Why? What's he done now?"

"I don't really know," Hannibal said. "But I do know his car is abandoned on a little side street. It's been sitting there for two days."

"Abandoned?" Queenie stared into Hannibal's dark lenses and for the first time he thought he saw genuine concern in her eyes. "Where is it?"

"A few blocks from Gana's place."

"Jesus. I hope nothing's happened to the big lug."

"Well, when you go chasing after thieves…" Big lug? Hannibal hadn't heard that phrase since he was watching old movies with his mother back in Germany.

"If it's by Gana's, then it can't be too far from here," she said, pulling a white satin windbreaker out of the closet. "Take me to the car." When Hannibal didn't move, she clamped her eyes shut and added, "Please?"

Hannibal led her out to his Volvo, telling himself that there might be some useful information inside the vehicle. Maybe Ben took notes during his surveillance of Gana, or maybe he had a lead on the money. If Gana's fortune was indeed stolen, he needed to know the source to finish his assignment. Queenie was playing things close, but if he did her a favor or two, got on her side, she might tell Hannibal who she worked for and how much Gana stole.

While he drove, Queenie stared out the window, examining every face that passed as if it might be her husband. She may have been both the brains and the guts of this team, but it appeared that Ben was the heart. She seemed lost without him.

She was getting antsy when they pulled into the block where Hannibal had twice passed the Saturn. Traffic was lighter in midafternoon and he rolled very slowly down the street, looking for the fire hydrant that was his landmark.

"Come on," Queenie said when they were a little more than half way down the block. "Where is it?"

Hannibal couldn't answer. The little brown Saturn was gone.

-14-

"Oh my God, where is he?" Queenie asked, shaking another cigarette out of her pack.

"He probably just came back for the car," Hannibal said. "And you're not going to smoke in my car."

"No, no, no," she said. "If he was OK, he would have called. He wouldn't let more than twenty-four hours pass without calling me." She stared at the dashboard for a second, realized that what she was looking for wasn't there, and fumbled for her matches.

"The car shouldn't be hard to find. Hey, did you hear me?"

Queenie managed to get the matchbook out of her pocket. She rolled down her window and struck a match. Hannibal's right arm snapped out, his gloved hand closing around the match and cigarette, snatching them both away.

"You are not going to smoke in my car," he repeated. "Now, does Ben own the car?"

"The Saturn? That's my car."

"Great," Hannibal said, making another turn to get pointed back toward the Cochrans' hotel. "Do you carry a copy of the registration?"

"The registration stays in the car."

"Too bad," Hannibal said, tapping buttons on his steering wheel. The car speakers put out the sound of numbers being pressed on a telephone.

"Are you making a phone call?"

"Yes, I'm about to report your car stolen. I have a friend who's a chief of detectives with a nearby police department and I think he could put some emphasis on it. This would have been a lot easier with the VIN number."

"Oh. Hey, is that number on the insurance card? I've got that in my purse."

"Good girl," Hannibal said just before making the telephone connection. When the answer came from the other end, Hannibal said, "Orson? This is Hannibal."

"That was quick. You get something out of the wife?"

Rissik's remark made Hannibal regret that he had the phone on speaker. Queenie opened her mouth to speak, but Hannibal held up a hand to silence her.

"I got sidetracked, but it's related, and I need your help."

"So what else is new?"

"Here's what's new," Hannibal said. "You're not the only one still interested in that particular death. I've got a prime suspect and somebody else was following said suspect before I came on the scene."

"I see. And is our follower a mob guy?"

Hannibal looked at Queenie. Her eyes grew to saucer size and her breathing became shallow panting. He took the deer-in-the-headlights response to mean that Ben did have organized crime connections.

"Don't really know, pal. But I think if we find the missing car it might yield some forensic evidence that could lead right back to my suspect and then I think we could possibly tie him to that killing."

After a pause, Rissik said, "Could? Possibly? You know, Jones, you and me we play this game where you BS me for what you think is a good reason. You pretend to be doing something for me, to help the law, and I pretend to believe you."

"Aww, you're breaking the illusion, Chief."

Rissik chuckled. "Yeah, and I promise never to do it again. I just wanted to make sure you knew that I knew."

"Seriously, Orson, I promise you that I'll never ask you to do anything you'll regret later," Hannibal said. He could feel Rissik nodding on the other end of the phone. He figured that his friend was just clarifying the ground rules, which he thought was important in any long-term relationship.

"OK," Rissik said, "What can you give me on the missing vehicle."

"I got the registered owner's name and address. I got the year, make, model, color, and VIN number of the car. But right this minute, I'm also fighting my way through midtown traffic so if you promise not to ask any embarrassing questions, I'll let the missing guy's wife give you the details."

"Good," Rissik said. "I can get a description of the man too, just in case he's sitting in a cell or a hospital somewhere under a wrong name."

"Cool." Then Hannibal turned to Queenie. "Go ahead. Just talk to the dashboard. Read what's on the insurance card and tell him whatever else might help."

* * * * *

Hannibal just pulled up in front of the Ramada because he didn't want to park. If he parked, Queenie might think he wanted to chat with her and he didn't really want any more of her company. There were types of women Hannibal just didn't like being around. That list included lonely women, lying women, greedy women, women who smoked, and women involved in ongoing cases. Queenie Cochran was at least four of those types rolled into one package, and she was a good candidate to go five for five.

"Just come up for one drink," she was saying. "Just long enough for me to get settled in. I'm kind of, you know, without Benny around."

"I understand but I have things that I have to get done if we're going..." Hannibal was interrupted by the telephone ringing. He tapped the button, wondering if Rissik could have already found the missing car, perhaps in a city impound lot.

"Hannibal? How you doing honey?" Cindy's voice coming out of the speakers caused Queenie's mouth to drop open and her eyes to swing from side to side the way eyes sometimes do when people are caught someplace they know they shouldn't be.

"Hang on a minute, Cindy," Hannibal said, staring at Queenie. "I have a client here, but she was just leaving."

Queenie took the hint better and faster than he expected, waving good-bye and closing the door with care rather than slamming it. Did she feel as if she had been caught poaching on another woman's preserve? Had she been trying to?

"OK, we're alone," Hannibal said, pulling away from the curb. Except for the Russian wiretap, he thought.

"Your client's a woman? What's the case?"

"Missing husband," Hannibal said, diving under a yellow light and pointing his car toward home. "Actually it's related to the bigger case I told you about."

"Right. Well, I just wanted to touch base with you about tonight."

A tiny Mini slipped in front of him, making him miss the light and trapping him at a corner clogged with pedestrians. "Seriously, honey, this case has me so tied down..."

"Don't sweat it, lover. I wanted to let you know I'll be looking at a couple more houses when I leave the office."

The light turned green, but the walkers didn't seem to notice. "After work? Why can't you do all this during the day?"

"Well, dear, some people just won't let you in their homes unless they're there."

Hannibal slowly nosed into the intersection. "Well, I hope you see something you like. And don't forget to eat something."

"Don't worry. After we check the houses, Reggie said we could stop someplace for something to eat while we go over some paperwork."

"Reggie?" Hannibal said, slowly trying to part the tide of humanity in front of his car, using his bumper. "Is that the Realtor?"

"Yeah. Reggie Johnson. Didn't I tell you? He's being real sweet to spend so much time on me."

The old woman really couldn't move any faster. The light changed. He was stuck behind it again. "Damn it!"

"Hannibal?"

"Not you, sweetheart," he said. "The traffic."

"Oh, okay. Well, listen, I just wanted to let you know what was going on. Much to do, and I know you're busy too. Talk to you tomorrow, baby. Love you."

"Love you too, babe. Talk to you later." He disconnected and the music returned. The light turned green.

"Damn it!"

Not the traffic.

* * * * *

This time Hannibal didn't even bother to resist Ivanovich. He went home, changed his clothes, and went straight to his office. He was greeted by an upraised pistol. Ivanovich sat behind the desk as before, headphones on. Hannibal locked the door behind himself and walked straight toward Ivanovich. He reached behind the desk, turned off the stereo, and planted his palms on his desk.

"This ain't working," he said. "I got to be able to work in here, you got to get on with your life someday, and we both need to be able to relax. So, let me tell you how this is going to work. Let's agree that you could kill me anytime you want to. You know it, and now I know it. But you don't want to; because I'm the only man on earth who might get you the answers you want. Right?"

Invanovich leaned back and gave a tentative nod.

"Besides, you kill gangsters, and I'm not one of them," Hannibal said. "Nobody cares about them, so life's pretty easy after the fact. If you kill me, you'll be on the run for the rest of your life. Second, I fucked up in here last night. It was a mistake to go for your pistol. It wouldn't have changed anything if it had worked. You've still got people on Cindy, and I won't risk her life. So let's agree that if I do anything stupid again, your boys will take her for that long walk and you know I couldn't stand that. So I'll stop trying to figure a way around your control position and focus on getting the goods on Dani Gana. Once I do, you can pull your dogs off my woman's tail. OK?"

Ivanovich gave another slow nod, but his expression was still unsure.

"Cool. So you can put that thing down now." Ivanovich didn't move. "Or don't. But I got to get back there to check my messages. Look, we have safeguards in place so we can trust each other. Or at least pretend to."

Ivanovich stood, slipping his gun into his waistband.

"Thank you," Hannibal said. "One more thing. I can't eat Chinese one more time. Why don't you order us a pizza while I take care of some of this administrative crap? Then after we eat I'll give you a full report on what I learned today. I think I made a little progress."

Ivanovich called in their order while Hannibal went through his mail. Then he listened to his voice-mail messages and responded to several e-mails. By the time he had finished with those minor jobs a delivery boy was knocking on the door. Hannibal paid the boy and carried the scorching hot cardboard box to his desk. Then he returned to his seat and Ivanovich pulled the guest chair to the desk. Hannibal cranked the stereo up again. Over pizza and sodas, Hannibal shared the events of the day. He had not spoken to Nikita Petrova's widow because the Cochran lead seemed more promising. They continued to discuss the case as the vodka came out again. Ivanovich filled his glass twice for every one Hannibal emptied, yet Hannibal felt the effects more. As the alcohol relaxed him, his conversation became more direct.

"On the basis of the available evidence, I got to tell you I'm still not convinced that Viktoriya's father killed himself. However, I am willing to accept on faith that you didn't kill him."

"So you believe me?" Ivanovich asked as he poured more liquor into Hannibal's glass.

"Until and unless the evidence calls you a liar," Hannibal said, picking up his glass and swallowing half its contents. Ivanovich emptied his and refilled it.

"Well, it does not really matter. This is not about me. This is about Viktoriya."

Hannibal could feel the industrial beat of the music deep in his chest and it seemed to strengthen him. He pointed at Ivanovich, working to keep his words clear and distinct. "That, my Russian friend, is bullshit. Bull. Shit. This is all about you and your ego. You think you're Sir Lancelot or somebody. You think that saving this fair, innocent flower will somehow redeem you. Admit it."

When Ivanovich shook his head, Hannibal thought he could smell the man's despair. "If I could fix myself I would try, but it's too late for me."

"Jesus, man, you listen too much of that Nine Inch Nails crap. Or maybe it's just a Russian thing to be so damned bleak. You think you earned all that angst? Shit. You ever heard of Corrosion of Conformity?" Hannibal got up, and started scanning the CDs in the rack on the wall.

"I know this band," Ivanovich said, perking up as if they had struck a point of commonality. When Hannibal found the disc he wanted, he replaced one of the CDs in the player's five-disc tray with the band he had just named.

"There's a line in one of their songs that I believe. 'In time, what's deserved always gets served.' That goes for you and Viktoriya too. I'm telling you, if this was about the girl it would be a whole different case."

"Different how?"

Hannibal sipped his drink again. He didn't taste it so much as he felt it. His tongue, he thought, was getting numb. Perhaps this was a message from his body that he had had enough.

"I'll tell you how," Hannibal said, carefully sitting back down. "I'd be trying to get a more rounded view of her world. I'd be checking her mother more closely to see if she was running toward something or away from something else. And

I'd definitely check out her mom's new fellow, this Yakov character."

"Yakov?" Ivanovich asked. "Yakov Sidorov? Big bushy eyebrows?"

"That's the guy." Hannibal said. "You know him?"

"Know of him?" Ivanovich jostled Hannibal aside to open his photo album. After flipping a few pages he came to a collection of what Hannibal would call party shots. Men and women were dressed up, drinking, laughing, and, in some of the pictures, playing cards. The fun was happening in a pretty fancy place with what looked like red silk covering the walls. He ran his fingertips over one of the photos. It was creased with age, as if someone had carried it around a while before putting it in the album for safekeeping. The picture featured a younger Viktoriya Petrova staring right into the camera, while her mother stood behind her, looking away at a man with such love in her eyes he had to assume it was her husband. He looked to be a jovial sort, and he was dark. Not dark like Gana or Hannibal, but like Omar Sharif in his prime.

"Here he is," Ivanovich said, pointing to another photo. "He was Nikita's doctor and, I believe, his friend as well. In fact, Sidorov was a doctor to many in the business."

"Mob doctor," Hannibal said. "There's always a guy who's inside but not really. A guy who doesn't feel the need to report the gunshot wounds he treats, and if a patient doesn't want to go to the emergency room after a beating or stabbing, well, he won't press the point."

"Exactly. He was treasured for his expertise but more for his discretion."

It was the man Hannibal had met all right, and from the pictures it was clear that he really was a family friend. His eyes slid over the photos almost as if they formed a motion picture of another time, another place. But what place?

"These all appear to be taken in the same swanky club. Where are they?"

"The Russia House, up on Connecticut Avenue. The best bar and restaurant in the city if you happen to be Russian."

"And I see there is gambling too."

"Well, there are private rooms." Ivanovich said, turning a page. "If they know you, you can always get a room for your group. This is where you go to play preference. See? Here. It is the game for serious card players in Russia."

"Whoa!" Hannibal sprang to his feet, and regretted it immediately. He felt dizzy for a moment, but focused on the new photo to steady himself. "Who is that guy? The one in the middle of the table."

"I do not know him."

"Everybody else sure does," Hannibal said. "Dr. Sidorov, Petrova, and isn't that Gana standing behind him? I thought he was new to the area."

"He left Washington years ago," Ivanovich said. "I never expected him to return."

Hannibal's index finger circled the photo. "Look at that. Sidorov, Gana, Petrova, they're all looking at that guy in the middle."

"They must all be friends," Ivanovich said. "I admit I never looked that closely at this one but, he almost looks like the leader of the pack here."

"Yeah, or at least the center of attention." Hannibal said, tapping the picture with his fingertips. "And that woman practically on his lap, she's clearly more than a friend."

"The blonde?" Ivanovich asked.

"Yeah, but she's a redhead these days. You can't miss that body. That girl is Queenie Cochran."

- 15 -
Saturday

Finding a parking place anywhere near the Russia House was a challenge. The yellow marble edifice sat just north of Dupont Circle, on the corner where Florida Avenue crossed Connecticut. That intersection was surrounded by triangular and trapezoidal blocks formed by streets crossing at awkward and bizarre angles. Parking was even more difficult for a man whose head was pounding due to a vicious hangover. Still, walking toward the stone monolithic that housed the Russia House, Hannibal considered the conversation that had led him there to be even more challenging. He had made the call from his office, with Ivanovich looking on.

"Well, good morning," Raisa Petrova had said. "You are my very first caller of the day. And who might you be?"

"It's Hannibal Jones, Mrs. Petrova."

"Oh." Her voice dropped a full octave. "Well, have you called to apologize?"

"Excuse me?"

"I thought maybe you had come to your senses. Have you finished cross-examining my son-in-law?"

"Ma'am, I spoke to Mr. Gana and we are not in conflict over anything," Hannibal said in his most placating voice. "I'm sorry if I upset you, but now I'm authorized to tell you what this is all about."

"Oh, so there's more to the story?"

As he expected, the hint of a mystery got her in a listening mood. "Yes ma'am. The truth is, we're looking into the circumstances of your husband's death. I didn't tell you right away because I didn't want to get your hopes up about anything. Naturally, we had to consider every possibility. Now we're trying to gather more background information."

"I'm not sure I can tell you much." He could hear her clinking the teapot against her glass and the sound of liquid pouring.

"I do understand, ma'am," Hannibal said, trying to be gentle. "We don't want to inconvenience you any further. But I would like to speak with Dr. Sidorov. If you could help me contact him, that would be a huge help."

"Yakov doesn't know any more than I do," Raisa said.

"I understand he knew a great deal about your husband's health," Hannibal said in a soft, understanding tone. "He may be able to help us understand why, well, why things happened the way they did."

Raisa took a deep breath and spent five or six seconds letting it out. "Yes, he may be able to help you with that. But I don't know when he will be home. He spends a lot of time at that club. The lounge, he calls it."

"Club?" Hannibal glanced at Ivanovich. "Do you mean the Russia House?"

"Why, yes," Raisa said, but he heard the surprise in her voice. "In fact, he's picking me up in a few minutes to go over there."

"I see," Hannibal said, not seeing at all. "But the restaurant isn't open for any meal but dinner."

Raisa almost snorted in skepticism. "That is for the tourists. If you know the right people, you go as part of a private party. Yakov will spend most of the day there, playing his card games. For some, it is like a drug. It sucked away my Nikita's soul and now it has Yakov's as well."

"Maybe I could meet him there."

"Perhaps," Raisa said, "if you were expected."

"Your help would be very much appreciated, ma'am."

When Hannibal hung up, Ivanovich asked, "You still think he committed suicide?"

"Not now," Hannibal said. "But she sure wants me to. That's the only reason she's pointing me to Sidorov, so he can tell me how much pain Nikita was in. But that's OK, as long as I get to question him under friendly circumstances."

"Why Sidorov?"

"Well, he seems to know all the players and might know something about your man Gana's past."

"But why not go back to the mystery woman, this Queenie? She already knows you."

Hannibal shook his head. Everyone's a detective, he thought. "Well, let's see. She's got her husband following Gana. Apparently, there's a pile of money in the balance. And she's working hard to disguise her Russian background. Everything about this broad tells me she'll lie to me about anything. I think I'm more likely to get the truth out of the doc."

All of that flew back through Hannibal's mind as he knocked on the door a few minutes after one o'clock. Dressed in his regulation black suit, wearing his Oakley sunglasses and black leather gloves, Hannibal was accustomed to being treated like some snooping government official. When the stocky man wearing an apron around his waist opened the door with an irritated expression on his face, Hannibal knew this time would be different.

"Didn't anyone tell you to use the back entrance?"

"I think you've got me confused with somebody else," Hannibal said, presenting his card. "I'm here to join Dr. Sidorov's game. I believe Mrs. Petrova told you to expect me."

The man at the door at least had the grace to blush as he swung the door wide. "I am very sorry. Simple mistake. Please come in and follow me."

Hannibal's guide led him through the lounge, which was as opulent as Ivanovich's photos had suggested. The red wall covering was what he thought Cindy called silk damask, and Russian paintings were displayed just far enough apart to not be too showy.

A flight of narrow stairs brought them to a more private but no less elegant room. Hannibal and his guide stopped in front of the elaborate oak bar that dominated one end of the room. The furniture was ornate, and in a style Hannibal couldn't name. Someone had positioned blocks of mitered green marble around the room with great care. Potted palm trees sat between cozy couches and low coffee tables. The three card tables looked too smooth and shiny to insult by sliding playing cards over them, but the people seated around them didn't seem to mind.

Each table held four players, all of whom looked across at their partners while they played but hardly glanced at their opponents. A thin cloud of smoke hung over their heads, raised by what Hannibal's nose told him were strong and probably foreign cigarettes. The play was quiet, and their fairly formal dress gave the impression of a serious tournament. The night before, Ivanovich had given him an overview of the play, which struck Hannibal as a simplified form of bridge. Having grown up playing spades and hearts, Hannibal figured he could sit in without much training. But he didn't expect to that afternoon. The faces he was scanning for were missing.

"I don't see Dr. Sidorov," he told his guide.

"That is because he is not here," a female voice said behind him. Hannibal turned to see a stately woman in a black, strapless formal gown - the kind of gown Hannibal didn't think anyone wore before dinnertime. She was perched on a bar stool and offering him a half smile. Her dark hair was up in a chignon, accentuating her height. Her thin eyebrows and long ascetic nose seemed at odds with full, red lips. He thought she was blessed or cursed with a cold beauty, the kind men love to admire from a distance but are afraid to touch.

"Good morning. My name is Hannibal Jones and I was to meet Dr. Sidorov here."

"He'll be back," she said. Then, almost as an afterthought, she added, "I am Anastasiya Sidorov. His wife."

Hannibal did not allow his surprise to show as he held his hand out. "A pleasure to meet you. Now that I look more closely, I do recognize you."

She touched her fingertips to his, and he was glad he was wearing gloves. Women don't become this cold without reason, he thought.

"Have we met before?" One eyebrow arched in disbelief.

"No, ma'am," Hannibal said, reaching into his jacket. "I have an old photo of your husband, and I think you are in it too."

This was too easy, he thought. He placed the photo on the bar. Anastasiya looked down, sipped her vodka, and smiled. He thought the smile was not so much for the picture as for the past it called up.

"This was taken right here," she said. She was standing beside Yakov in the photo. Gana stood to Yakov's left, behind the mystery man and Queenie. On the other side of them, Nikita Petrova was just close enough to be in the picture.

"Yes," Hannibal said, "taken right here. And whoever took it managed to get two lovely ladies in the photo. You and..."

"Renata." Anastasiya said in her light, musical tone.

"Renata?"

"Renata Tolstaya," she said with a heavy sigh. "You are interested in her?"

"Not really. But I did want to talk with your husband about some of the other people in the photo."

Anastasiya looked Hannibal up and down. Then she turned away toward the bartender. "You need a drink," she said over her shoulder. "Misha, please bring this fellow with the colorful name some vodka. He will have..." she looked at Hannibal as if measuring him anew, and then returned to the bartender, "He will have some Jewel of Russia to start. On Yakov's bill."

"Is that a good brand?" Hannibal asked, sliding onto the barstool beside her. She had apparently decided to have a real conversation with him. "I will admit to being pretty ignorant about vodka, although lately I seem to have developed a taste for it."

She turned back to him and gave a full smile, resting her chin on her palm. "It is a true Russian vodka and one of my favorites. They have about fifty different vodkas here and there is only one way to know which you like most."

Hannibal lifted his glass and sipped, just to be polite. Then he sipped again. It was an entirely different taste from the vodka he had shared with Ivanovich, not nearly so harsh, but it still flamed on its way down his throat. "I didn't know it was supposed to be chilled. Much better. And this is really, really smooth."

"I see you have been drinking cheap vodka," Anastasiya said. "No one should drink cheap vodka."

"I'll keep that in mind. Do you know when your husband will be back? I wouldn't want these folks to get the wrong idea." Hannibal smiled, knowing that the card players were ignoring them completely.

Anastasiya's smile faded, and she fished in a small clutch purse to pull out a cigarette. "You needn't worry. And Yakov should be back very soon, unless of course he decides to stop over. He went to drive Raisa home." Her tone told Hannibal where the coldness came from.

"I see. I thought she came to play cards too, but I guess she doesn't like to stay as long as you do."

Anastasiya made a show of fitting the short cigarette into a holder. Hannibal spotted a heavy porcelain lighter on the bar and held its flame forward. She blew out a thank you with her first puff of smoke.

"You are a gentleman. A vanishing breed in this country. Your woman is very fortunate." Hannibal neither confirmed nor denied the existence of a woman in his life. She looked as if this was a disappointment. "Raisa didn't come to gamble. That was her husband. She came today so she could ask Yakov for money in person."

"Money?"

"They are close," she said. "You need more to drink. Misha, do you have some of that Kremlyovskaya chocolate in the freezer? This one needs his horizons broadened."

Hannibal sat quiet until his second drink arrived, planning to nurse it until he left the building. A two-ounce shot was plenty of alcohol for him right after lunch, and that was the way they seemed to pour in this place. But he was curious enough to pick up the new glass. It looked the same, but the smell was a startling difference. He tasted slowly, his eyes widening behind his glasses.

"It really is chocolate," Hannibal said. "Chocolate vodka. I'll be damned."

"Life is full of surprises," Anastasiya said. She looked happy to have pleased a man. He wanted to give her another chance.

"So, Raisa Petrova asked your husband for money."

"Ten thousand dollars," she said, making the words sound like profanities.

"Whoa. They must be very close indeed."

Behind Hannibal, a familiar voice said, "We are very old friends, and I promised Nikita that I would take care of her."

Hannibal spun on his stool and stood to shake Yakov's hand. "Sir, I've been waiting for you. I was hoping to learn a bit more about some of your old friends. I hope Mrs. Petrova told you…"

"Look at this photo," Anastasiya said, interrupting Hannibal by thrusting the picture between the two men. "Do you remember those times?"

Yakov leaned back to focus on the picture. "Oh my. Look at that. There's Boris and Renata Tolstaya. I haven't thought of them in years."

"You loved me then," Anastasiya said. She stood quickly, but lost her balance and fell forward into her husband's arms.

"Sir, if I could have just a couple of minutes," Hannibal began.

"Did you give it to her?" Anastasiya asked. "Was she worth so much?"

"I think you started a little early today," Yakov said. Then to Hannibal, "I'm sorry young man, but I think I need to get my wife home now. Raisa seemed to have more to tell you, though. Perhaps you should speak with her again. I will be happy to meet with you another time."

"You could probably find him at her house," Anastasiya said as Yakov began easing her toward the staircase. "But you would not. You are a gentleman."

-16-

Hannibal let the Black Beauty wander the Dupont Circle area for a while before he set a solid course for the Petrova house. He knew he wanted to talk to Raisa, but was not sure what he wanted to ask her about. It seemed clear now that she knew more about Dani Gana than she was telling, and the truth about Gana was his primary objective. On the other hand, the mystery surrounding Nikita Petrova's death was calling to him. His first impression was that Nikita was universally respected and liked within his little criminal universe. But the deeper Hannibal dug, the more people turned out to have a motive for killing Nikita, including Raisa if Mrs. Sidorov's suspicions were accurate.

He parked across the street from Raisa's house and got out of his car with one thought at the top of his mind. No one he had met on this case was stupid, and even the women seemed well practiced in duplicity and capable of anything.

A tap at the door yielded silence for a good thirty seconds. When he heard movement, it was a shuffling gait, not the energetic steps he expected. When she opened the door, Raisa was in heels and a tasteful gown. He assumed she had not changed from what she wore to the Russia House that morning.

Invited into the house for the first time, Hannibal was struck by how much the décor reminded him of the Russia House. Not just the paintings but the frames too gave the impression that this woman longed to go back in time and live in tsarist Russia. She seated him at the kitchen table and poured for them both from a china teapot. After taking a long drink, she looked at Hannibal as if anticipating an inquisition and not really caring to avoid it. At that moment, Hannibal had no desire to play the game.

"Mrs. Petrova, are you all right?"

"I am fine," she said into her teacup. "It is just that, well, she's gone."

"Viktoriya?" Hannibal asked. When she gave a sullen nod, he asked, "Gone where?"

"Gone with Dani. Gone from my life."

Raisa Petrova had the furnace running and kept the house quite warm. That didn't stop Hannibal from feeling a chill run down his spine. Had she expected them to stay there with her? Was she counting on Gana's money to support her, or was she simply missing her little girl?

"Never mind," Raisa said, waving her hand to brush the subject, or perhaps her daughter, away. "You have spoken to Yakov, I suppose, and now have more questions of me about Dani. Well, go ahead and ask them."

Hannibal nodded and pulled out the same photo he had shown the Sidorovs. He laid it on the table between them and watched Raisa's face. She brightened for a moment, and slowly reached down to stroke her finger over Nikita's smiling face.

"This was taken in the Russia House, years ago," she said. "Where did you find this? How did you get it?"

"I'm a detective," Hannibal replied.

That earned a genuine smile, and Raisa reverted to the woman he first met. "Yes, of course. You have your sources and all that. Well, thank you for showing me this photo. It takes me back. But why are you showing it to me?"

Cindy's safety and Hannibal's privacy depended on his exploring how long Raisa had known Dani Gana and what his relationship was to the others in the room that night. But when he went to point to the photo, his finger moved of its own accord like the pointer on a Ouija board to the central figure. He had to follow his instincts.

"Can you tell me who this fellow is?"

"The big man with the little round belly and almost no hair left?" Raisa said. "That's Boris Tolstaya." There was now an edge on her voice, slicing at Tolstaya's memory.

"I take it you knew him."

"He was a friend of Nikita's from the army," she said, shaking her head. "Big gambler, and investor for the Red Mafyia. Like Nikita, he was one of Yakov's patients."

"A tight little group," Hannibal said, surprised at how casually she was talking about her husband's mob connections. "A couple of war vets, both tended by the same doctor. And if this Tolstaya was handling mob money, I can see how he was able to support your husband in his efforts to keep things running smoothly."

"Support him?" Raisa slammed her empty cup down on the table hard enough for Hannibal to fear it would break. "He destroyed my poor Nikita. Between them, those two paved the path to his destruction."

"I don't understand," Hannibal said. He looked at the picture again, hunting for any sign that these men were anything but friends.

"Tolstaya was a gambler," Raisa said. "One of those jovial men who make you laugh all the time. But he was a gambler who got my poor Nikita hooked on that hateful habit. He pretended to be a friend while he took everything we had, one hand of cards at a time." Her breathing became halting. Hannibal reached out across the table with a gloved hand and spoke in a very soft, even tone.

"The debt."

"Yes," she said, looking up in surprise. "How did you...oh. That's right. You are a detective." She had no way to know he had spoken to Rissik, but she seemed ready to trust him. She wrapped a hand around his.

"So Tolstaya took all of your husband's money," Hannibal said. She nodded. "But you said the two of them destroyed him. How was Dr. Sidorov involved?"

Her face fell in on itself and Hannibal could see tears in there trying to get out, yet she hesitated. She stared into

Hannibal's face, so he slid off his sunglasses. Her head snapped back in surprise. After a moment, she seemed to relax and a small smile emerged.

"They are so blue," she said. "Like fine porcelain."

"Not always," Hannibal said. "But you were going to tell me how Dr. Sidorov contributed to your husband's downfall."

"Not him," she said, shaking her head. "But he introduced the downfall of our marriage. He never found out that I knew, but I found it just two weeks before the end."

"Found it?" Hannibal asked. She was rocking in her chair now, clinging tightly to his hand as the tears began to flow at last.

"The letter. The love note he wrote to Anastasiya Sidorov."

The ring of Hannibal's cell phone split the air like a lightning bolt, charging the air in the kitchen. Raisa turned with a napkin to her face, and Hannibal pulled his phone out to stop the noise as quickly as he could. It was a new phone that did a lot more than Hannibal needed it to, but the one thing he could do with confidence was to push the right button to answer a call. When he said hello, he heard an unexpected voice.

"Jones. I have something for you," Anthony Ronzini said.

"I'm with Mrs. Petrova right now," Hannibal said.

"Well, you sure don't want to have this conversation in front of her."

-17-

It was difficult for Hannibal to pull away from Raisa Petrova, but he knew that this call could hold the final piece of the puzzle that would free Cindy from potential danger. He apologized for his haste, got to his car, and got on the road toward home. Then he pushed the button on his cell phone to dial the number returning the last incoming call. Ronzini answered.

"Jones?"

"Yes."

"Delete this number from your phone. I'll wait."

Hannibal wasn't sure what to think, but he complied right away.

"OK," Hannibal said. "It's gone." Was this a way of saying he didn't trust Hannibal to have his private phone number. Probably. But to take his word for it that he had in fact deleted the number was also an expression of trust.

"Good. I must say this little exercise has been fun. I begin to see why you found this Dani Gana character so interesting."

"Is he really rich?"

"Could be," Ronzini said. "My man at the Provident Bank says he opened his account with $256,000 from an account in Morocco."

"Morocco?" Hannibal swerved to avoid a little Mini whose driver was in a great hurry to get up on the ramp to I-395. "I suppose an Algerian might keep his money there. Of course, so might a Russian mobster. I wonder if we can find out where the money was transferred from to get into the Moroccan account."

"Not likely," Ronzini said. "They're a lot like the Swiss. The Arab Bank of Morocco holds a lot of oil money and a lot of sheik money. And they are very big. Whereas some banks boast of half a billion dollars in assets, the Arab Bank paid a half billion dollars in interest over the last nine months."

Hannibal nodded. "Well, as far as I'm concerned, that tells me where his money came from."

"Good, because it would take you weeks or months to get any more. And it's too late for my man at Provident to get anything else."

"Too late?" Hannibal asked. He stopped at a light behind three other cars. "I don't understand."

"The account is closed," Ronzini said. "Gana withdrew the entire balance, in cash, just before the close of business yesterday afternoon."

* * * * *

Hannibal explained his latest discoveries to Ivanovich in his office over a pot of fresh coffee. He had hung up his jacket, pulled off his tie, sunglasses and gloves, and rolled up his white shirt sleeves. Ivanovich moved to the visitor's chair, leaving the desk chair for its actual owner. Hannibal could only hope that agreeable attitude would hold as he shared all he had learned that day. Once he had filled two big mugs with his Kenyan blend he turned down the booming heavy metal Ivanovich had started and gave him a thorough report. Ivanovich sat quietly.

"So, that's it then," Ivanovich said at last. "He has married her and taken her off to some mysterious place. It doesn't sound as if he has made contact with any of his old friends and from what you've told me, even Mrs. Petrova has no idea where they've gone."

"That's about it," Hannibal said. "He didn't give us much time to investigate." He watched Ivanovich shrink a little bit.

He sat with his elbows on his thighs and his head dropped forward as he stared at the floor. To maintain perspective, Hannibal tried to imagine how many people this man had killed in his criminal career. It didn't help. Without a gun in his hand, he no longer looked like a killer. All Hannibal could see was a man in despair. But that was Ivanovich's problem. Hannibal had his own.

"Listen, Aleksandr, I think I have done all that you asked of me that first night. I feel like I've kept my part of the deal. How about calling your dogs off Cindy?"

Ivanovich looked up and Hannibal returned his gaze in the most nonthreatening way he could. In the sudden stillness, the speeding guitars seemed to kick into a higher gear. He didn't know what was going on in the mind of this very dangerous man, but he knew he couldn't push the subject.

"There is another bottle of vodka under the desk," Ivanovich said. Hannibal rolled his eyes and reached for the bottle. When he thumped it on the desk, Ivanovich added, "You will want to celebrate." He pulled a very slim cell phone out of his pocket, flipped it open, and pressed a button. When someone answered, he said something Hannibal could not hope to understand. Ivanovich nodded a couple of times, said a couple more words, and then closed the phone and put it away.

"I have told them that it is finished."

"Thank you," Hannibal said. He understood what Ivanovich had just given up. Now he was powerless. Hannibal poured into their two glasses, stood up, and handed one to the man who was now his guest instead of his captor. Ivanovich accepted the glass and took a small sip.

"Now, unless we are to have an Old West gunfight, I must ask you for a favor instead of making demands. It will be easier for me if I can stay just a little longer, until the sun is down."

"I can live with that," Hannibal said, grabbing his glass from the desk. He held it up. Ivanovich stood and tapped his glass against Hannibal's. Then both men upended their glasses, draining the liquid down their throats. Hannibal clenched his eyes tight as it went down.

"Aleksandr, I want you to know that I understand why you did what you did," Hannibal said. "In your spot I might have tried to blackmail someone the same way. And I really am sorry that I couldn't get enough evidence of Gana's game, whatever it is, to maybe take it to Mrs. Petrova before he disappeared with the girl. But now you need to let it go and get back to your life."

"My life?" Ivanovich said it with a smirk. "What life? I am a hired killer. Everyone fears me. No one..." He didn't finish the sentence, just dropped back in the chair, looking past Hannibal. "Do you know how far this has gone? Just how damaged have I become?"

Hannibal didn't have the answer to that one, but he could see that the scars on this man's soul ran very deep.

"Hey listen, Aleksandr, why don't I get something in here for us to have for dinner, one more time?" When Ivanovich smiled back at him he said, "Good. I'll order something form the Chinese place, but first, there is one other call I have to make."

Hannibal wasn't sure what he intended to tell Cindy, but he knew he had to let her know that there was a reason he had gone two days with hardly any contact with her. He thought he also wanted to ask a few questions about that real estate agent with whom she had been traveling the city. He might even want to invite her over to meet the man who caused all that grief.

But as he reached for the telephone, it rang.

"Hannibal? It's Orson Rissik."

"Orson?" Hannibal said. "You calling to find out what I learned today? It wasn't much that can help you."

"That's not it," Rissik said. He seemed to be speaking more slowly than usual. "Did you speak to Mrs. Petrova today?"

"Chatted with her in her kitchen this afternoon," Hannibal said.

"Well, I hope you got everything you were hoping for from her."

Hannibal's eyes narrowed and the hair rose on the back of his neck. "Why?"

"You just might be the last person to see her alive," Rissik said. "Except of course for whoever shot her."

-18-

Hannibal quickly suited up for business again. While he was tying his tie, Ivanovich went into the next room and returned in a nondescript sport coat.

"It was Dani Gana," Ivanovich said while Hannibal pulled on his gloves. "He realized that he could not take Viktoriya away and leave a loose end like her mother to hunt him down one day."

"Let's not jump to any conclusions," Hannibal said. "My police contact says I'll be allowed to survey the crime scene because I could tell if anything was stolen. While I'm there, I might find a clue that would help me find out where Gana took off to."

Ivanovich put a hand on Hannibal's shoulder. "Why are you doing this? I have released you from any obligation."

"That's right," Hannibal said, sliding his Oakleys into place. "And that means this is no longer about you. Now it's about the girl. If you're right and Gana had anything to do with this, she's in danger. If it was a near-miss by one of his enemies, she may be in even greater danger. Either way, she probably doesn't know her mother is dead. I need to find him and tell her what I know so she can make an informed decision about whether she wants to stay with this guy."

"Then I'm going with you."

Hannibal shook his head. "Bad idea, Aleksandr. Not only will the place be crawling with police, but anybody who really thinks you killed Nikita Petrova will be out for blood now that Raisa has been murdered. Whoever your enemies are, they'll all be out tonight. Just let me go find out what I can."

* * * * *

When Hannibal pulled up across the street from the Petrova residence that evening, every light in the house was on, including lights on the front and back porch. The front door and upstairs windows glowed like the eyes and mouth of some ghastly jack-o'-lantern. Neighbors probably thought there was a party going on inside, but he knew the opposite was true. As he pushed the fob button that locked the doors, he made a conscious decision to leave his guilt out in the car. Yes, he had stirred up some old stories that might better have been left alone. And yes, he might have inadvertently fingered Mrs. Petrova if someone was looking for her, or if someone thought she knew something that should not be shared. Of course, he didn't know any of that. The suspect pool was running over. Both of the Sidorovs appeared to have motives. Russian mobsters may have decided to silence her before she said the wrong thing to Hannibal. Or, for all he knew, Ivanovich's theory was correct.

The walk up the steps to the door seemed twice as long as it had before. When he arrived, Rissik was there to meet him. They nodded, then Hannibal got to the matter at hand.

"Where is she?"

"Backyard, just past the patio," Rissik said. "Neighbor kid found her when he was cutting across the yards to visit his girlfriend."

Hannibal digested that information and considered all it might imply. He really didn't want to see her dead, but he supposed it was necessary. After a deep breath, Hannibal stepped toward the house. Rissik took his arm to stop him.

"Local people have done a lot of looking and collected forensic evidence. The body is still in place, but the medical examiner will be here soon to pick it up. This is not my case, Jones. I'm only allowed to be here as a courtesy, because of the connections to the husband's death. You are here as a favor to me."

"Bottom line?"

"You can look around the house for anything that might be significant, based on what you know. Do not touch the body. Understand? Do not take anything out of the house. And do not discuss what you might see with any member of the press."

"I won't embarrass you," Hannibal said. Rissik nodded. Hannibal opened the door and went inside.

The house was as he had left it, a little cluttered, ornately decorated, warm and friendly with hardwood floors and a great room serving as both living room and dining room, separated by beautiful pocket doors just like the ones that separated the rooms in his own apartment and office. A small squad of detectives scurried around the four finished levels.

As he entered the kitchen, the smell told him she had been preparing dinner. A look at the stove and the bowls beside it told him why the smell was so strong. Cabbage rolls were already prepared and mushroom soup was in process. Someone had interrupted her. Red spatter on the counter between the stove and the door told him where the crime took place. Two drops on the floor between the stove and the door implied she had moved pretty quickly afterward.

Crickets made the backyard garden sound like a Hollywood jungle. Hannibal walked down a narrow cement path toward the flashlight in a patrolman's hand. The boy in the uniform looked as if he would start shaving any day now. He kept his light on the body, maybe hoping it would keep the bugs away until the city's angels of death arrived to spirit her off to the city's purgatory where she would wait in a drawer until others moved her to her final resting place.

Raisa Petrova had gone outside in her dressing gown and mule slippers with a scarf over her hair. Hannibal thought that only a life-threatening situation could make her do that. She lay face down on the winding cement ribbon with one arm stretched forward, as if after falling she had decided to try to swim the rest of the way. The spreading stain on her back surrounded a small hole in the dressing gown and, he assumed, her back. It was a very small hole. Of course, a hole in your back doesn't have to be very big to let all the life leak out. Sometimes it just takes a while. In this case, it took almost ten yards.

Her face, turned to one side, was not placid. Her jaw was set in the stubborn way he saw it in life. She seemed to smirk at him for a moment, the shadows dancing on her face. Hannibal realized that the light had shaken. He looked up at the young cop who was standing over what was sure to be his first corpse.

"She reminds me of my grandma," the cop said, looking ashamed of his own reaction.

"Me too," Hannibal said, although he didn't make the connection until the cop spoke.

Back inside, Hannibal tightened his gloves on his hands and started to explore the lady's bedroom. The décor gave the room an overwhelming femininity, with silk and satin on the bed and candleholders on every available surface. Music boxes and jewelry boxes cluttered the dresser and chest, and fresh flowers filled a crystal vase on the windowsill. A smiling photo of Nikita Petrova stood guard on the night table beside her bed.

The room carried the slight smell of lavender, and that scent grew ever stronger as he approached the bathroom. Even there, candles and mythological figurines held sway. Hannibal gave the bathroom the onceover, but he expected to find what he was looking for in the bedroom.

Drawers creaked like old knee joints when he pulled them open. He wished he hadn't known Mrs. Petrova as he flipped through her most personal clothing items, but he had no choice. Important personal papers could be concealed anyplace. Music boxes and jewelry boxes added up to a dozen good hiding places and Hannibal checked them all, surprised at how little jewelry of value he found. Then there were the knickknacks, some of which held hidden compartments.

Finally, he got down to the nesting dolls. A wooden woman's top half lifted off to reveal a different woman inside. Inside that woman hid yet another different woman. Just like real life, Hannibal thought. It was inside the third one that he found tightly rolled papers. The top page was what he was looking for: a handwritten note in a scroll-heavy feminine hand, addressed to Nikita and signed by Anastasiya. Unfortunately, those two names were all he could read. The rest of the writing was in Cyrillic characters, so he couldn't verify the content. Not that it mattered. The fact that Raisa felt the need to hide the note told him all he needed to know.

Two sheets down he came to a prize he didn't expect. This letter was in English, and it was addressed to Raisa. The letterhead, first in Arabic, then in French, and finally in English, was that of the Arab Bank of Morocco. For a business letter it was long and wordy, which Hannibal assumed was what happened when you translated Middle Eastern business language into English.

Music boxes proved useful to pin down the edges of the letters. Once they were secured on the dresser, Hannibal pulled out his cell phone. After only three false starts he managed to photograph the documents. Then he rolled them up, replaced them in their hand-carved hiding place, and carried it out to the front door. The air had turned brisk while he was inside. He found Rissik sitting at the table where Hannibal had first met Yakov Sidorov. Hannibal stood beside Raisa's chair, but decided not to sit down.

"I told you not to take anything," Rissik said.

"I'm just bringing this to you." Hannibal removed the top half of the wooden woman, revealing the rolled papers. "There might be a valuable clue to the murder in here."

"Really?" Rissik said, accepting the doll. "Something that points to motive?"

"I think so. There's a note to Nikita from a woman named Anastasiya Sidorov. It's in Russian so I can't tell you what it says, but based on what Raisa Petrova told me, I expect it's a love letter. Now, if Raisa confronted the other woman, or threatened to tell her husband..."

Rissik nodded. "Yeah, that could speak to motive. Thanks for the lead. And hey, it looks like there was an adult daughter. Any idea how we can contact her?"

"Afraid not, Chief," Hannibal said. "But if I hear anything about her, I'll let you know."

* * * * *

By the time Hannibal got back to his office, Ivanovich had emptied the last bottle of vodka and it was too late to order more. Not that Hannibal minded. Coffee was much more to his taste right then. He brewed a fresh pot while he filled Ivanovich in on his final visit to the Petrova house.

"You don't really think Anastasiya Sidorov would murder Raisa Petrova, do you?" Ivanovich asked, slouching into the chair and sipping his coffee.

"Not really," Hannibal said, fishing an electric wire out of a desk drawer. "Raisa found that letter before Nikita died. Why would she wait until now to confront Anastasiya? Besides, she didn't even try to get around to the front door. She died trying to get to the rental house. Did she think she might find help there? Or was she trying to point us toward her killer?"

"So, you finally see the light. The shooter was Gana."

"Maybe," Hannibal said, fumbling to plug a cord into his cell phone. "At least I might see a reason for it now."

Ivanovich moved to stand behind Hannibal, looking over his shoulder at the computer screen. "What do you have there?"

"It's a letter from a bank. The Arab Bank of Morocco to be exact. The same bank Gana transferred a quarter million dollars out of."

"It looks as if the bank was sending her periodic payments," Ivanovich said, scanning the letter and records Hannibal also photographed. "Gana?"

"I rather doubt the bank will name the accountholder," Hannibal said. "But these documents make it pretty clear that she wasn't authorized to do anything with the account."

"Yes," Ivanovich said, pointing to the screen. "And this letter seems to be the bank officially telling her that the account is now empty, so no more payments will be forthcoming."

"Right. If this account did belong to Dani Gana, then it looks as though Raisa may have effectively sold her daughter to Gana for a monthly stipend. If that theory holds, then Raisa might not have been too pleased when the money ran out. Suppose she threatened to tell the girl the truth?"

Ivanovich slapped his palm down on the desk. "He killed her to keep Viktoriya from learning his filthy secret. Now we must find her, to make sure she knows why her mother let this animal marry her."

"We?"

"You have got to find them," Ivanovich said, his fists clenched and shaking with rage. "Find her and get her to safety. Then I will take care of Dani Gana myself."

"Look, I do think she needs to know the truth, but…"

"I am not trying to blackmail you," Ivanovich said, palms forward and brows raised. "Please, let me hire you. I will pay you. In fact, I had planned to pay you anyway when our business was over. I have a good deal of money saved up, money I hoped one day to use to give Viktoriya a good life."

Hannibal read the documents on his screen more closely to avoid Ivanovich's eyes. "Look, Aleksandr, I'm worried about the girl too, and I will help you find her and Gana if I can find any leads to their whereabouts. But I won't set up a guy for you to take him out. We clear?"

After a deep, heavy sigh, Ivanovich said, "I understand. The important thing is to save Viktoriya from this monster."

"It looks like she was getting about five grand a month until last month," Hannibal said. "Nice pay for doing nothing, but not exactly wealth untold. Hard to believe a woman with old-school values would give up her only child for this."

"Who knows how badly she needed the money," Ivanovich said, resting a hand on Hannibal's shoulder. "I didn't know this man Tolstaya, but I know that Nikita gambled with him. Constantly. He may have been in a great deal of debt to the man."

"Enough to kill him for?"

"Maybe," Ivanovich said, "but dead men don't pay up. More likely Nikita killed himself, but to a man like Tolstaya that would not make the debt go away. He would take away everything the surviving wife had and if that did not pay off the debt, he would demand more."

Hannibal sat back, resting his elbow on the arm of his chair and his chin in his hand. "Sure would like to question that guy. But I've got no idea where he is. And I don't know if anybody knows where Dani Gana took off to with his new bride."

The ring of the desk phone surprised them both. Hannibal glanced at his watch, confirming that it was awfully late for someone to be calling. After eleven, he would normally let the machine take it. But right then, he wanted to know who had something important enough to call him about at that hour. When he answered the phone, the speaker was surprised to hear him.

"Hannibal?" Rissik asked. "What are you doing in your office at this time of night? I intended to just leave a message."

"You can't have a break in the murder already," Hannibal said. "Besides, it isn't even your case."

"Not about the murder. Your other matter."

Hannibal had to think a moment. "Oh, the car. They found the car?"

"Yeah, I just got the call," Rissik said. "They found the car, kind of smashed up. And they found the owner. He's kind of smashed up too. They took him to Georgetown University Hospital and I guess they decided to keep him."

-19-
Sunday

Like writers and artists, detectives often do their most important work when they appear to be doing nothing. Hannibal knew he looked idle, sitting there in the morning sun, staring down at his desk. His desk was almost covered by pictures taken from Ivanovich's album. The photo featuring Boris Tolstaya was front and center, with other pictures taken in the Russia House surrounding it. All the pretty ladies were in their evening gowns and the men in suits or, in Dani Gana's case, a tuxedo. Something was nagging at the back of his mind, and he knew that the answer lay someplace in those photographs.

Ivanovich sat a steaming mug of coffee beside the photos. The aroma told Hannibal that his houseguest had found the Hawaiian kona beans. After a sip, he let the nutty, woody flavor linger on his tongue before swallowing.

"Do you intend to visit Cochran in the hospital?" Ivanovich asked. He had slept on the guest bed in the room beyond the office again. Both men seemed to know they were in this together until it was finished, one way or another.

"It was too late to go up there last night," Hannibal said, "but yeah, I'll go talk to him today when I'm sure he's awake."

"You do realize that Gana did this."

Hannibal sighed and looked up from the photos. "Yes, Aleksandr, that is my current theory. I think Gana must have caught Cochran spying on him and beat his face in. Then he probably loaded the man into his own trunk, bound and gagged, and drove the car over to that side street. He probably knew that if it sat there for any length of time, unlocked, someone would steal it. They did. But it didn't go to a chop shop as he likely expected. Some joy-riding kid took the car, smacked it into a tree, and left it there. Cochran was lucky they found him back there."

"Is there no evidence of all this?"

"Only my stupid eyes." When Ivanovich gave him a quizzical look, Hannibal said, "When I went to the house, I heard the girl scream and rushed in. I saw Gana with blood on one hand, and there was blood on the back doorsill. I figure he had just returned."

"And Viktoriya screamed when she saw him with blood on his hand," Ivanovich said, finishing the thought. "You were so close but could not know."

"Yeah, just like with this," Hannibal said, turning back to the pictures. Ivanovich nodded, pushed the visitor's chair over by the big front windows, and sat with his coffee. A minute of silence passed before Ivanovich spoke again.

"You know my people were watching your woman very closely."

"Yes," Hannibal said, not wanting to explore that subject.

"They saw you watching her that day."

"I had to see her, Aleksandr," Hannibal said. "I know you understand that."

"Yes, I do. Who is the man?"

"What man?" Hannibal asked, trying to keep his focus on the pictures.

"The man she went into that house with. You saw him."

"Oh. He's nobody. Just the real estate agent."

"Really?" Ivanovich asked, sipping his coffee and crossing his legs. "I didn't think real estate agents took their clients to dinner."

"Look, that's just a courtesy." Hannibal's head snapped up toward Ivanovich, his eyes blazing. "I'm telling you there's nothing between them. He's just the hired help." He opened his mouth to say more but other thoughts arrested his attention. He turned back to the photos and slapped his palm down on the table.

"Of course," he said, almost shouting. "They all but told me when I was there. Sit tight, Aleksandr. I've got to run to the Russia House. It turns out you were right all along. Dani Gana is nowhere near who he says he is."

* * * * *

The same man answered the door when Hannibal arrived this time, so getting into the Russia House was no problem. He was surprised to learn that this fellow was called Billy. Before Hannibal could ask, Billy told him that the Sidorovs were not there, and were not expected that day. Yes, Billy had heard about poor Mrs. Petrova and no, no one could believe anyone would want to hurt her. When Hannibal asked to speak to the manager, Billy showed him to a small office that was a good deal more austere than the rest of the establishment. A wide man with bulging forearms growing out of his rolled up sleeves walked around his desk to shake Hannibal's hand. His jovial, ruddy face was topped with a thatch of hair that had the texture and color of straw.

"I appreciate you taking the time to speak to me Mr..."

"Call me Mike," the manager said with the slight trace of an accent. "Everyone else does. And any friend of Dr. Sidorov is always an honored guest here."

Mike sat at his oaken desk with the Tiffany lamp at one side and poured two glasses of a brand of vodka Hannibal didn't recognize. The label said Turi.

"This is Estonian," Mike said. "Exceptional clarity and smoothness. Good for the mornings."

For the mornings? Hannibal thought. They drink it like coffee. When he pulled out the photo, he saw surprise in Mike's eyes.

"I've been looking for one of the men in this picture, and I realized this morning that I've been going about it all wrong. The clue has been staring me in the face ever since I came here yesterday. Your man thought I should go to the back entrance."

"I am so very sorry for that," Mike said. "He was ignorant and that is not how we are here. I can have him disciplined."

"No, no," Hannibal said, raising a palm. "I didn't say that to complain. It just made me aware that you don't get too many guests here who are, well, people of color. Do you?"

"Our clientele is mostly Russian nationals and Eastern European immigrants," Mike said, looking nervous. "We do not discourage any type of person from eating and drinking here. Some just don't come."

"That's the thing about this guy," Hannibal said, laying the photo on Mike's desk and pointing to Gana. "He's not a guest, is he?"

"Gary? No. He was tending bar that night." He looked up and then back down. "It is true that the help are often, as you say, people of color."

Hannibal brushed Mike's defensive remarks away with a wave of his hand. "Gary?"

"Well, Gartee was his actual name," Mike said. "We often give our people nicknames that are more American."

"Like Billy—and Mike."

"Yes, just so," Mike said with a grin.

"Funny," Hannibal said. "I know this fellow as Dani."

"Danny?" Mike sat back in his chair and slid thumbs under his suspenders. "I don't remember anyone calling him that. Only Gary. And I know that Gartee is his real name because I hired him myself."

"You seem to be the man I should have been talking to all along," Hannibal said. "Do you know the other people in the photo? This woman, for instance?"

Mike sat back again, this time with his big arms crossed. "Sir, I always try to be helpful, but I do need to know what is your interest in our clients."

Clearly, questions about the hired help were not an issue, but the paying customers were different. Hannibal looked back at the door, then turned to face Mike and pushed his glasses up tighter on his face.

"Tell me, Mike, do you know Aleksandr Ivanovich?"

Mike's voice lowered. "I know of him."

"Well, he is the one who has asked me to look into this matter," Hannibal said. "He hoped I could take care of this inquiry for him but if it proves necessary, he can come and talk to you himself. Would you prefer that?"

Mike licked his lips, his eyes darting from side to side. His face looked pale in the soft light of the Tiffany lamp. When he spoke, his words were soft. "I don't think that it will be necessary for him to trouble himself. You and I, we can take care of this."

"I thought so," Hannibal said with a broad smile. "Now this woman. I know her as Mrs. Ben Cochran."

"That's right," Mike said. "Although at the time this was taken she was living with this man, Boris Tolstaya."

"I see," Hannibal said. Mike's eyes were wide, as if he was eager to answer another question. Hannibal thought he should not leave him feeling unfulfilled. "Looking at this photo, one could get the idea that this Tolstaya was the ring leader. Did he gather these people together? The Sidorovs, the Petrovas?"

Mike swallowed. "I can't really say who the leader of the ring was. I do know that it was Dr. Sidorov who brought Mr. Petrova and Mr. Tolstaya to the club."

"So this was Yakov's posse?" Hannibal asked. Mike looked confused, but the question was rhetorical. "Yeah, but you brought Dani Gana, aka Gartee, to the party. You say you hired him to work here?"

"I like to give students a chance," Mike said with an emphatic nod. "He was one of the Howard University students who waited tables and tended bar."

"When did he leave and where did he go?"

"I don't know where he went," Mike said, picking up his glass and swallowing half its contents. "I really don't. But I know when he left. We were talking about it today after we heard the awful news about Mrs. Petrova."

"Not sure I see the connection," Hannibal said.

Mike downed the last of his vodka and stared into Hannibal's eyes. "It was almost spooky. I mean, Nikita Petrova dies. Gary resigns the next day. The day after that, Mr. Tolstaya leaves the city, never to return. Three years later, you come in, asking about the Tolstayas. The same day, Mrs. Petrova dies. And now, the next day, you return, asking about Gary."

"Yeah," Hannibal said, looking back down at the photo. "Spooky."

* * * * *

Howard University sits like a modest houseguest at the northern edge of LeDroit Park, one neighborhood in the District that gives visitors the feeling of stepping into an earlier era of the city's development. When he lived in New York, Hannibal heard all about Harlem and its renaissance. But when he moved to Washington, he learned that this little neighborhood was the real center of African American intellectual and cultural life until about 1950. This was where black doctors, lawyers, professors and businessmen lived. Many of them taught at Howard. Fifty years later, the area had a bit of a split personality. Parts were badly run down, but younger people who could appreciate the area's heritage and distinct architecture were moving in to try to revitalize it.

Howard itself was exactly what Hannibal thought a college campus should be. Huge brick, colonial looking buildings and well-treed walking paths gave him the feel of Philadelphia in 1776. Ten steps past the main gate, Washington, DC, disappeared from sight. In the middle of the city, this little settlement was a complete escape from urban life. Hannibal shook his head, thinking of how much he would have loved this higher learning experience rather than the combination of correspondence courses and nights at City College that brought him his degree. For now, he would just hope it was the place where he could confirm who Dani Gana really was and where he was from.

He was very pleased and only a little surprised to find the registrar's office open on the weekend. He doubted it was really necessary, but he knew they made up jobs to find excuses to pay students who needed financial aid. It was obvious that the young woman in charge of the office that day was a student. Her round, dark face wore a bright smile and big, inquisitive eyes. She had pulled her hair back and wrapped it with a rubber band, where it puffed out into a soft, fuzzy ball. She asked, in exacting English, if she could help him.

"Yes, ma'am. I'm trying to find one of your alumni, a man named Gartee Roberts. Do you have any record of where he may have gone?"

"I'm sorry, sir. We sometimes have forwarding addresses, but we don't make them available to the public." Her smile never wavered.

"Look, I'm a detective," Hannibal said, displaying his identification. "I'm trying to track this man down to make sure he gets what's coming to him as a result of the recent death of an older relative."

"I understand, sir," the girl said with unrelenting pleasantness. "I wish I could help."

Hannibal nodded. "Is there a rule about telling me where he was from? Or his last known address while he was a student? That would at least help me to verify that I'm looking for the right young man."

He matched her smile for smile and after a few seconds, she turned to her computer and started tapping on the keyboard. Hannibal stood by making a show of patience. The girl seemed to get lost in the monitor and he feared for a moment that she had forgotten him and was playing a video game. Then he saw her face pull back in surprise.

"Sir, when you say, where he came from, do you mean originally, or..."

"Both." When it was offered, he would take all the information available.

"Well, originally, he was from Liberia City, Liberia," she said. "But he came here from UVA." Not just a different name, but a different country of origin as well. And he had studied at the University of Virginia before moving to Washington. Hannibal was considering the significance of that fact when the girl made a hmph sound, that sort of surprised sound that people make when they want to tell you something but know you probably wouldn't care. Of course, Hannibal did.

"What's that?" he asked, leaning over the counter to see the screen.

"Oh, I was just thinking how predictable some people are," she said.

Scanning the screen, Hannibal's eyes hit a familiar name. "There, on his schedule. Krada. Is that professor Jamal Krada?"

"You know Dr. Krada?" she asked. "I was laughing because he's from Africa and he gets all the African students. Myself, I want to learn America, so I try to get all the American instructors."

"You know, I think you've got the right idea, young lady," Hannibal said. "In fact, I think I'll go talk to Dr. Krada right now. I'd like to know just how close he gets to his African students."

-20-

Hannibal was peeling down Sixth Street to duck under a yellow light when she answered the phone.

"Hello, Mrs. Krada. It's Hannibal Jones. Is your husband home this afternoon?"

"Yes," she said, in the tone she might use if she wasn't sure what the right answer might be. "Hold on and I'll go get him."

"No need," Hannibal hastened to say. "I'm kind of in the neighborhood and I wanted to thank him in person for his help. Please tell him I'll be there in a few minutes."

"I...all right."

"Thanks," Hannibal said. "I look forward to seeing you again."

"Oh. Um. Yes. Good-bye."

Hannibal was just wondering if there was a school to learn how to train your woman that well when his phone rang.

"Hey, honey," Cindy said. The cheerful wave she sent through the phone was riding on a tide of weariness.

How you doing, babe?" Hannibal asked. His anger at Krada evaporated for the moment. "And how goes the hunt for the million-dollar dream house?"

"The hunt is kicking my little Latin ass, sugar," she said. Hannibal heard a pencil scratching on a pad. "I've fallen so far behind at work that I'll be here in the office all day and most of the night just trying to catch up."

"Jesus, on a Sunday, babe?"

"Just wanted you to know," Cindy said.

"It's sweet of you to let me know, babe. I'm still working that same case, so no worries."

"All right," Cindy said. He could tell she was multitasking, and let a couple of seconds of dead air pass. "And I won't be looking at any more houses for a day or two. But I still haven't seen my dream house. We'll sit down tomorrow night and go over a few more prospects on paper to see what's worth going to see." She said it almost as an afterthought, as if meeting another man at night was not really worth mentioning. Hannibal felt his anger welling up behind its fragile wall again.

"Yeah. Well, listen, let me go ahead and get back to work," he said. "Maybe I can wrap this up before tomorrow night. Maybe I can join you."

"Oh." He swerved around a slow pedestrian, hearing the writing stop for a moment. "I guess. I didn't think you were interested in the house thing, but if you want to."

"I'm here, babe," Hannibal said as he pulled into the Krada driveway next to a navy blue Lexus. "Let's just see what happens."

Hannibal got out of his Volvo and looked over the roof at Krada's car. If Krada drove a Lexus LS, he wondered what his wife drove. As low as his expectations were, peering into the garage doors still disappointed him. The two-car garage was empty. Nina Krada was certainly home, so it appeared that she didn't have a car at all.

The front door flew open and Jamal Krada came flying out toting a briefcase and wearing a frown. He was halfway to his car before he realized that Hannibal was already there. With one hand on the car door handle, he faced Hannibal while his face tested a number of expressions, as if he was trying to decide on his reaction.

"Dr. Krada," Hannibal said, striding toward him, "I'm glad I caught you. I wanted to ask you about a man I'm looking for. He may be using an assumed name, but I have a photograph."

"Look, I am a very busy man," Krada said, yanking his door open. "My wife was wrong to tell you I was available. I need to get to the university right now." He sat in his leather seat and slid his key into the ignition. Hannibal reached into his jacket to retrieve the photograph while his right hand gripped the top of the car door, preventing it from closing.

"Yeah, yeah, busy. That Sunday afternoon class you've just got to get to. Right. But for now you can just confirm that you know this man I'm looking for. He goes by Dani Gana now, but you might have known him as Gartee Roberts."

Hannibal held the photo at Krada's eye level. After one hard but unsuccessful yank on the door, Krada looked at the picture. His eyes went up to Hannibal's, and returned to the photo, before he sat back in his seat, facing his windshield.

"Yes, I know the man. He was a student of mine here. That must have been three or four years ago. I have no idea where he is now."

"What about the rest of this crew?"

"I've never seen any of the others before in my life," Krada said. "May I go now?"

Hannibal released the door and Krada slammed it shut. He started the car, slammed it into gear, and pulled back out of the driveway. In seconds he was gone. Hannibal wondered if Krada was being evasive or just plain lying. If he was in contact with Gana, he could be part of the cover-up.

While Hannibal stood beside his car, Nina Krada opened the door and took a tentative step outside. Her eyes scanned the world, looking for evidence that her jailer was returning. She stepped down the three front steps on bare feet, moving as if she was sneaking out. She walked toward Hannibal even though her eyes never touched him. She stopped beside him, pressing her upper arm against his, as if for warmth. She looked at the photo in Hannibal's hand and grimaced, then raised a hand and touched one face with a fingertip.

"Her."

Hannibal looked at her nervous eyes. "You know this woman? You've met Viktoriya Petrova?"

Nina nodded. Hannibal waited for her to talk.

"He has these parties," she said, staring into Hannibal's collarbone. "He invites all his students. Many of them are also African. I have to serve them. They are children, but I have to serve them."

He could feel her resentment. She must have felt that she had to serve them like a servant girl in her master's house. He could imagine Krada showing off his importance to these young students while his wife brought them snacks and drinks and cleaned up after them. At that moment, Hannibal wished that Jamal Krada had killed someone, so he would have an excuse to beat the man's face in.

"Nina, are you saying this girl attended your husband's parties?"

"Yes," she said. "He wanted her." Her finger stabbed Gana's face.

"So they were schoolmates," Hannibal said. "Thank you, Nina." She smiled at him and, on an impulse, he kissed her very softly on the cheek. She beamed back at him the way a dog does when you pat its head. Hannibal got back into his car. She watched as he backed out of the driveway.

-21-

Like Hannibal's building, the old brownstone had once been someone's home. Now it was divided into a number of apartments that college students shared. As he parked across the street from Dani Gana's address during his college days, Hannibal thought that luck was with him at last. An older black man sat on the stoop with his feet two steps down, watching everything in his little slice of the world. His hair was now a gray laurel wreath that reached three quarters of the way around his head, leaving the front open. His top front teeth were gone.

This was almost certain to be the man Hannibal wanted to see. He crossed the street, walked up the steps just high enough to put one foot on the stoop, and offered the older man his hand.

"How you doing, brother? My name's Hannibal and I'm betting you're the owner of this place."

The return shake was firm and energetic. "What's up, there? No, I don't own the place, I'm the super. Folks call me Junior."

"The superintendent? Even better, man. I needed the man who runs things."

"You with the insurance?" Junior asked.

"Me?" Hannibal chuckled. "Oh, hell no. I just need some help. A guy who used to live here might be in some real trouble. I figure you're in and out of the building whenever anything breaks down, so you have to know what's going on in there on a day to day basis. Am I right?"

"Well, I can probably tell you a little about every young man who's lived here in the last ten years." Junior shuffled over a few inches on the stoop.

"I kind of figured you could," Hannibal said, sitting on the stoop beside Junior. "I think if you see this guy you'll know him right away. I think his name's Roberts."

Junior accepted the picture that Hannibal had begun to think of as the class photo. He could see Junior's mind working behind his clouded yet perceptive eyes, taking in the faces and backing down their ages.

"Yep, that's him all right," Junior said with a smile. "Had a wild ass first name. Yeah, Gar-tee."

"Yep, that's the guy," Hannibal said. "You act like you might have known him."

"Oh, yeah." Junior laughed. "I usually get to know the boys." A student burst through the door behind them. Junior and Hannibal shuffled to opposite sides to let him pass. "That there is Sonny Woods. Plays baseball, studies archeology."

"Really?" Hannibal said, leaning his arms on his knees. "And what was young Mr. Roberts into?"

"Him? His thing was history," Junior said, smiling his open smile. Hannibal caught the tang of cheap wine on his breath. "Crazy about history, that boy. And what a talker. Jesus."

Hannibal laughed along. "What did he talk about?"

"Wild, crazy stories," Junior said, shaking his head at something he must have heard years ago. "He was a runaway, you know. Spies were chasing him, from his real home, back in Liberia he said. Like, how would a guy from Liberia have a name like Roberts, right?"

Hannibal shook his head, wanting Junior to continue. The super didn't know Liberia's history, that the African nation was founded by free blacks from America in the mid-1800s. But Roberts was a history major, so he would know that history well. It seemed the odds were about even that he really was from Liberia, but Hannibal could see how that might be the lie and Algeria the reality. Right then, it didn't seem to matter much. Either way he was a liar, and there were more pressing questions to ask.

"I guess he talked a lot about where he was from," Hannibal said. "Did he say anything about where he was going?"

"Not a word." Junior leaned to one side and took his chin in his hand. "You know, he left in a hurry, all in one day, smack in the middle of the term. Maybe somebody was after him after all."

"So he left suddenly," Hannibal said, staring forward trying to see Gana's future path.

"Uh huh. In fact, I think it was them two helped him pack. I'm thinking they drove him away too."

Hannibal's head snapped around to share Junior's view of the photo. The cracked nail of Junior's index finger indicated the central couple.

"These two?" Hannibal asked. "You sure, Junior?"

"Brother, you don't forget a woman with a body like that one," Junior said, grinning again. "And the man's name stuck in my mind. Boris, just like the little guy in *Rocky and Bullwinkle*. Kind of looked like him too, only taller of course."

So they go back to his college days, Hannibal said to himself. Then to Junior, "You sounded surprised that he left."

"Oh, yeah," Junior said. "I'm surprised he left the girl behind. He was crazy about this broad, Vicky. He always said he was going to go off, get rich, and come back and marry that girl. So I guess he's out making his fortune somewhere, huh?"

"Maybe," Hannibal said. "And I just might know somebody who knows where the fortune was supposed to come from. The more I hear, the more I want to find Gartee Roberts."

"Well, when you do, say hello for me," Junior said.

* * * * *

The short drive to Georgetown University Hospital gave Hannibal just enough time to think about what he wanted to say to Ben Cochran. A brief telephone call confirmed that Cochran was awake and able to receive visitors. Hannibal hoped that Cochran was getting plenty of pain medication, but then cursed himself for the thought. He didn't really want the man to be injured and in pain just so he would be easier to question. Besides, after having his head handed to him by Gana, he might be more than willing to share the truth even about personal matters like how he ended up with Boris Tolstaya's woman.

Hannibal had spent too much time in hospitals to suit him, almost always visiting someone who did not deserve to be there. Hospitals always seemed too bright to him, as if someone thought the light would kill germs. Or maybe it was just all that white. Walking down the sterile halls he knew he would never get accustomed to the smell. Why, in the high-tech twenty-first century, did hospitals still have to smell like alcohol. Did they even use alcohol anymore? Maybe the odor was all in his head.

At Cochran's door Hannibal took a moment to remember him as he had seen him last: vital, alive, and frightened. Then he walked into the room. There were two beds, and Cochran's was nearest the door. His watery brown eyes wandered to Hannibal and one eyebrow lifted toward the bandage on his forehead. His sandy brown hair was a loose mop scattered around the pillow. His nose was swollen the way noses are when they've been broken and reset. The purple around his left eye and split lips told Hannibal that he had been worked over by an amateur driven by anger, someone not well versed in the science of hurting. Hannibal rested a hand on Cochran's arm, careful not to disturb the tube running into it.

"Hey, man. What happened to you?" Hannibal asked.

"Walked into a door." The right corner of Cochran's mouth tried to support a smile. Hannibal didn't credit him much for brains, but he had to admit the man had more heart than expected.

"How?" Cochran asked. It took Hannibal a second to guess the full question.

"How'd I find you? Gana disappeared and I hoped you could help me find him. Didn't see you around anywhere, so I reported your car stolen. Cops found it, and you." Cochran nodded his thanks. Then his eyes focused past Hannibal. He tried to pull them back but it was too late.

Hannibal spun around and almost bumped into Queenie Cochran.

-22-

"It's hard to see you as a Renata," Hannibal said. He settled into the cafeteria booth with the two cups of coffee.

"I'm as American as you are," Queenie said, cupping her hands around her cup. "I grew up right here in the District. It's not my fault my mother gave me that Old Country name."

"And you ran as far from your culture as you could, didn't you?" Hannibal looked at the cowboy boots and blouse, tight jeans and bottle-red hair, searching for the Eurasian features he knew they must hide. "But you couldn't run far enough away to keep from marrying a Russian man, could you?"

"Ben?" Queenie sipped her coffee. "Ben's Polish. And thank you, by the way, for helping him. I heard what you said in the room just before I walked in. If you hadn't been looking for him, he might be dead right now. Do you know what happened to him?"

"Sure I do." Hannibal leaned in, tired of being nice to this woman who seemed obsessed with deception. "Dani Gana caught him snooping one too many times and beat the crap out of him. His blood was all over Gana's hands afterward. I saw it on Gana's backdoor sill after he got home. He had to wrap his right hand, and after seeing Ben's face I can see why. So whatever you wanted to trade Gana's picture for, that's what cost Ben that ass whipping. And I didn't mean Ben anyway when I said a Russian man. I was talking about Boris Tolstaya."

Queenie blanched and her lower lip started to quiver. Hannibal just figured this to be her second line of defense.

134

"Boris was Mother's choice," she said, her voice so low it was almost lost in the babble of other diners around her. Hannibal was suddenly aware of how crowded and how noisy the hospital cafeteria had become.

"Why Boris?"

"Why?" she asked. "He was an important man in the Russian community. He had lots of money and was very old school. And he was a constant gambler. You know, that was fun for a while."

The coffee was hot but weak and rough. Hannibal drank it to give his hands something to do. "So, Boris was Mother's pick. He was a player, a gambler, rich, influential, and fun. Ben Cochran appears to be broke, and kind of weak. How does a fellow like Ben win you over from a man like Boris Tolstaya?"

"With a straight flush," Queenie said, pulling out a cigarette.

"What?"

"Boris bet me in a poker game." Her face clouded up, but she regained control while searching herself for a match. "He always treated me like an object, and I took it, you know, because of everything else. But that night, that was too much even for me."

"You can't smoke that in here," Hannibal said, taking Queenie's arm. "Let's go outside for a few minutes."

She looked a bit unsteady so Hannibal took her arm and walked her out of the cafeteria. The cigarette between her fingers seemed to give her strength, even unlit. Hannibal didn't think the past could shock her any more.

"Would I be right if I said that Boris made his money from involvement with the mob?"

"The mob?" Queenie asked. "I'm not sure I know what you mean by that term. Boris was half-owner of a brokerage firm. He handled investments for a lot of prominent people. I know he didn't ask a lot about the investors. I know that he skimmed money from their investments and never paid taxes on it. Does that make him a mobster?"

"That depends," Hannibal said, holding the door for her. "If he takes money from criminals and makes it legitimate for a fee then yes, I'd say it does. If he just swindles ignorant investors, he might just be a plain old crook."

They walked west, and Queenie squinted into the afternoon sun as she smoked her cigarette. Hannibal let her mind and emotions rest for a while. As a kick boxer, he understood fatigue and figured he'd give her three minutes between rounds. Reservoir Road took them into Glover Archibald Park, replacing the modest row houses with greenery. It was quieter, but Queenie didn't seem to notice the change of scenery.

"So, why are you trying to photograph Dani Gana? Or rather, why did you send poor Ben to do it?"

"Ben and Dani are the only two men who ever beat Boris," she said. "Ben beat him fair and square and won me. Dani took his money. I'm not sure which hurt him worse."

Hannibal thought he knew, but it wasn't the answer she wanted. "How did Dani get his money? He wasn't a player. He was a waiter."

"Boris had a huge ego," Queenie said, chuckling. "Dani knew how to play on that ego. His real name is Gartee Roberts, you know. He knew how to spot a mark and rope him in. He got investors for Boris. Later, he started handling some of the funds. He seemed to be able to get money in and out of the country. Maybe that's just 'cause he's from someplace else."

"I can guess the next step," Hannibal said. "Dani started skimming from the funds Boris was skimming, right?"

Queenie stopped, and Hannibal missed the click of her boot heels on the path. "By the time Boris missed the funds, Roberts had somehow sucked a couple million dollars out of the accounts. You should have seen Boris's face when he figured it out. God, he was furious."

"You were with both of them for a while, weren't you?" Hannibal asked. Again Queenie went pale, which surprised Hannibal. She must have thought no one would guess.

"I got used to being treated with respect."

"But you were also used to the money," Hannibal said. She started walking again and he followed. "You knew the money was gone and you knew who had it. You figured if Ben could get a slice of it that that would be your ticket to freedom from Boris."

Queenie stepped away from the path out into a small patch of open grass. Dogs seemed to be everywhere, unleashed and maybe unwanted, yipping at each other but she ignored them. When she turned to Hannibal, her eyes were lowered in what she must have thought was a seductive expression.

"It was pure luck that I found out that Roberts was back in town, now calling himself Dani Gana. I figured if we had a picture of him we could threaten to send it to Boris, who would surely kill him if he knew where he was. Then, we could force him to give us half of the money he stole from Boris." Her eyes went down, then back up to Hannibal's. "It is still a good plan. Ben is sneaky, but he's not strong enough to confront Dani Gana. You are a stronger man. When Ben recovers, he can find Gana again for us. And maybe, for half a million dollars..." Her right hand lightly touched Hannibal's sleeve.

-23-

Hannibal spent only a minute or so considering how half a million dollars might impact his relationship with Cindy. He could pick up the check wherever they went. He could fly her to the Bahamas for a couple of weeks. He could pay for half of her dream house.

Then he raised his right hand and got a very gentle grip on Queenie's right hand, moving it down and away from his arm.

"And if Gana said no?" Hannibal asked, staring down into her eyes. "Would you then take the photo to Boris? Would you sentence Gana to death?"

"He is a thief. And Boris Tolstaya is still my husband."

"Uh huh." Her self-righteousness was as thin as the wisps of smoke rising from her cigarette, which was also almost burned out. "And feeding him Gana would put you back in his good graces, wouldn't it? I get a feeling old Ben would be left in the dust if things went that way."

"Don't say that."

"Why not?" Hannibal asked. "It's the truth, isn't it? You saw a two-way bet and you took it."

Queenie took a step back and looked at Hannibal as if for the first time. He could see her reevaluating, rejecting her original judgment of him, and deciding just what kind of sucker he really was. When she shook her head, he wondered how accurate her new evaluation was.

"If you help us, I will never have to face that option," she said. "And I will commit to staying with Ben. He's the man who loves me, after all."

"That's big of you," Hannibal said, turning back toward the hospital.

"Besides, there is the matter of the million dollars we could split."

"I don't want your money," Hannibal said, in part to convince himself, "but I sure want to get to Gana and Viktoriya before your ex does. If he is mob connected, they'll never make it out of the area on a plane or train or bus. Gana's car is in the shop so he'd have to rent one to drive. The Russian mafia would have an eye on them too. So they're probably still in town."

"He has no friends, no contacts," Queenie said, trailing along. "They would go to her mother for help."

"Didn't you hear?" They stopped when Hannibal realized they were back at the hospital entrance. "Her mother's been killed. Probably by Boris's boys getting close to the trail."

"Then there is no one left they can trust," Queenie said, dropping her cigarette and grinding it into the sidewalk.

"Maybe for him," Hannibal said. "There might be one person left she can rely on, and I'd better find him fast." He turned toward the parking lot.

"Wait," Queenie called. "What can I do?"

"You need to get up to that hospital room," Hannibal said over his shoulder. "There's a man up there who needs you."

* * * * *

Hannibal imagined that on a Friday or Saturday night, with the acid jazz booming, the Russia House lounge would be a virtual clubhouse for Washington's Russian and Eastern European community. But on Sunday, just after the official opening at five pm, it was just a good place to sip vodka and soak up the atmosphere.

As soon as Hannibal walked in, the bartender pointed him to the far end of the bar. He slipped past the collection of patrons, most looking too grim to be having a good time, and slid onto the empty stool beside Yakov Sidorov.

Yakov raised his bushy eyebrows, but his surprise soon faded. He nodded and turned back to his drink. Hannibal signaled the bartender, careful not to smile any more than any of the other somber drinkers.

"Jewel of Russia," he said, in a tone that said it was his usual brand. He faced forward while waiting for his drink. When it arrived, he sipped just a little of his vodka and nodded at the glass. Yakov slid a plate across the bar to the space just to the side of Hannibal's glass. The platter held a pile of small dumplings. Hannibal nodded his thanks and picked one up. A bite told him they were stuffed with potatoes and onions and a meat that was not quite chicken. He looked at Yakov.

"Smoked duck," Yakov said. "These are the best pierogi in the Western Hemisphere." Then Yakov got one for himself and dipped it in the cream in a nearby bowl. Hannibal tried it and found the sauce quite spicy. This beat the hell out of bar peanuts.

"You've heard about Raisa," he said when his mouth was empty. It was not a question. Yakov nodded.

"A tragic loss," Hannibal said, "and I don't even know if her daughter has been notified. Where is Viktoriya?"

"With Gartee Roberts," Yakov said just before draining his glass.

"Where have they gone?"

Yakov shrugged his shoulders and picked up another pierogi.

"I thought if her mother didn't answer the phone she might call on you."

"I wish it were so," Yakov said. He waited just long enough for the bartender to fill his glass before snatching it up and drinking down half the contents. "The girl is like a daughter to me. But she does not realize what she has gotten into by marrying this man."

"You were against the marriage?"

Yakov nodded. "I tried several times to convince Raisa to forbid their union."

Hannibal emptied his glass. He hadn't noticed the slight sweetness in the Russian vodka before. Things are so often different the second time you consider them. Yakov was not part of Gana's support system as the old photographs implied. Other connections now became possibilities. What if Gana wasn't paying for the girl at all? What if Viktoriya was insurance against revenge from someone close? Or taking care of her could be payback for something else. When he turned to Yakov, Hannibal spoke very softly.

"You broke with Gartee Roberts because he is somehow connected to Nikita Petrova's murder."

"He and Boris Tolstaya," Yakov said. His dour face looked close to tears. "I am the reason they all met. I introduced Boris to Nikita. It seemed natural since they both had health issues from the war. But yes, now I am sure that he and Roberts had something to do with Nikita's death."

When Hannibal turned to the bar, his glass was full again. He took another sip of vodka. "Raisa must have known. Why else would she accept payoff money from Roberts? Gana. Whatever."

"Roberts?" Yakov stopped, his glass held halfway to his mouth. "No, Raisa would never have accepted money from him."

"Sorry, Yakov, but your friend Nikita didn't leave much behind when he died. How do you think Raisa has been taking care of herself?" The room noise was getting louder. To Hannibal it was more like white noise than usual because most of it was in a language he didn't understand. Yakov Sidorov leaned close as if he feared someone might overhear them even in that noisy setting.

"Raisa Petrova was blackmailing Boris Tolstaya." He shook his head with grim finality. "She found out somehow, and she knew that Boris was the evil one. When he left town right after Nikita's death he took Roberts with him, but I don't think he wanted to go."

"Yes," Hannibal said, turning his head to look very closely into Yakov's reddened eyes. "He was evil, and you are the man who brought him in here and introduced him to Nikita in the first place."

Yakov finally downed his drink, but Hannibal suspected that his body and mind were already numb. Maybe that was his objective. He stared at his glass.

"Boris Tolstaya was a powerful, dangerous man," Yakov told his empty glass. "I invested with him and did very well. Then I gambled with him. I lost. A lot. This, you see, was his way to gain control of people. And this was the leverage he used to force me to bring him here, to introduce him and Renata to certain people who were influential in the local Russian community. People like Nikita Petrova."

"Come on, Yakov," Hannibal said, brushing Yakov's shoulder with the back of his fingertips. "You knew Tolstaya was a snake, yet you introduced him to Nikita. I could understand steering strangers to him, but how could you do that to your good friend?

The room was filling up, and a few strangers stared at Hannibal after his outburst. Yakov lowered his voice and leaned in closer. "After Nikita betrayed me, it was easy."

"Betrayed you?"

"With Anastasiya." It was almost a whisper, which Yakov chased back down his throat with more vodka.

Hannibal returned his gaze to the bottles behind the bar to give Yakov some privacy, to let his grief and his guilt fight it out in peace. He had brought the Tolstayas into the picture, but he didn't seem to have anything to do with Gartee Roberts. Tolstaya must have met the name-changing waiter in the club and seen something there he could use. Or maybe Roberts saw something he could use.

It appeared that Anastasiya's suspicions were just her projecting her own weakness onto her husband. The more likely truth was that he tried to look after Nikita's surviving wife and daughter out of guilt because, one way or another, introducing Tolstaya to Nikita had led to Nikita's death. And now he had failed to protect poor Raisa. Now he, like

Hannibal, was worried that Viktoriya would be lost as well, but where was she?

Beside him, Yakov Sidorov jumped as if he had received an electric shock. When he began fishing in his jacket pockets Hannibal realized he must have a cell phone set on vibrate. Yakov fished the phone out, glanced at the screen display, and then pressed it against his ear. He mumbled softly into it, but ended the conversation with, "Of course, child, as soon as possible."

Hannibal could only imagine one person he might call "child" and faced Yakov with an expectant stare. The older man didn't hesitate.

"It was Viktoriya. She needs help right away."

"Is she OK?"

"For now, yes. But Dani Gana has been shot."

-24-

Ten minutes later, Hannibal was merging onto Route 50 East. The good news was that once he crossed into Maryland he knew that even the higher speed limit, sixty-five miles per hour, was just a suggestion and the high occupancy vehicle left lane was in effect 24/7. With Yakov sitting beside him, the Black Beauty was now an HOV. The bad news was that Viktoriya had called from a hundred and twenty-five miles away.

"Why Rehoboth Beach, for God's sake?" Hannibal asked.

"When she was younger, her parents would take her there in the summer," Yakov said, clutching the seat as Hannibal pressed the Volvo up past eighty-five. "They vacationed at Rehoboth because Ocean City is too crowded. Are you familiar with the little town?"

"As it happens, I am," Hannibal said. "Rehoboth beach is the biggest of Delaware's Atlantic resorts, part of a continuous line of seashore tourist areas, like Dewey Beach and Bethany Beach. They each kind of have their own personality. The Coffee Mill is in Rehoboth. That's the little shop I order my custom ground coffee from. Without the summer beach traffic in my way, I can make it there in just about two hours."

"Fine. As long as we get there alive."

The wide, level road took them to MD 404, which turned into DE 404 as they crossed the state line. While the sun inched lower in the western sky, Yakov Sidorov talked about his youth in Mother Russia, his brief meeting with Nikita Petrova in Afghanistan, and his journey to the United States to make his fortune. His patients were almost all Eastern Europeans who paid in cash. He asked no questions except those related to their health and for their part they never argued about his rates or threatened to sue him for malpractice.

The sun was just thinking about surrendering to the night as Hannibal cruised down the wide Main Street, lined with most of Rehoboth Beach's two hundred shops, twenty or so hotels, and about as many bed and breakfasts. He circled the big gazebo at the beach end, still not finding a parking space. When they did find a meter without a car in front of it, they were three blocks from the ocean.

Viktoriya had asked Yakov to meet her on the wooden boardwalk, a mile or so of eateries, games, hotels, and eclectic shops. Beyond the railings the umbrellas on the white powder sand beach were disappearing one by one, and lights winked on in front of shops as the night life was about to kick off.

"I see why so many vacation here," Yakov said as they walked past colorful storefronts and restaurant tables on front porches. "The town is charming, with a certain artistic appeal."

"Yes," Hannibal said. "Quiet, clean and safe. Although maybe not so safe for everyone."

Sharp salt air wafted in with the tide on a persistent breeze. The two men walked slowly, staring into the alcove entrances of the minigolf courses and arcades.

"Viktoriya should be easy to spot here," Yakov said. "The style here seems to strongly favor short hair on women."

Hannibal smiled. "Yeah, well you might not know that Rehoboth Beach is also becoming one of the mid-Atlantic's most popular gay and lesbian getaways. Think of it as South Beach, north."

Yakov opened his mouth to respond but Hannibal stopped him with an elbow in the ribs. He pointed toward a food counter where Viktoriya stood with both hands wrapped around a container of boardwalk fries. She was balanced on heels with tiny straps circling her ankles. The shoes were wrong for the beach, and the satin shorts and camisole impled she had left someplace in a hurry. Her shiny black tresses whipped in the breeze, waving them in. Her mouth dropped open as they approached. When they were within reach, she hugged the older man, but her wary eyes never left Hannibal. The embrace was strong, but brief.

"How do you know Uncle Yakov?" she asked.

"I thought he could tell me a bit more about your husband," Hannibal said. "We were talking when your call came in."

"We need to see him," Yakov said. "If Dani is wounded, he will need immediate attention."

She drew back into the corner of the counter. "Dani's gone and I don't know where."

"What do you mean gone?" Hannibal asked. "Is he alive?"

"He was when I saw him last."

Hannibal nodded, and turned to Yakov. "We obviously have much to discuss. We need to go sit down someplace and have the girl bring us up to date. And I know just the place.

* * * * *

Rehoboth Mews was not much more than an alley a couple of blocks from the boardwalk. It was a narrow walking path from Main Street to the next street perpendicular to the ocean and held five or six small shops. Hannibal had an account at one of them, The Coffee Mill. He didn't visit often, but the manager recognized his name from the monthly shipments.

"Hannibal Jones," she said, barely tall enough to see over the counter. "It's always a pleasure filling your orders. Rather a surprise to see you at this time of year."

"Maybe, but I'm sure glad you stay open year round. I need drinks for my friends here, but mostly we need a quiet place to sit. And I think you can provide that."

Within five minutes, Hannibal, Yakov, and Viktoriya were seated at one of the outdoor tables. Strings of oversized Christmas tree lights decorated the doors and crisscrossed from the buildings on one side of Rehoboth Mews to the other.

Hannibal would have felt trapped if they sat inside the coffee shop, but sitting in front of it was different. Despite having storefronts on both sides, Rehoboth Mews was little more than a narrow alley, reserved for pedestrians. That meant that people could only approach from two directions and Hannibal could watch both ways with ease. Hannibal had splurged on cups of Jamaican Blue Mountain for himself and Yakov. Viktoriya had requested a frappuccino.

"Now, tell us what happened to Dani," Hannibal said.

She slurped at her straw, peeking out from under her hair at Yakov. He nodded. She spoke.

"Well, we wanted to go someplace to have a little sort of honeymoon, you know? Dani didn't want to fly anywhere, said he was just sick of traveling and besides, there were nice places right nearby. I mentioned the beaches up here, where my folks used to bring me, and he thought that was perfect. So, he asked me to rent a car."

"Didn't want to do that himself, eh?" Hannibal asked.

"He had stuff to do, you know? Had to settle up with Mama and do bank stuff and, you know. Stuff. So anyway, I get this big old four by four because he doesn't want to leave any of his stuff behind. We pack it all up and drive up here."

Hannibal let the rich flavor roll around his mouth, swallowed, and smiled at the girl. He hadn't heard her say much before and was surprised to find that Valley Girl inflections could fit with the first-generation Russian-American accent.

"You didn't talk to your mom before you took off?"

"No, he did," she said, waving the question away. Yakov clenched his eyes shut tight, which startled her. "What?"

Yakov shook his head. "Please. Continue."

"Okay, well we get here and he rents us a little house, kind of divey place eight or nine blocks from the ocean. Said it belonged to a friend, you know, so we would stay there as a

147

favor. So I says, 'What, are we broke?' and he points to this duffel bag. So I open it, you know?"

"And it was full of cash," Hannibal said, rolling his eyes to the sky.

"Yeah. How'd you know?"

Hannibal waved a palm to erase her question. "Can we skip to the part where Dani is shot?"

"Oh, God." As she continued, Hannibal could almost see her heart pounding faster, shaking the material of the tight camisole. Her voice actually quavered a bit and she looked down as if trying to avoid an ugly sight. Maybe she was. "I was out in the kitchen making us some iced tea. I heard the doorbell ring and I figured it must be the owner because who else knew where we were, right? So I hear Dani talking to somebody and I figure I'll be polite and pour a third glass of tea. Then...." She closed her eyes and shook her head as if she still couldn't believe her own senses. "Then I hear this pop, like somebody set off a firecracker in the house. I'm curious, so I go out into the living room."

Viktoriya's lips curled in and the tears finally came. Yakov laid a protective arm across her shoulders. She stared up at Hannibal's lenses as if asking if this was enough. He kept his face impassive.

"When I get to the living room, Dani is alone. He's sitting on the sofa holding his chest. I thought he had a heart attack or something. Then I saw the blood dripping out from under his hand. I scream but he says he'll be OK. I run to the phone in the bedroom to call 9-1-1."

"But he didn't want that," Hannibal said.

She looked at Hannibal with the wide eyes of surprise. "You're right. He said an ambulance would bring police into it and that would be trouble. I should call Mama first. So I called home, but there was no answer. It just rang and rang. I was so scared. So I called you, Uncle Yakov. He didn't want anyone to come to the house, so I told you I'd meet you on the boardwalk. So then I felt a little better, anyway. But when I went to tell Dani what was going on, he was gone. I heard the SUV pull away out front. I think he thought I was in danger as long as he was with me."

"You poor girl," Yakov said, gathering her into his arms.

Hannibal didn't think she was in any danger, but he wanted to be sure. "The duffel full of money?"

"Gone too," she said. "Maybe they shot him for it."

As good an explanation as any, Hannibal thought, although if her story made any sense, the shooter didn't have time to find the right bag. It seemed more likely that Dani took the money with him.

"What a horrible day for you, my child," Yakov said. Hannibal thought he knew where that conversation was going, and he wanted to forestall it a bit. He pulled out the photo he had shown everyone else.

"This might help us find Dani's attacker," Hannibal said. "Who else do you recognize in this picture? That's your husband in the back there."

"Yes, standing behind Uncle Boris," she said. Yakov moved his arm and sat back, his mouth slack. "Yes, Uncle Yakov, that's Uncle Boris and Aunt Renata."

"And Danny went by Gartee Roberts at that time," Hannibal said.

"Gartee? What the hell kind of a name is that? I never heard him called any other name but Dani."

Hannibal chose not to challenge the obvious lie.

"How did you know the Tolstayas?" Yakov asked.

"Another disappointment," Viktoriya said, slurping the last of her drink out of its cup. "I was a big North Africa freak in college. Uncle Boris was going to take me on a trip to see Algeria where he has some business connections. Papa was all for it for a while, but then he backed out of it. That was right after I met Dani. He was working for Uncle Boris. He ended up getting the trip to Algeria."

Yakov took Viktoriya's hand, painting his face with a gloss of sincerity. "So many losses and disappointments. And now..."

"Listen," Hannibal said. "Yakov has something he needs to tell you. I'm going to walk down the path a little way and make a call, OK?"

In the doorway to a little clothing store that was now closed, Hannibal called Orson Rissik.

"Jones?" Rissik growled into the phone. "I know this can't be Hannibal Jones. He would never call me at my home on a Sunday night. He knows better."

"Sorry to bring business into your house," Hannibal said. "Please apologize to Mrs. Rissik for pulling you away from your real life."

"If there was a Mrs. Rissik she'd tell you to piss off. But this is still my personal time and you better have a murderer in custody to be calling me now."

"That I don't have, Chief, but I thought you'd want to be first to know the latest on this Petrova case. Or cases, I suppose."

"Oh." Hannibal heard a brief pause, and then Rissik said, "Let me get a pen." When he got back, he was all business. "All right, what have you got for me?"

"Here's how it lays out," Hannibal said. "Nikita and Raisa Petrova have a grown daughter named Viktoriya."

"Yeah, tell me something I don't know."

"Well, she recently married," Hannibal said. "They came to Rehoboth Beach to honeymoon, which is where I am now."

"And I need to know this because...?"

"Because the husband's been shot. His name is Dani Gana, also known as Gartee Roberts." Hannibal spelled both names and waited for Rissik to confirm that he had them. "He's run off, maybe to draw danger away from the girl, but I don't think he's likely to get far with a sucking chest wound. I'm watching the girl since she might be next on the hit list, but can you get with Maryland police and put out a missing persons on the husband? You might save a life, and might even make some sense out of the murder of the parents."

"I'm with you," Rissik said. "Give me your exact location. And, hey, I'm glad you called me before the Maryland guys."

In the time it took Hannibal to give Rissik a few more details and end the conversation, Yakov had done his grim duty. Hannibal walked back to the table to find Viktoriya's face buried in Yakov's shoulder while her body shook with heavy sobs. No one could be surprised. Three years ago she lost her father under suspicious circumstances. She was hardly married a day before someone shot her husband. Now she had learned that even before that, her mother had been murdered. It was a series of emotional body blows that would bring any sane person to her knees.

Hannibal returned to his seat, swallowed the last of his coffee, and waited for Yakov to look up.

"I understand that this is a very difficult time, but we can't stay here and she can't go back to that rented house."

"Oh God, no," Viktoriya said. "And I can't go home now that I know... I know..."

"Of course not," Yakov said.

"Besides, if anyone is looking for her, they'll have her mother's properties covered."

"Looking for me?"

"If they were after the money, they might think you've got it," Hannibal said. "We don't want to take any chances."

"My place?"

"Not if the hunters know all the players," Hannibal said. "We need to get her to a safe, neutral place. I think Dani had the right basic idea, but I want her closer. So we go back to the District and book her into a small, innocuous motel."

Hannibal stood and the other two followed suit. The evening was turning cool so they walked briskly to his Volvo. Hannibal opened the back door for Viktoriya. As Yakov slowly lowered himself onto the front passenger's seat, Hannibal's cell phone rang. He took the call standing beside the car. It was brief. After he put his phone away, Hannibal opened the back door and waved Yakov out.

"We need to talk," Hannibal said.

-25-
Monday

Mornings were getting tough for Hannibal, but he figured that was due to the amount of drinking he had been doing in the last week. He admitted to himself that it might also have to do with the twisted case he was working on. He had gotten in pretty late the night before and gone straight to his apartment to get some sleep. Now, tying his tie, he stared into the mirror and remembered the conversation he had with Yakov Sidorov the night before.

"I'm afraid you have another nasty job ahead of you," Hannibal told Yakov, with one eye on Viktoriya in the car. "The locals have already found Dani. In his rented vehicle. Dead from a second gunshot wound."

"Oh no," Yakov said. "She can't take any more."

"Not that it matters that much, but they didn't find the money," Hannibal said. "If the hunters got it, maybe the danger to her is over."

Yakov nodded. "True, but is it not just as possible that Dani hid the money someplace before he died?"

"I'm afraid so."

That had led to a very difficult drive back to Washington, after a quick stop for Hannibal to run in to the rented house and pick up a few of Viktoriya's necessities. By the time Hannibal got her checked into a low-profile motel, delivered Yakov into the hands of his worried wife and got himself home, Hannibal needed a solid night's rest. Now he was ready to get back to work as soon as he got something to eat. He grabbed a carton of milk, a box of cereal and a couple of bowls and headed across the hall, figuring he could eat while he updated Ivanovich.

Walking into his office he found Ivanovich in the second room, topless, working out on the heavy bag Hannibal kept hanging there. Based on the musky smell, the bag work must have started quite a while earlier. He registered Ivanovich's smooth musculature and upper body definition, as all fighters do when they see another in training. This would be a hard man to put down, Hannibal thought, and wondered if his guest had been working out every day.

"Good morning," Ivanovich called, wiping his face with a towel and returning to the office. "There is a message on the phone from a Chief Orson Rissik. What happened to you yesterday? Do you have any news?"

"I'm sure you'll consider it good news," Hannibal said, setting the bowls on his desk. "Viktoriya is now a widow."

"You killed the bastard?"

"No, Aleksandr, I didn't kill the bastard, but somebody did." Hannibal settled into his desk chair, dialed Rissik's number and poured cereal into the bowls. Ivanovich poured two cups of coffee and placed them beside the bowls.

"Now she is all alone in the world," Ivanovich said. "She is lonely and defenseless. Where is she?"

"She's in a safe place," Hannibal said, pouring milk into both bowls. "Eat your breakfast."

"You must take me to her," Ivanovich said, walking around the desk to stare down at Hannibal. Hannibal held up his palm as the call connected.

"Good morning, Orson. What can I do for you?"

"First and foremost, you can tell me where this Queenie Cochran is. She's wanted for questioning in connection with her husband being hospitalized and now in connection with the death of your missing man, Dani Gana."

"Afraid I don't know her whereabouts," Hannibal said, glancing at Ivanovich's impatient eyes. "I left her at the hospital, planning to go up and visit her old man."

"Yeah, well she never did go back up to visit him again," Rissik said,

"It might help to know that she's from this area," Hannibal said, "and that she was known as Renata Tolstaya before she married into the Cochran name."

"That should be useful," Rissik said. "You know, if we put our heads together we might be able to make sense of these cases."

"I think you're right," Hannibal said, returning Ivanovich's stare. "Tell you what. As soon as I grab a quick bite to eat, I'll come on over to your office and we can compare notes."

Hannibal could feel Invanovich's impatience as he hung up the phone.

"What?" Hannibal asked.

"Viktoriya," Ivanovich said, eyes wide as if his question was obvious.

"What about her?"

"You know where she is," Ivanovich said, in an accusatory tone. "I need to see her. You have got to take me to her."

Hannibal sneered up at him. "No, actually, I ain't got to do shit."

Ivanovich gripped the front of Hannibal's shirt with both hands. "You will take me to her."

Hannibal sprang to his feet, his right fist cocked at his side, his left hand holding Ivanovich's wrist, his teeth bared, his breathing fast and deep. The two men stood with their eyes less than five inches apart.

"You want to go?" Hannibal asked. "We going to do this right here, right now? I'm saying the girl needs some time alone, to get her head together before she starts having to deal with your lovesick puppy routine. You think you can beat her location out of me, then bring it, bitch, and we'll see who gets up when we're done. Otherwise, back the fuck off."

Ivanovich locked eyes with Hannibal for five long seconds before taking a small step backward. Hannibal released his arm to point a finger in Ivanovich's face while looking at him out the corner of his eye.

"Push me like that again, mother fucker and it's on. Now shut up, sit down, and eat your cereal."

* * * * *

Hannibal was comfortable in Orson Rissik's office because it was one of the most orderly places in the universe. There was never any paper on his desk except in the OUT box or the one marked HOLD. Hannibal had never seen anything in his IN box. The three framed citations hanging on the wall to the left and right of the desk must have been put there using a T-square and a laser sight. And he loved the poster just behind Rissik's head. It showed a pelican trying to eat a frog. His head already in the bird's mouth, the frog had reached out and wrapped a hand around the pelican's throat, preventing it from swallowing him. A caption under the picture said "Never Give Up." That defined Rissik better than any citation or award ever could.

In front of the poster, Rissik leaned back with his hands clasped behind his head.

"So my old murder case has spawned not one but two follow-up cases, eh?"

"Well, either that or this is one damned unlucky family," Hannibal said.

"I'm betting you've got a theory."

"Natch, Chief." Hannibal stood up and handed over the group photo, pointing out the man in the center. "This guy. Boris Tolstaya. I like him for the original murder. The one that's officially a suicide."

Rissik accepted the picture, staring at his new target. "Enlighten me. Motive?"

"Take your pick," Hannibal said. "One scenario says that Nikita Petrova owed this guy a substantial gambling debt. I can substantiate that by at least two eyewitnesses. When he refused to pay, Tolstaya had him thrown off the roof."

"Weak but workable. You don't usually kill a guy who holds your marker, you want to hurt him and scare him. But maybe something went wrong. Next?"

"Try this," Hannibal said. "The daughter, Viktoriya, says Tolstaya wanted to take her on a trip to some exotic Africa country. She was up for it, but Daddy refused. Maybe Tolstaya wanted her bad and when Nikita put the chill on the idea, he went off his nut."

"That's weak too," Rissik said, "but together they might add up to a reason to find this guy for questioning."

"I figure that could spin into a reason for the wife's death too," Hannibal said. "Not sure about the husband, Gana, AKA Roberts, but maybe when I get a positive fix on who he really is I can tie it all up. Right now, I'm not even sure what country he's from."

"He's a foreigner, right?"

"One way or the other," Hannibal said. "Gana is from Algeria. Roberts is from Liberia. Will the real African immigrant please stand up?"

"Have you checked with the embassies?"

"Orson, they won't tell me shit. I have no official government status. I'm not even a cop. Or have you forgotten that fact?"

"You ain't, but I am." Rissik smiled and pushed a button on his intercom. "Hey, Gert, could you stop in here a sec?" Then to Hannibal, he said, "As far as I'm concerned, any resident foreigner using an alias could be a terrorist. You got any other leads on this guy?"

Hannibal thought for a second about giving up everything he had to Rissik. It was uncomfortable, but he couldn't come up with one good reason not to.

"A girl in the Howard registration office told me he transferred in from UVA's history department. If she's right, maybe they can be the tie breaker on where this guy really came from."

"It's worth a shot," Rissik said.

A few seconds later, a brunette of indeterminate age in a gray suit with the skirt hanging three inches below her knees paced in. She was a little heavy, but well proportioned and would have seemed tall if not for the sensible shoes. She stopped in front of Rissik's desk so precisely that Hannibal half expected her to go to parade rest.

"It's a multipart assignment," Rissik said. Gert flipped open a notebook and held a pen at the ready. Rissik pushed the photo forward across his desk. "First, scan this photograph in. Separate out the man in the middle and the man standing behind him, and enhance them as much as you can." He placed a sheet of notepaper on top of the photo.

"That top name is the guy in front. Check the usual databases and see what we can find on him. The next two names both belong to the guy in back. Fax his photograph and the names to these two embassies and see if anybody can tell us for sure who he is and where he came from. Then send his face and names to the University of Virginia registrar and see if they can find me a professor who had this guy in class. He'd have been a history major. That's it. Any questions?"

"No sir. I'm good," she said.

Gert did an almost military about-face and hurried off to complete her assignment. Hannibal's eyes tracked her out the door, but he said nothing. When he turned back, Rissik raised his eyebrows and tilted his head as if asking if Hannibal had a question. He did, but he would not ask anything about Gert.

"So, do we know anything about Raisa's murder? Forensic evidence maybe, or a substantial clue?"

"Not much you could work with," Rissik said, "but there was one point of interest. The murder weapon was unusual."

"Really?" Hannibal said. "I figured a small caliber automatic, like a .22."

Rissik shook his head. "Even smaller and faster. Our guys say it was a .17-caliber bullet that poked that hole in Mrs. Petrova."

"Seventeen?" Hannibal slid to the edge of his chair. "That's mostly a rifle round, but this was done in the house at handgun range. I think Ruger chambers an automatic for that caliber. And I think Smith and Wesson has a revolver, but these guns are for popping squirrels or target matches, not murders. Unless…I guess a head shot would do the job."

"Yeah these things would poke through the skull but probably not exit," Rissik said. "Make a hell of a mess rattling around in there too. Really quite logical for in-city assassinations."

Hannibal nodded. "Yeah, except in this case the shooter went for center mass."

"That tells me this perp didn't know what he was doing," Rissik said.

"And that's part of what makes me want to reject the whole mob murder scenario. Besides, there are plenty of people who could have personal motivations for her death."

Rissik's intercom buzzed. "Sir, I have a Dr. Van Buren on the line. He's head of the history department, University of Virginia."

"Put him through," Rissik said. "I'll leave it on speaker for my guest." After hearing the right set of clicks Rissik said hello and introduced himself.

"This is Eric Van Buren," the tiny speaker said. "I am very short on time, Detective, but I understand you need information about a former student of mine in relation to an investigation?"

"Yes," Rissik said, "I appreciate you calling back so fast."

"The dean kind of encouraged my cooperation," Van Buren said.

"Yes, well I'll try to keep this brief. I hope the photo we faxed you is clear. We're having a little difficulty finding background on this man because he has apparently changed his name and personal history. Did you know him as Dani Gana from Algerian, or Gartee Roberts from Liberia?"

"Well, that's the thing," Van Buren said, and Hannibal sat forward on his chair. "I'd have to say neither. I remember this young man; he was an excellent student. But I knew him as

Hamed Barek and he had come to this country from Morocco."

-26-

Orson Rissik let several seconds of silence pass after he disconnected the telephone call. Hannibal wondered if their thoughts were the same. He was considering that 97 percent of all crimes had simple solutions. They were acts of passion or greed, generally committed on impulse without much thought or planning. Occasionally one would come along that showed some cunning on the part of the perpetrator, a professional criminal who thought he had figured a way to beat the system. And then there was that one case in a hundred that was genuinely convoluted, usually because one evil person had tried to outsmart another evil person and had somehow ended up involving a third. This was beginning to look like one of those.

The intercom buzzed again, shaking them both out of their wandering thoughts. This time Rissik picked up the handset and held it to his ear. Hannibal smiled. If it was unrelated police business, he didn't really want to know anyway. But when Rissik hung up and stared at him he figured the news was connected to their shared case.

"Our luck is turning, Jones," Rissik said. "We might have a lead on the Tolstaya girl."

"You found Queenie?"

"No, and we never would if that was all the name we had," Rissik said. "But after you gave us Renata Tolstaya we had something solid to chase. Her maiden name turns out to be Mikhailov, she is from DC, and her mother still lives in the area. We even have an address."

Hannibal slid to the edge of his seat. "You know her daughter would run home if she had nowhere else to go. Mom's seen her for sure. You bringing her in?"

"I don't think so." Rissik shook his head. "There's a minor record, and hints of more mob connections. But they're just hints, and we got nothing we could charge her with. Besides, she's part of a culture that tends to be pretty uncomfortable with authority figures, you know? Honestly, I don't think she'll talk. At least, not to a cop."

He left the comment hanging in the air until Hannibal rose to the bait. "Sure, Chief, I'll be glad to help out. Let's ride over there and see what the lady might be willing to share."

* * * * *

Rissik was not the kind of man to talk when talk wasn't necessary. That's why Hannibal was following the Honda Civic for a few minutes before he realized that Rissik wasn't headed toward the District, and a few more before he knew they were Maryland bound. They drove north on I-95 and in a little more than an hour they pulled up in front of an unimpressive apartment building in Baltimore.

Hannibal thought that Baltimore had an even larger African American population than The District, but there were pockets of resistance. They parked in one, a little area surrounding the Holy Trinity Russian Orthodox Church around the corner on East Fairmount Avenue. It was a street of older brick buildings with big windows and narrow stoops. Black iron fences stood guard in front of the houses, the kind with spearhead points on top. A hand pulled a curtain aside to watch him when he walked up to Rissik's car. Rissik rolled down his window. Hannibal leaned on the roof of the Civic.

"You didn't say she lived in Baltimore."

"You didn't ask."

"So did you clear this with your Baltimore counterparts?"

"Clear what?" Rissik asked. "I'm not even here. You're pursuing your own investigation, aren't you?"

Hannibal nodded. "Yeah, I guess I'm on my own. But if I turn up any good leads that could point to Viktoriya's whereabouts…"

"You can count on full police support," Rissik said. "She's a material witness who might be able to shed light on three murders and one serious assault. Now go do what you need to do."

As he walked up the steps to the front door, Hannibal was not sure what that was. Should he offer to help this woman's daughter? Threaten her with legal action? Was this to be an interrogation? Or would he gain more with sympathy and a soft tone?

The woman who responded to his knock nearly gave him a jolt of déjà vu. In the time it took her to ask, "Can I help you?" the feeling changed to a peek into Renata Tolstaya's future. This woman's hair was the same fiery red, except that the quarter inch closest to her scalp was mousy brown. The cobwebs spreading from the corners of her eyes told her apparent age, as did her slightly stooped posture. Her lipstick matched her hair but was uneven on her lower lip. She had the same robust figure as her daughter, but while her waist was only a little thicker her bust and hips had swelled to almost cartoon proportions. In a housecoat and mule slippers she was surely everything Queenie feared growing into.

"Mrs. Mikhailov?" he asked, not feeling right using her first name. "My name is Hannibal Jones and I'm here trying to help your daughter, Renata."

"Renata? Is she all right?" Mrs. Mikhailov's eyes flared with fear, then settled back into their natural lethargy.

"I'm not sure," Hannibal said. "I think some bad men may be after her."

"Are you the police?"

"No ma'am. I was working with her husband, but he's been hurt and I'm just a little worried about her. May I come in?"

She teetered on the edge of decision, looking to Hannibal for help. He did so by saying nothing more, just smiling and working at not being threatening in any way. Old Country

162

women were predictable in some ways. She could be defensive, she could even be aggressive when she had to be, but she could not be rude. She had no choice but to invite him in.

Hannibal was startled by the similarity between this apartment and the home of Mother Washington, the black woman who was a pillar of his own community. As in Mother Washington's modest house, the passage of time had dulled the paint and faded the wallpaper, but otherwise the apartment was immaculate. All the furniture was overstuffed and reupholstered more than once, in the kind of eclectic decor that comes from collecting pieces one at a time at bargain prices. There was no portrait of Jesus, but a large crucifix dominated one wall in the living room and he could see a similar one in the kitchen.

"Would you like some tea?" Mrs. Mikhailov asked, falling into her usual hostess role.

"I appreciate the offer," Hannibal said, "But I really should make this quick. I think I need to find Renata soon, before whoever went after her husband goes after her. He's still in the hospital but she hasn't visited him. That's why I wonder if she's OK."

Mrs. Mikhailov said, "Well, I haven't seen her in months." But her eyes wandered down and to the right, and Hannibal was gratified to meet one person after so many days who was not a born liar.

"Oh, but I'll bet you've kept her room for her, just in case she comes home." He walked deeper into the apartment with the woman following him. If she was like most women living alone, the open door led to her own bedroom. The closed door had to be Renata's room. He walked in before his hostess could object. He was standing in the middle of the room by the time she spoke.

"You can't go in there. It's private," she said, but it was a weak protest.

Standing in the center of the room, he looked around slowly. Instead of the expected musty smell of an unused room, he was surprised by a faint smoky odor. Surprised, because the room wasn't merely neat, it was spotless. Too bad. If Mrs. Mikhailov weren't such a good housekeeper, small clues wouldn't be so obvious.

The ashtray beside the bed had been dumped, but not washed out. The ash at the bottom was not loose but ground in from someone stubbing out a cigarette. The bed was made and the pillow had been fluffed up. Hannibal bent to sniff the pillow. The odor of Renata's Marlboro or Winston was still there in the pillow. Two stray red hairs clung to the pillowcase. He carefully lifted the longer hair, using his first two fingers as tweezers, and stood up straight. His eyes continued to roam the room.

"So, she was here last night. Are you saying she didn't tell you where she was going?"

When Mrs. Mikhailov stayed silent, Hannibal decided to try the photo on her. He wanted to know if she recognized Dani Gana or Viktoriya, but before he could actually ask anything her face twisted into a mask of hate.

"It is him. You're here for that monster, Boris Tolstaya." Then she turned away as if she was looking for someplace to spit.

"No ma'am. I don't know this man. In fact, for all I know he could be the source of the danger. What can you tell me about Boris?"

Mrs. Mikhailov didn't look like she was quite ready to trust him, but he had at least found a subject she was willing to talk about. The rage bubbling up out of her was thick and heavy.

"I can tell you that he is an evil, despicable man. I can tell you that he seduced my poor Renata with money and power and stole her away from Benjamin."

"Benjamin? Ben Cochran? I'm sorry, I thought it was the other way around."

Mrs. Mikhailov shook her head and looked at her feet. "Benjamin loved her, would do anything for her. But this monster stole her away. Somehow, Benjamin got her back.

164

And now you see the result. Boris has found them, poor Benjamin is in the hospital and Renata has run off in fear. She would not tell me where she was going. She was trying to protect me."

Hannibal could understand why Renata would not have told her mother that her return to the man she loved had come about through the turn of a card. And her assumption that Boris had hurt Ben made sense too. If Renata's plan had worked, there would have been an interesting irony in them getting money from Boris for helping him find Dani who appeared at this point to be his traitorous partner. All of that moved Boris up on the list of suspects for any of the murders.

"Ma'am, if I can't find Renata maybe I can make things safer for her," he said. "If you know where I can find Boris Tolstaya, maybe I can convince him to leave her alone."

"You would face this man?" she asked, looking into Hannibal's eyes. "He is powerful and dangerous. You don't know."

"Ma'am, these people don't scare me. I deal with his kind all the time. Just help me get face to face with him."

* * * * *

Hannibal felt as if the entire neighborhood was staring at him as he returned to Rissik's car, but in fact he knew that only one old woman might be watching through one of the big windows. He got in, but couldn't stop looking around.

"So, a lead on Renata Tolstaya?" Rissik asked.

"Not really, but she did give me some dirt on Boris Tolstaya. Apparently he and his partner, one Ivan Uspensky, own a securities firm and do a lot of money laundering for the Red Mafiya."

"Yeah, Boris is a real bad guy," Rissik said, starting the car. "You ought to steer clear."

"You know about this guy?" It was more a demand than a question.

Rissik was unruffled. "The FBI has an open file on him. He and Renata are under investigation for income tax evasion."

"And you didn't tell me any of this why?"

"Look, this is a genuine bad guy," Rissik said. He looked at Hannibal with an expression that Hannibal didn't recognize. "Do you know that the Red Mafiya scares the FBI more than the Italians, the Colombians, the Yakuza, anybody? Heroin smuggling, weapons trafficking, mass extortion. These guys, Tolstaya and Uspensky, apparently set up here in the Dulles Corridor to funnel the cash flowing down from the casinos in Jersey and up from the strip clubs in Miami Beach."

"Yeah? So? Am I supposed to be scared or something?"

Rissik gripped the wheel with both hands as he eased through traffic. "See, that's why I don't tell you this stuff. Because you are a knucklehead. You're always stepping in some shit. I mean, you see the shit lying right there on the sidewalk, right there, and you step in it anyway."

Now Hannibal thought he recognized the expression on Rissik's face. "I'll be damned. You're for real. You're worried about me. I'm touched, Chief, I really am, but you know I have to follow this lead. If this is all about Tolstaya getting ripped off, the bodies are going to keep dropping until he either recovers the cash or he lands in jail. The way I see it, Viktoriya Petrova will never be safe unless I make one or the other happen. And the next step is to get face to face with Ivan Uspensky and see what he says about the Russian mob and his old buddy Boris."

"You know I can't back you up on this," Rissik said.

"Don't sweat it," Hannibal said. "I know where I can get some backup."

-27-

Like Silicone Valley in Southern California, the Dulles Technology Corridor is not so much a location as a concept. Hannibal had heard the terms "netplex" and "high tech colossus" in reference to the area, but to him it was simply a commercial zone out by the airport.

Driving down the Dulles Toll Road he wondered if the businesses that set up on either side of this minor highway had set out to form an unrelated conglomerate of research, technological, and development oriented companies, or if it had just happened. He recalled some startling statistics: thirty thousand businesses and more than a half million of Northern Virginia's jobs were stuffed into these futuristic buildings, and he didn't know if he was in Herndon or Reston or Falls Church or if perhaps the Dulles Corridor had its own ZIP code.

Sitting beside him, Ivanovich said, "You know, he may recognize me." He tugged at the lapel of his navy blue suit, checking to make sure his jacket hung properly to conceal his pistol.

"I'm counting on it," Hannibal said. "Having you behind me will make me a player in his eyes, and that might make him want to cooperate."

"And if it does not?" Ivanovich asked as Hannibal eased his Volvo onto an off ramp. "We are hardly in a position to challenge him. If he decides we represent trouble he could make us disappear like that." He snapped his fingers for emphasis.

"Well, that will make it an exciting day," Hannibal said with a smile.

The sprawling Worldgate complex was built by a land development company called Monument, and the different sections were numbered. Hannibal followed the signs toward Monument 3 Worldgate and rolled into the parking garage beside the building that housed Rice, Staff & Spike Securities. Before getting out of the car he reached into the glove compartment for a spare pair of Oakley sunglasses. Ivanovich nodded and slipped them on as he got out of the car.

Instead of heading for the elevator Hannibal led them outside to stand in front of the building for a moment to gather his thoughts. He wondered what army of immigrants maintained such beautifully landscaped property, almost a hundred acres of industry conducted almost entirely on paper and in computers.

"So this is where organized crime hides these days," he said, "three or four miles from one of the country's busiest airports, surrounded by Fortune 500 companies in one of the fastest growing, wealthiest locations for economic development in the country."

"This," Ivanovich said with a smirk, "is where organized crime has always hidden. Shall we go face the lion in his luxurious den?"

The two men entered the building and walked straight to the security guard's desk. The uniformed guard looked up in surprise, probably because these two had crossed the faux marble floor without the usual clacking shoes usually make. Ivanovich, true to his character, looked everywhere except at Hannibal. Hannibal focused only on the guard, who looked and sounded Somalian.

"Good afternoon. Buzz up to RS&S and tell them that Hannibal Jones and Aleksandr Ivanovich are here to see Mr. Uspensky."

"Is he expecting you?" the guard asked in a singsong, offkilter accent.

"We don't have an appointment," Hannibal said, "but I suspect that he is expecting us."

In the following three minutes a handful of people walked through the wide hall, each wearing an identification badge and the scowl that is the real badge of the modern office worker. Hannibal and Ivanovich signed in and a guard prepared their visitor badges. Then, three men in well-cut suits who looked familiar to Hannibal stepped out of the elevator. Not that their faces were familiar, but their body language and posture were unmistakable. They varied from six foot three to six foot five and all had wrestlers' bodies and bored Slavic faces. Two of them stopped six feet away while the third moved forward until he was staring down into Ivanovich's face. Hannibal saw no change in either man's expression.

"Aleksandr," the taller man said.

Vladimir," Ivanovich returned.

Then the tall man broadened his view to take Hannibal in as well. "Gentlemen, if you will follow me."

Hannibal found their escorts to be both polite and professional. In the elevator, one of the men watched Hannibal, one watched Ivanovich, and the third watched the doors. When they stepped into the carpeted, paneled hall on the appropriate floor, two stood on either side of a door while Vladimir faced them, looking almost embarrassed.

"I am sorry, but I must ask you if you are..."

Hannibal held up a palm, and then opened his jacket. Vladimir reached in and pulled the pistol from under Hannibal's right arm. Then he turned to Ivanovich, who stood with his hands folded in front of him.

"No," Hannibal said. "You take nothing from him."

"Aleksandr," Vladimir said, "I have to."

"Only if you are prepared to literally take it from me," Ivanovich said. None of these men showed any emotion on their faces but Hannibal could taste the tension in the air. These two men had history, but now they were sizing each other up again, testing and probing in some way below

Hannibal's level of perception. He looked at the two door guards and chose the one he would take out if things went sour, and watched Ivanovich because he somehow knew that the loser would speak first. He was surprised when Vladimir turned to address him instead of Ivanovich.

"He can't go in."

"I go where he goes," Ivanovich said, his voice snapping out in defiance.

"Not necessary," Hannibal said, tuning out the three strangers and holding Ivanovich's eyes with his own. "He won't hurt me; he just wants to feel safe himself. Just stay near this door. And if you hear anything that doesn't sound like friendly conversation, I know you can take these three assholes out." Then he looked up at Vladimir and pointed at his chest. "And you know it too."

Hannibal walked between the two towering bodyguards, opened the door, and stepped into wonderland. The carpet was deeper, the paneling changed from laminate to cedar, and the desk set to one side of the football field of an office offered its occupant a commanding view of the toll road that led to Dulles International Airport. The paintings were not prints but real oils. Classical music wafted in, just loud enough to notice. It was all meant to impress. Hannibal faced the desk and let the man behind it see that it had worked.

"Ivan Uspensky?"

"And you must be Hannibal Jones," the man said, standing and offering his hand. The handshake was warm and firm, but taking the man in caused Hannibal to linger with it. Uspensky could have been Tolstaya's brother, another big man with a little round belly and almost no hair left. The difference was that while Tolstaya's photo showed wisps of black hair, the few strands remaining on Uspensky's head were blond. This man was likely on the godfather level even if he wasn't, he was surely a senior captain of contemporary industry. Hannibal decided on deference and courtesy.

"Thank you for making the time to see me."

"How could I not?" Uspensky said. "You are clearly a man of some influence. You have Aleksandr Ivanovich."

Hannibal smiled and nodded. "He opens doors. I only want a few minutes. By the way, I love the name of your brokerage firm. Tell me, who are Rice, Staff and Spike?"

Uspensky smiled, regaining his seat and opening a humidor. "Those are just common words chosen at random. They are meant to send the message that the company is very American. I can see that you are a man who understands the importance of appearances. Now, is this to be a chat, an interview, or an interrogation?"

Hannibal selected one of the cigars. "Just a friendly conversation. You can help me with my current investigation. First, I'd like to make sure I'm pursuing the right man."

He handed over the photograph he had been carrying for the last couple of days. Uspensky took it, laid it on the desk and stared down at it while clipping the end off his cigar. He lit it with a Zippo lighter and took a first puff, all the while gazing at the picture as if trying to find some inner meaning in it.

"Yes, this is my business partner, Boris Tolstaya at the center."

"And do you know the man behind him?" Hannibal asked.

"I believe that to be Gartee Roberts, an African who I think may have worked with Boris on a project."

Hannibal nodded and settled into the overstuffed armchair by the picture windows. "Well, that fellow you knew as Roberts is now known as Dani Gana. He was murdered recently. His widow is in hiding, in fear of the killer."

"Obviously I wouldn't know anything about that," Uspensky said, his face the embodiment of innocence. "I didn't really know this Roberts, or Gana, or whatever. In fact, I think I only met him once."

The sweet cigar smoke reached out to Hannibal, reminding him that he was holding a similar weapon. He glanced at his cigar, but decided to tuck it into his inside jacket pocket. Not looking up, he said, "He was more Boris's friend, I guess. I'd sure like to discuss it with him."

Uspensky's laugh was a raucous bellow. "Oh, I bet you would. And believe me, I wish I could help you, but I haven't seen Boris in weeks."

"I guess it took him a while to find Roberts," Hannibal said. "I think Roberts may have stolen money from Boris. That would make it easy to put the murder on Boris. The thing is, once Boris found Roberts, I figured he'd come back to work."

Uspensky stopped laughing. "I think you got that a little mixed up. Funds disappeared all right, right about the time Boris did."

"Boris?" Hannibal sat forward, his feet sinking into the deep carpeting. "Well, that kind of makes sense. Our boy steals money that's already been stolen, figuring the original thief, Boris, can't go to the cops or even to the mob to report it."

"Look here, Jones," Uspensky said, resting both elbows on his desk. "You got Ivanovich backing you up. That makes me think you are not with the police. But it would be polite for you to confirm this."

"I assure you I'm no kind of cop or fed. No affiliation with law enforcement of any kind."

Uspensky nodded. "Now the question is, are you connected?"

"If you mean to some sort of criminal organization, like perhaps the Red Mafiya, I have no connections or affiliation there either. You can check me out."

"I'm inclined to believe you," Uspensky said. "I guess you're here asking for information, for help. Come over here and let me school you."

Hannibal stood and went to the front of the desk. Uspensky clutched his cigar between his teeth and spread his meaty hands on his desk to lay it all out for Hannibal.

"You see, the securities business isn't much different from the casino business. Sometimes people bet big. Sometimes they do it on the margin, which means they actually bet, or invest, more than they have. Sometimes when they do that they lose. We have to carry that debt, and sometimes those debts can add up because of interest."

"I'm familiar with this type of debt," Hannibal said. "Interest can get quite high."

Uspensky nodded. "Yeah, sometimes. And sometimes people don't want to pay. Now Boris, he liked to keep his hands clean. He meets this Roberts guy, and this guy is smooth. So Boris has the kid handle some of the collections. He was collecting and stashing some of these funds."

"Stashing?" Hannibal asked.

"Hey, you're a businessman," Uspensky said. "Nobody reports all their income to the IRS, right?"

Hannibal did, but he just nodded and smiled.

"Well, that side of the business was kind of subjective. Sometimes Boris would give the big losers a little discount if they did things for him. And sometimes he'd collect an extra percentage point from those he could squeeze it out of. And sometimes when he did that, he would do some creative bookkeeping. You getting any of this?"

"Oh my God," Hannibal said, his face scrunching into an open-mouthed smile. "Boris was embezzling from his own business. He was stealing from you. Gana wasn't hiding from the mob, he was just hiding from Boris. Boris is the one hiding from the mob."

"That kind of hangs together," Uspensky said, blowing a big cloud of smoke at the ceiling. "If you got it right, it sounds like Boris caught up with the little African thief and that means he might have my money back."

"So, you don't know where he is."

"No," Uspensky said, "but nobody can hide forever. You're a pretty clever detective, Jones. You'd have to be to follow a trail from that old picture to me. And you got Ivanovich at your back. There could be a fat finder's fee if you was to find my old partner and let me know where he is. He left here with a sizable sum. I'm just saying."

"How much money are we talking about?" Hannibal asked.

"A sizable sum."

Hannibal nodded and walked very slowly toward the door. When he wrapped his hand around the knob, Uspensky asked, "Well?"

Hannibal turned and smiled. "It's a very tempting offer, but that would turn our friendly chat into a business conversation. And, no offense, but you're not the kind of guy I really want to do business with."

* * * * *

Once he got the car back on the Dulles Toll Road, Hannibal pushed a button to call a familiar phone number.

"Rissik."

"Hey, Chief," Hannibal said. "I just wanted you to know that a friend and I just paid a visit to Ivan Uspensky and are on our way home with our skins intact."

"Really?" Hannibal could hear him leaning back in his office chair. "You learn anything useful?"

"I think the visit did shed a little more light on Dani Gana's murder, and maybe on all three."

"Glad to hear it," Rissik replied. "It's kind of late in the day for you to visit here, but stop by my office in the morning so we can compare notes. You tell me what the Russian money man says, and I'll tell you the interesting connection my people turned up that ties Dani Gana's death to the murder of Raisa Petrova."

-28-
Tuesday

Sitting in his car, in the parking lot outside of Rissik's office, Hannibal made a rare early-morning phone call. He was facing eastward, watching a thin wisp of clouds trying in vain to hide the red-tinged rays of the autumn sun. With all the windows down he enjoyed a pleasant cross breeze that carried the sweet scent of late-blooming lilacs growing nearby. The cool air against his skin brought a smile as he listened to the phone ring at the other end.

"Hello?" a somewhat impatient voice finally said.

"Hey, babe. How is your morning looking?"

"Hannibal?" He could hear Cindy's voice shift into a sweeter mode. "I can't remember the last time you called me before I left the house for work. What's up?"

"Well I'm nearing a turning point in this case and I realized that I miss you. Do you realize that we haven't gotten together in a week?"

"Wow, it has been a week," she said, sounding surprised. "The caseload has been fairly heavy, and you know I'm still scoping on the perfect house. But there's always room in my schedule for my honey."

"That's what I wanted to hear," he said, lowering his voice to make her press the phone closer to her ear. "What are you doing for lunch today?"

He endured a brief pause while, he assumed, she checked her calendar. "Today? Nothing I couldn't move."

"Great," Hannibal said. "How about I pick you up around noon and we step down to your favorite little Thai place?"

"In the mood for something hot, eh?"

"Yeah," Hannibal said, "but I'll settle for lunch with you. Maybe after dinner I can get something hot."

They spent several minutes teasing their way toward good-bye. As Hannibal finally cut the connection, he saw a familiar silver Honda slide into its parking space. He raised his windows and went to meet Orson Rissik.

"This is a surprise," Hannibal said, checking his watch. "I always imagined you as an in-by-seven-a.m. kind of guy."

"No, I'm the in-by-eight-a.m.-but-usually-stuck-there-until-eight-p.m. kind of guy. How are you doing?"

"Not bad, all things considered," Hannibal said, holding the door open for Rissik and following him inside. "Now, you said you had some new evidence on the two murders?"

"Geez, can't I even get into my office?" Rissik asked. "Besides, I want to hear what you got yesterday first."

Both men said good morning to Gert as they passed her desk. Inside Rissik's office they found a pot of fresh coffee. Rissik poured for both of them, and then sat at his desk.

"Fair enough," Hannibal said after tasting his coffee. It wasn't gourmet in any way, just good, solid coffee. "Here's what I think I know. Chameleon Boy, otherwise known as Dani Gana, was Boris Tolstaya's courier. Tolstaya was coleader of an investment firm either run by or at the very least doing business with the Russian Mafiya. The firm might have been skimming from the clients, which is a bad idea if they were laundering mob money. Tolstaya was skimming from the firm, an even worse idea. Dani was skimming from Tolstaya, which, as it turns out, was even stupider. I think Tolstaya killed Dani for stealing."

"That all makes sense, and gives us enough motive for us to get serious looking for Boris Tolstaya," Rissik said. "And if he can be convinced to turn state's evidence, we might even get to poke a hole in the Russian mob."

"I'm glad I could make you so happy, Chief," Hannibal said. "And nobody in uniform could have gotten that stuff. Now, about your news…"

"Oh yeah," Rissik said, leaning back with his hands on the back of his head. "The murder weapons."

"What about them?" Hannibal asked, annoyed that Rissik felt the need to be dramatic.

"Oh. You remember that the bullet that went through Mrs. Petrova was an unusual, small caliber? Well, the bullet that took Dani Gana out was the same. They found it in the vehicle. I had asked the Maryland boys for the report and when I read that, I got on the horn with them to let them know about Raisa's case."

"Got to be the same gun," Hannibal said. "And I can see how Boris might have taken out Mrs. Petrova if she wouldn't give up her daughter's lover. But why the tiny gun?"

"I can see it if he's really a gambler and businessman," Rissik said. "Easy to conceal, right? And real quiet."

Hannibal's nod was more vigorous than usual because his cell phone was vibrating in his jacket pocket. He excused himself and pulled it out.

"Mr. Jones? It is Yakov Sidorov."

"Yakov?" Hannibal looked up at Rissik. "What's going on? Is Viktoriya OK?"

"Fine, fine," Yakov said, "but I need to talk to you."

Hannibal again looked at Rissik, who said, "Go ahead. We're done here and I've got lots to do now, thanks to you."

Hannibal smiled, nodded, and headed for his car.

"Yakov, what's the problem?"

"Do you know a man named Krada? Jamal Krada?"

"Yeah, but how do you know him?" Hannibal asked as he walked across the parking lot.

"He called my cell phone, asking all sorts of questions about Dani Gana. He said he knew you."

That brought Hannibal up short and he stopped beside his car. "What? How'd he get your number?"

"He said he got it from Gana, who was one of his students. He said he had lost contact with his student and wanted to know if I could put him in touch with him."

"What did you tell him?" Hannibal asked, getting into his car and yanking the door shut.

"Nothing," Yakov said. "I just said I did not know what he was talking about. This man I did not know and who was I to tell him his student had been killed?"

"You did the right thing," Hannibal said, checking his watch. "I have to be in the District for lunch anyway. I think I'll swing by Krada's house and tell him in person."

* * * * *

Krada didn't look happy when he opened the door, but he also didn't look as arrogant as he had before. Hannibal judged him to be a private man. He would not like too many people knowing his business, especially if one of them was a private investigator. He looked up at Hannibal like a boy who had been caught peeping in the girls' dormitory window.

"So this Sidorov person felt the need to drag you into this," Krada said.

"Actually, he said you mentioned my name to try to get him to talk to you," Hannibal said. "So the truth is, you dragged me into this. And I'd like to know why you were so concerned."

Krada offered a noncommittal grunt and walked back into the house. Hannibal followed him to the same seat he had occupied on his first visit. The house carried the faint lemon scent of furniture polish. Had the woman been up cleaning the house this early?

As he sat, Mrs. Krada floated into view wearing a caftan in muted colors and carrying a carafe of coffee. As she poured for the two men, Hannibal rose from his seat and said good morning. She did not respond verbally, but he saw color come to her cheeks as he sat back down. How did a woman come to be so unaccustomed to simple courtesy in twenty-first century America?

"So why were you so concerned?" Hannibal asked Krada as his wife faded into the background.

"Well, Gartee was always taking chances," Krada said. "I have worried that he would attract too much attention and they'd find him."

"That would explain his changing his name to Dani Gana," Hannibal said, not asking whose attention Gana would not want to attract.

"Exactly," Krada said, sipping his coffee. "He never understood how determined those feds could be."

Hannibal nodded. "FBI," he said, sipping and staring out the back door.

"Immigration," Krada said, correcting him, and then raising his eyes in surprise. "Wait. You didn't know, did you?"

"So he was in country illegally," Hannibal said. "And he shared that knowledge with you, along with the phone number of one of the first friends he made in this country."

"Yes, as have many of my students," Krada said. His eyes seemed to soften somewhat, and he stared down into his cup. "Sometimes they have no one else to turn to, and they need a fatherly figure. I stay in touch with a few, as I did with Gartee."

"Yes, I should have seen that right away," Hannibal said. "It explains how he was able to toss off the answers to all of your quiz questions. You gave them to him before I got there. That was clever."

"Was I wrong to try to help him keep his secrets?" Krada asked. "If so, I was not alone. Sidorov would tell me nothing. But you said you had some news to share." He ended the sentence on an up note, like a question. His expectant expression made Hannibal's next words more difficult to say.

"I'm afraid I don't have good news. I'm sorry to tell you that Dani Gana, Gartee Roberts, is dead."

"Dead?" Krada almost spilled his coffee putting the cup down. "How?"

"He appears to have made some enemies far worse than the INS," Hannibal said. "I'm afraid he was murdered."

Krada's gaze returned to the inside of his cup. He seemed to need a few seconds to take the news in. Not knowing what to say next, Hannibal finished his coffee and waited.

"When I spoke to him last, Gartee was about to get married," Krada said.

"Yes, they did marry," Hannibal said. "In fact, I think you knew the girl. A Russian girl, Viktoriya Petrova."

Krada's eyes went up as if he was searching his memory. "Viktoriya? Yes, I think I may have met the girl back when Dani was still attending classes. This must be terribly hard on her. Is she all right?"

"She's fine," Hannibal said, "and safe and sound under Dr. Sidorov's care."

"Well I hope he can protect her," Krada said, "in case whoever went after Gartee goes after her. Perhaps I can offer a safe haven."

"I appreciate the offer," Hannibal said, standing, "but I think I have a better idea of how to make sure she's safe. And if I move right now, I'll just about have time to take care of that chore before my lunch date."

Hannibal shook Krada's hand at the door and called good-bye to his wife just to see the annoyed look on his face. He was still smiling at his ability to get under Krada's skin when he started the car and his phone rang at the same second.

"All right, Rissik, are you lonely or something? You can't have learned anything about old Boris in the time since I left your office."

"Nope, but one of yesterday's pigeons has come home to roost."

"News about Dani Gana?" Hannibal asked as he backed out of the driveway.

"Gana's a dead end. As a matter of fact, so is Gartee Roberts. Thank goodness you tracked the boy back to Hamed Barek. That appears to be a real person. And you're not going to believe who he really is."

-29-

Hannibal pulled up in front of his building long enough for Ivanovich to run out and hop into the passenger seat. As they pulled away, Ivanovich again straightened his suit coat. A bad habit, Hannibal thought, for a man who is always concealing a firearm. Others will know that he is armed.

"Note this gesture of trust," Ivanovich said. "You call. I come, with no idea of where we may be going."

"I'm taking you to Viktoriya," Hannibal said, never taking his eyes off the traffic. "You can stay there until I straighten this whole thing out."

"Thank you," Ivanovich said. Then, after a beat, "Why?"

Hannibal smiled, and turned up the stereo. Steely Dan boomed out, Donald Fagan calling their attention to the glory of the royal scam. "Don't worry, you'll be chaperoned. But I think her late husband's enemies may be even bigger and more varied than I thought before, and I want her protected right while I'm out tying off the loose ends."

"You have news?" Ivanovich asked, taking out a handkerchief and laying it on his lap.

"Well, I found out this morning that Dani Gana, AKA Gartee Roberts, was in the country illegally."

"INS is no trouble," Ivanovich said, drawing his weapon. "They rarely find anyone unless there is heavy political pressure."

"I also now know that Hamed Barek is his real name. And Rissik just called to tell me that Barek is a Moroccan ambassador."

"I see." Ivanovich watched the road while he disassembled the pistol in his lap. "Possible international intrigue in relation to the mob money. Yes, there may be more professional people involved."

Hannibal rolled up onto the beltway pointed north as he went through it all. "So this Barek, a diplomat from Morocco, steals money from the Russian mob. He vanishes, by which we can assume he goes home with his fortune, which can neither be traced nor claimed by the previous owners. But then he returns to the U.S. Why?"

"Is it not obvious?" Ivanovich asked, pushing the slide back onto his gun's receiver. "He came back for her. She shines in a world full of ugliness."

"Yeah, yeah, yeah," Hannibal said. But as he pulled into New York Avenue, he wondered if Ivanovich might be right. After their first meeting Hannibal suspected Dani Gana of planning to con a helpless young girl out of her virtue and her father's fortune. Could Gana have been, in reality, no more than a lovesick hustler risking it all for the woman he fell for in college?

Hannibal pulled off of I-495 and into Capital Heights, just outside of the District, as Steely Dan declared that they had found their home at last. He didn't think so. Technically, they were in Maryland but as is so often the case, there was no clear line between the little town and Washington. Watching his mirrors closely he pulled into the parking lot of a pink, two-story building with a Motel 6 sign over the entrance. Ivanovich got out of the car at the same second he did. Both men scanned the area carefully, verifying that they had not been followed.

"You brought my Viktoriya here?"

"Inconspicuous, out of the way, and the last place anyone would expect to find her," Hannibal said, deciding to let the "my Viktoriya" pass for the moment. He led the way up the exposed stairs to the landing surrounding the building. They walked around to the back of the building. Hannibal knocked on a door and called out his own first name. He heard two locks turned and the door opened a crack with the security bar still in place.

"Yakov, if it wasn't me, that security device wouldn't stop anyone from shooting you," Hannibal said. "Just let us in, all right?"

To call the room modest would have been a kindness. The carpet was new but cheap, the wallpaper was intact but dull, and the curtains were sun-faded. But the room was clean and the flowered bedspreads lent a bit of brightness.

Viktoriya lay on the second of the two full beds. Her hair was splayed out like a black silk fan across the pillow as she dozed. She lay atop the covers in a white peasant dress that was definitely not what Hannibal had seen her in before.

"Tell me you didn't let her go shopping."

"I went out long enough to buy her some clothes and other necessities," Sidorov said. "I was careful."

"I hope so," Hannibal said. "The people looking for her now could be very, very good."

Sidorov snorted. "I grew up in the shadow of the KGB. I know how to be careful."

"Who knows you are here?" Ivanovich asked, watching Viktoriya's chest rise and fall.

"No one," Sidorov said, waving at Ivanovich to keep his voice down. "Not even my wife. I would never endanger my Viktoriya."

"She looks awfully quiet," Hannibal said, sitting on the unoccupied bed.

"I've given her a mild sedative," Sidorov said. "She became upset."

As if to contradict him, Viktoriya opened her eyes and looked around the room with unfocused eyes. When her gaze did settle on something, it was Hannibal or perhaps her own reflection in his glasses.

"Uncle Yakov?"

"I am here, child," Yakov said.

"Everything is fine," Hannibal said. "You're safe and sound."

Her eyes clouded up. "But my Dani. Dani is gone. I waited. He came back. But now he's gone."

"I won't let anything happen to you," Ivanovich said, stepping into her view. She visibly started.

"Aleksandr?"

"He's just here for extra protection," Hannibal said.

"I know," Viktoriya said through a soft smile. "Everyone always wants to protect me. Daddy. Aleksandr. Even Uncle Yakov back when I worked for him."

Hannibal and Ivanovich both turned to stare at the older man.

"During college, she was my receptionist for a short time," Sidorov said. Then his cell phone interrupted him and he snatched it out of his jacket.

"Yes, this is he," Sidorov said in a professional tone. He kept talking as he pulled out a notepad. "Yes. Yes, of course. And the patient?" The conversation continued and Sidorov scribbled at a furious pace on his tiny pad, ripping off pages and writing again. Hannibal lost interest and turned to the big windows. He had placed his bet on obscurity but right then, inside that little room, he felt trapped and cornered. An enemy who located them would have no trouble disposing of them all.

Sidorov closed his phone and put it away. Then he sat at the little table under the gaudy hanging lamp and nodded to himself for a few seconds before he spoke.

"Do you believe in divine providence, Mr. Jones?"

"Is this a trick question?" Hannibal asked.

"That was my service," Sidorov said as a smile blossomed on his face. "I told you that Boris Tolstaya had health issues, although I have kept his confidentiality as to the type or severity of his problem."

"So?" Ivanovich asked.

"Boris is under the care of another physician," Sidorov said. "This new doctor called my office for Boris's medical records. The girl called for my permission to release the records. Of course, while she was speaking with the other physician, she updated our patient records. And that included Boris Tolstaya's current address."

-30-

Hannibal felt a surge of electricity shoot up his spine as he took in this news. It sucked the air out of his lungs but then drove him to his feet. Tolstaya—killer, threat to Viktoriya, holder of the missing fortune—was the finish line and Hannibal was driven to dash toward it. Ivanovich, ahead of him by a small margin, already had a hand on the doorknob.

"No," Hannibal said, grabbing Ivanovich's sleeve. The Russian turned blazing eyes on him and for the first time Hannibal saw the killer inside the man.

"Because of him, Viktoriya is in danger," Ivanovich said. "But not for long."

"And if he's not working alone?" Hannibal asked. "Will you take your revenge while his followers storm in here and take out the girl?"

"What would you have me do?" Ivanovich asked, his eyes flicking toward Viktoriya. "I am a hunter, not a protector."

"Well, for just a little while we're going to have to exchange roles." Hannibal pulled out his wallet and dropped bills on the dresser. "Go downstairs and rent the room next door. Then stay out of sight and watch this door. Watch the landing. Watch the stairs. Watch the parking lot. If you want to keep Viktoriya safe, you'll be looking everywhere except at her. Got it?"

* * * * *

All the way across town Hannibal had thought about nothing except what he might find when he arrived at the address Sidorov gave him. Boris Tolstaya might be holed up alone, or he could have an army of Eastern European thugs with him. He could greet Hannibal as the smooth gangster he appeared to be in his photos or as the hardened killer Hannibal now suspected him of being. He might panic, or he might offer money for Hannibal's silence. It didn't matter. All Hannibal really wanted to do was to establish his location as a certainty, appraise the relative risk he presented, and call Rissik to take him into custody. With any luck, he would squeeze the location of the money out of Tolstaya and return it to Uspensky to end any chance that people would hunt Viktoriya. After he got the man to admit which murders he had committed, of course.

Doubt didn't begin to creep into his mind until he was parked two houses from Tolstaya's residence. The house was a modest rambler in suburban Silver Spring with a small yard and stained vinyl siding. He felt very close to the answers he had been seeking for days. He also felt very close to death. A wise man would call the police right then. Hannibal drew his Sig Sauer, charged the slide back, clicked the safety off, and slid it back into his holster.

Hannibal expected a long wait after he rang the doorbell. It seemed unlikely that Tolstaya would know who he was. He might suspect police, but they wouldn't send a lone man to the door with no vest. He might be expecting his doctor or a delivery boy. In any case, Hannibal would have only seconds to make him feel safe. He figured he would start with one truth that should not be threatening, that Yakov Sidorov had sent him.

It would be hard to say who was more surprised when Renata opened the door. Hannibal knew immediately why Boris had been so hard to find. She was able to rent a house as Renata "Queenie" Cochran without raising any alarms while police watched for activity in the name of Tolstaya.

"Nice to see you," Hannibal said, watching Renata's red-rimmed mouth hang open. "Should I be surprised? It seems your loyalties flow rather fluidly."

"Ben is safe, and he doesn't need me anymore," she shot back, searching the street behind Hannibal. "How did you find me?"

"I'm alone. And Dr. Sidorov sent me to check up on his patient. May I come in?"

Her eyes flashed from side to side as if she was searching for an alternative. Not seeing one, she stepped back. As Hannibal entered, she took his arm and guided him to the dining area. She sat and, seeing no one else, he sat also, but with his back toward a wall.

"Where is Boris, Queenie?" Hannibal asked. "Or is it Renata again?"

"Queenie, please," she said. "Even Boris calls me that now. He's in the backyard. He likes to be out in the sun."

Hannibal nodded. "He might not see a lot more of that. He must feel the net closing in on him after he got rid of Dani Gana."

Queenie leaned back, her brows reaching up toward her scarlet bangs. "Boris didn't get rid of anybody. He's not dangerous. He's running for his life. They'll kill him if they find him."

"You must mean Uspensky and the mob boys," Hannibal said. "Boris was your concern all along, wasn't he? Poor Ben."

Queenie's eyes went down to the table. Then, with a good deal of apparent effort, she raised her eyes to face his. Her brow wore deep furrows and her lower lip began a slight tremble. Hannibal thought he read sincere remorse in her eyes.

"You're right. I took advantage of Ben. I took advantage of his love because I knew he could help me try to get Boris's money back. If Dani had been reasonable, he'd have negotiated with Ben and we could have found out where he hid the money. But instead he..." She couldn't go on, so Hannibal filled in the blank.

"Instead he beat the man half to death. All because Boris couldn't take care of his own business."

"You have to understand," she said, straining not to shout. "Boris's life was at stake. These men in the Mafiya, you don't know these men. He had to stay in hiding. God, I need a cigarette."

"Well, before you fire one up, I'll just wander outside and have a few words with your husband du jour."

Hannibal walked slowly thorough the kitchen and turned sideways to peer through the window. The man in the yard was sitting on the far side of a wooden table with his back to the house. Hannibal couldn't see his hands. It was possible, he supposed, that the man was sitting there with a shotgun in his hand, waiting for trouble to call. There was really only one way to find out.

"Mr. Tolstaya," Hannibal called as he opened the back door. "Yakov Sidorov sent me to check on you. My name is Hannibal Jones."

"Sidorov," Tolstaya repeated, not moving. "He may be the only man alive smart enough to not want any of the missing money."

"Maybe," Hannibal said, stepping out into the sunshine, onto the neat, level lawn, "but it would sure make a lot of people's lives better if you returned it to its rightful owner." Tolstaya's mention of the stolen money left no doubt that he knew who Hannibal was.

"I am the rightful owner," Tolstaya said. "That money belongs to me. Gartee Roberts stole it from me, left the country, and changed his name."

"And that's why you killed him, isn't it?" Hannibal asked, stepping closer to the still figure. "That's murder number three for you, isn't it?"

The scent of grass that had been mowed that morning spoke to him of life, not death. Hannibal wasn't sure what he expected next, but it was not the sound of grass bending under rubber wheels and a subtle squeaking as Boris Tolstaya turned his chair toward his visitor and rolled closer.

"You can't pin Dani's murder on me," Tolstaya said. "You can't pin any murder on me."

He rolled his chair closer, into Hannibal's silence. The face was the one in the photographs of Boris Tolstaya, except that it was a little thinner. The black hair was a little thinner too. The change in his body was more profound. This man was half the size of the rakish gambler whose photograph Hannibal had been carrying around in his pocket. He wore a heavy sweater and slacks that hung on his frame. Two transparent plastic tubes snaked up from the back of the chair to clip into his nose. Tolstaya stopped just three feet in front of Hannibal. The left side of his mouth curled into a half smile.

"You didn't know," Tolstaya said. "Sidorov kept his word after all."

"I guess he did," Hannibal said. "What happened to you?"

Tolstaya laughed, a weak but real laugh. "You Americans. Always so direct. But you are right, you never learn anything otherwise. What has happened to me, Mr. Jones, is called amyotrophic lateral sclerosis."

"ALS," Hannibal muttered.

"Yes, the disease named after your baseball player Lou Gehrig," Tolstaya said, turning and rolling back toward the table. "I soldiered in Afghanistan at the same time that Nikita Petrova was there. I believe I was exposed to many of the same chemicals and toxins your soldiers faced during your Gulf War of 1991. Most escaped without harmful effects. Many did not. I am among them. It's neurological, you know. This wasting disease progresses quickly once it gets hold of you."

"I'd read that nobody knows what causes ALS," Hannibal said, sitting at the table opposite Tolstaya.

"I know," Tolstoya said. "Many soldiers know. Of course, they don't have much of a voice. No one survives this disease. There is no cure. I no longer have the strength to move my legs, Mr. Jones. My arms will be next and then eventually I won't even have the strength to breathe. I hope for only two things. One of them is peace and comfort until I die."

"And the other?" Hannibal asked.

"That my enemies never learn that I became so weak and helpless and died this way."

"By your enemies, I take it you mean your former mob partners," Hannibal said. "But I'm not sure I understand," Hannibal said.

Tolstaya took a deep breath and clenched his jaw. "That is because you think I am simply a gangster. You do not understand who I am."

Who was this man Boris Tolstaya, Hannibal wondered. He was a Russian gangster. Bu he was also a soldier stricken with a fatal disease. He was a lifelong keeper of secrets. He was an underworld figure who was at odds with his closest allies. And he was a man who seemed oddly at peace with his fate. Then the picture became clear. Boris Tolstaya was not concerned with dying, Hannibal decided, only with the nature of his death.

"Come on," Hannibal said, "there's no reason to keep secrets now, except maybe your location and your health situation. If I wanted to give those away, I would have already done it. I can keep those secrets for you until it no longer matters, but you can't just keep me in the dark."

Tolstaya nodded and his mouth formed an upside down U, the universal symbol for considering a new premise. He looked toward the house and the half-smile returned. "Ahh, what the hell. Yes, of course I mean my friend and partner Uspensky. But I cannot blame him, really."

"I don't know," Hannibal said, weaving his fingers together on the table. "In my circles, you don't kill a friend over money."

"It's not the money," Tolstaya said with a short laugh. "It's the federal charges. I did skim some money from the brokerage firm, you know. So did Uspensky. Between us, it was enough to allow the IRS to build a case for income tax evasion. Ivan fears that if they find me before he does, I'll turn state's evidence and help them send him to jail. And he knows that if they never find me, it still leaves him to take the fall. But if he found me, well, he could make me the fall guy. It would be easy to show evidence that I stole the money to avoid taxes."

"So, you're saying your low profile has nothing to do with Nikita Petrova's death, or Raisa's, or that of Dani Gana?"

Out the corner of his eye, Hannibal saw Queenie approaching slowly from the house. He stayed quiet until she stood beside the table. He could not interpret the look that passed between her and Boris, but it was not the look of love or hate or regret or obligation although it had elements of all of those.

"Is everything OK?" she asked.

"Everything is fine, my dear," Boris said. "Join us. The time for secrets between us is long past."

Queenie sat, but Hannibal felt that he was still Boris's focus. He would sit quietly and hear all that Boris had to say. As was so often true, he counted on silence to draw the truth out.

"I will tell you what there was between me and Nikita Petrova" Boris said, maintaining eye contact only with Hannibal. "First, we had the army experience in common. Then I worked with him to launder local Mafiya money through my firm. Then we gambled. He gambled poorly and he eventually owed me a great deal of money. This put me in the position to pressure him to turn a blind eye while I skimmed from the mob money he brought to our brokerage firm. That was all there was between us."

"That's a lie," Queenie said. "There was the girl."

Hannibal's brows reached for his hairline. He was astonished that Queenie would contradict Boris, especially with a third person present. Boris leaned forward, his eyes pressed together as if focusing all his power on Queenie's defiant face. His breath came in jagged gasps.

"What are you talking about?" Boris said, each word sounding like a separate sentence.

"You wanted his daughter, Viktoriya," Queenie said, her voice dropping into a deeper, more hateful register. "You wanted that child. You would have used her to clear his debt."

Boris's face, already pale and wan, fell like an underdone cake. His eyes stayed with Queenie but his gaze softened. His mouth quivered only for a brief second.

"You knew."

"Of course I knew," Queenie said. "And one night, at the Russia House, I told Raisa. I assume she told her husband. I know that Boris would not let you take his little girl away. Like everyone else, he loved her too much. I know that is why you and Nikita fought, that night. That is why you killed him."

"You can't know that," Boris said, raising a weak arm in protest.

"Of course I know," Queenie said, standing. "There was a witness. Dani Gana saw you kill him."

Queenie snapped to her feet, knocking over her chair behind her, and ran for the house, leaving a loud sob in her wake. She didn't seem concerned that Hannibal knew she was living with a philandering murderer, but she apparently couldn't stand to let him see her cry. Considering all the violence and double-dealing that circled Boris Tolstaya's life, it seemed odd that the moment felt so awkward. Hannibal let a few seconds of silence sit between him and Boris, but found more questions irresistible.

"So...you and Viktoriya?"

Boris smirked. "Not quite what my wife imagines. I wanted her help in the business. A beautiful, strong, and ambitious young woman can always be useful. I could see that she was attracted to the money and the power it brings. Sadly, her father never got past seeing her as a helpless little girl. She wanted to see northern Africa and made it clear in her clumsy overtures to me. I offered to send her to Algeria to make business arrangements there. But Boris, he stood firmly against me, even after I offered to wipe his debt clean."

"I'm surprised you would honor his wishes," Hannibal said.

"Fortune smiled, on him and me. I met Dani back when he was known as Gartee Roberts. He was also young and ambitious and attractive in his way. And he was attracted to the money. And he had family in Africa. In fact, his family ties reached high into the Moroccan government. So I sent him to Morocco with new clothes and enough money to get established. In short order he wormed his way into their foreign service. The test there gets easier the more you pay to take it, you see. And once he was working for the embassy, he could cross borders at will with however much cash we needed to move."

"So then Nikita had little to offer you to clear his markers," Hannibal said, shaking his head. "His death was pure and simple. A mob hit for unpaid gambling debts."

"Nikita's death was an accident," Boris said, his voice now softer. "I did not hate the man, and you know you can't collect from a corpse. We went to the roof to talk, Nikita and I and two of my associates from the firm. The conversation got rough. I had to discipline him. It was meant to be a beating, nothing more, to show him I was serious. He..." Boris paused for more labored breathing. "I didn't know how sick he was. How weak he was. It seems his injuries took far more out of him than anyone suspected."

"Oh, it was an accident, huh? I'm sure that made his widow feel better," Hannibal said.

"I took care of Raisa." Boris dropped his fist on the table with all the energy he had. It was a pathetic display of weakness that somehow made Hannibal feel a little better.

"She knew it was you," Hannibal said, standing.

"She found out somehow," Boris said. "Nikita left little money behind, but his wife blackmailed me for enough to keep her in her chosen lifestyle."

Hannibal stood, hands in pockets, staring down at Boris in disgust. "And that's why you had to kill her too."

Boris rolled back from the table, his shadow just reaching Hannibal's toes. He stared at his own knees, then held his palms wide and stared up into Hannibal's face as if preparing himself for crucifixion.

"Look at me," he said through clenched teeth, and then louder, "look at me. Who could I kill?"

Hannibal had to admit this truth. Within the last week Boris Tolstaya could have no more slipped into Raisa Petrova's house to shoot her than he could have hunted Dani Gana down in Rehoboth Beach.

"Nikita's death sounds more like manslaughter than murder, so why not just come clean and explain. Why should I keep your secret now? If you talk to the police, you can go to a decent facility where they can care for you properly."

"You will keep my secret because you know that whatever the police know, Ivan Uspensky will know soon. He believes that Renata and I both know the location of the missing fortune. Even if I am in custody he will find her and torture her for information she does not have."

"How selfless of you," Hannibal said.

Boris smiled, making it clear that he did not miss the irony in Hannibal's dry tone. "That is your reason for keeping my location to yourself. For myself, I prefer to keep my reputation intact until the end. Let them all think I am a killer. Renata can take care of me well enough between now and the end."

"How nice for you. But doesn't the Petrova girl deserve some justice?"

"Justice?" Boris breathed, and choked. "Really, Mr. Jones, what possible purpose could it serve for me to be in prison? Is it not sufficient that I am a prisoner of this chair?"

"Which brings me to the one remaining thing I don't get," Hannibal said. "Now that I know what she knows, I don't understand why Queenie is still here. She loves you far more than you deserve."

"You think so?" Boris turned his chair to face the back door more directly. "You have listened to my story, but not paid much attention to what you know about her. Renata believes that I know where the missing money is. And she

194

believes me when I say that I will share that information with her just before I die."

Hannibal looked back toward the door. "You didn't kill Dani Gana. You never even found Dani Gana. You don't have any idea where the money is, do you?"

Boris gave him a sly smile and turned his chair away from Hannibal and the house. Hannibal realized this sad, sick man was right about one thing. He was being well punished for whatever his crimes were during his life. It made him feel good to know that the random vagaries of fate didn't just strike the innocent.

With his back to Hannibal, Boris said, "I wish you luck, Mr. Jones. If you locate the money, at least my Renata and the Petrova girl will be left in peace. Now, would you please ask my wife to bring out my lunch? I'd like to stay out here in the sun."

"Lunch. Damn." Hannibal checked his watch, cursed under his breath, and moved quickly toward the house.

-31-

Hannibal's phone was calling Cindy's office before he pulled into traffic. The ringing didn't give him enough time to berate himself for letting the case push their lunch date out of his mind. He would have learned all the same information if he had arrived at Boris Tolstaya's rented house two hours later. Viktoriya would have still been under Ivanovich's watchful eye and the three victims would still be dead. But he would not have been calling Cindy more than an hour late.

When the phone clicked over to Cindy's voicemail, Hannibal hung up and called the office general number. After three more rings, the receptionist answered. He pushed under a yellow light, his mind elsewhere.

"Hello, Mrs. Abrogast. It's Hannibal."

"Hello, Mr. Jones," Abrogast said in her deceptively old-lady voice. "I'm afraid Ms. Santiago isn't in this afternoon. And I must tell you, she was not happy with you when she left here, young man."

"My fault," Hannibal admitted. "What did she say, Mrs. Abrogast?"

"Oh, something about being stood up, I believe. She remarked that she had canceled a lunch meeting with that nice real estate fellow to go with you instead."

"Really? Well, I sure feel bad about that," Hannibal said, voice dripping with sarcasm.

"Yes, well I don't think it will be a big problem," she said. "She'll meet him for dinner instead. At Bobby Van's, I believe. Nice place. Would you like to leave a message?"

"A message? No thank you, ma'am. Have a nice afternoon."

As he cut the connection he felt cold inside. A message? What message could he possibly leave? Mrs. Abrogast was right. Bobby Van's was not his idea of casual dining. It was expensive and classy, and well known for its top-notch prime rib. For a moment he considered hunting her down at court or wherever she was, but knew that would be close to impossible. Besides, if she was working, she would not appreciate his interruption. And besides all that, he was working too, damn it. He was on a case.

Or was he? No one was paying him to find the murderers or to protect the orphaned survivor. In fact, who knew how much paying work had passed him by while he was chasing Russian ghosts. Worse, this pro bono pursuit of answers no one else wanted was costing him the closeness he deserved to have with his woman. He wasn't sure why, but he felt obligated to share what he learned from the Tolstayas with Aleksandr Ivanovich. After that, he decided, it was time to return to his own life. Right then, he defined his own life as Cindy Santiago.

The drive back to Viktoriya's motel was uneventful despite the bank of dark clouds that slid across the sky to park overhead. Hannibal pulled between white lines among the very few cars in the motel lot and strolled to the building, scanning his environment as he climbed the exposed stairs. He didn't see Ivanovich during his long trip between his car and the door, but he was certain that Invanovich had seen him. A sharp breeze sliced through his suit jacket as he stood on the landing. He gave the door a couple light taps when he reached it.

Dr. Sidorov opened the door just enough for Hannibal to enter and closed it without locking it. Viktoriya handed Hannibal a mug of tea poured from the little coffee pot they had moved from the bathroom to the round table. Her dark eyes were still a little drowsy, as if they had not yet pushed all the way out from under the sedative. Having never seen her calm and relaxed, Hannibal looked at her as if for the first time.

Her skin wasn't simply fair. Her face glowed like that of a china doll. It cut a sharp contrast with the eyes that looked almost too big for her face and the rolling waves of hair like a black storm at sea. Her smile was inviting to be sure, but he wasn't certain if it meant to suck him in or chew him up.

"So tell me," she said, perching on the edge of the bed, "did you learn anything of value from Mr. Tolstaya?" Her voice was as soft as he remembered, but he had not noted that husky undertone before.

"Yes, tell us," Ivanovich said. Hannibal snapped around to find him just inside the door. He had slipped inside, unnoticed. He was very quiet of course, but Hannibal knew there was another reason he did not feel Ivanovich's entrance. For a brief moment, he had fallen under the same spell that held Ivanovich in thrall and, from all appearances, had called Dani Gana back from his African home. He sipped his strong tea while he took time to gather his thoughts.

"Well, I think I know the truth about Viktoriya's father," Hannibal said. He stood in the corner beside the door. Ivanovich sat on the nearer bed. Sidorov settled into a chair at the round table. With the audience assembled, Hannibal figured he'd better just get on with it. "Boris Tolstaya admitted to me that he and Nikita argued about the money he owed. The argument became violent."

"No," Viktoriya said. "Uncle Boris wouldn't kill Father."

"Not on purpose," Hannibal said. "I think he just got carried away, and your father was weaker and sicker than anyone knew."

Viktoriya clouded up, and buried her face in her hands. Ivanovich stood to get closer, but stopped short of putting an arm around her. After watching her body shake with soft sobs for a moment, he turned back to Hannibal.

"So this was all about money after all?"

"Maybe," Hannibal said. "I think there may have been another factor. Boris's wife seemed to think he wanted

Viktoriya for himself, and was going to take off with her to Africa or someplace. Of course, if that was true, why would he introduce her to Dani?"

"He didn't."

Viktoriya raised her face when she spoke. Sidorov produced a handkerchief, which she accepted with a smile. Sidorov and Ivanovich looked at her the way the Tarleton twins watched Scarlett O'Hara in *Gone with the Wind*.

"You didn't meet Dani through Boris?" Hannibal asked.

"Oh no," Viktoriya said. "I met him in college. Actually, Professor Krada introduced us at one of his parties, and we dated for a while at Howard, but we kept it sort of quiet. It can be hard for a boy dating a white girl there."

Hannibal's eyes flashed to Ivanovich, then back to Viktoriya. "My mistake. I knew you went to parties with him at the college while he was a student, but I thought you met him after you yourself left school. You've really known this man longer than I thought you had. You didn't drop out because of meeting him at the Russia House, did you?"

"Oh no, of course not," she said. "I left school for the abortion. I was kind of surprised to see him again at the Russia House."

Hannibal watched the men's faces. It appeared that he was the only person in the room surprised by the mention of an abortion.

His mind returned to Viktoriya's ruthless husband. Had he gotten Viktoriya pregnant in college? Or what about Boris, whose wife believed he had a thing for her? Hannibal already knew that Raisa was prone to blackmail. Maybe the abortion produced another income stream for her until the blackmailer had had enough. It could be a motive for murder, but it didn't fit very well with Raisa and Dani being killed by the same weapon—unless Dani had embarrassed the folks back home and someone was sent to clean up all evidence of his transgression.

Before Hannibal could decide on the right way to ask who got Viktoriya pregnant, Ivanovich stood.

"Let us step outside for a moment."

Ivanovich held the door open for Hannibal and followed him outside. They walked toward the stairs with Hannibal in the lead. He assumed that Ivanovich wanted to protect Viktoriya from the obvious questions, but when they stopped he pulled out his wallet and handed Hannibal a check, folded in half. For the first he looked past Hannibal, avoiding eye contact.

"You have done your job honorably," Ivanovich said. "I know we did not meet in the best way, and that I took advantage of you, but once you made a commitment you did all that you agreed to do. I want you to know that I am also an honorable man. This is fair compensation for a job well done."

Hannibal nodded and slipped the check into an inside jacket pocket without looking at it. Now, even in Ivanovich's mind, the case was over. Hannibal nodded and shook his most recent client's hand. Ivanovich started back toward the room, but stopped when Hannibal did not follow.

"Will you not come in to say good-bye?"

"No need," Hannibal said. "Neither of them needs me in their lives anymore. And probably neither do you. I have strong ties to law enforcement and you don't need their interest rubbing off on you."

"I see," Ivanovich said with a wry smile. "And we all have ties to organized crime and you don't need those associations either."

"Look, I don't know what your future holds, and it's probably best that way," Hannibal said. "Just protect the girl for a couple more days until I can get in front of Uspensky and convince him that she doesn't have the missing money or know where it might be. Some losses you can recover and some you can't. I'm afraid he's just going to have to eat this one."

"She would be safe if you gave up Tolstaya."

"Yeah, maybe," Hannibal said, turning toward the stairs. "But his wife is there with him. Even if I was prepared to

200

throw Tolstaya to the wolves, I'm not prepared to toss Queenie out with him. Just watch her until you hear from me, OK? I've got my own life to take care of."

* * * * *

The clouds broke open just as Hannibal reached his car. The blackness leaned in, turning afternoon into night and the beltway into an elongated parking lot. Hannibal cranked Van Halen up as loud as he could stand it to blot out the sound of cold, watery fists beating against his roof and hood. He knew it wouldn't last long.

Only a light drizzle pattered on the street when Hannibal stepped out of the Black Beauty to inhale the sharp freshness of storm-cracked ozone. Inside his office, he stood in the middle of the floor for a few moments, enjoying the peace of having the space to himself for the first time in several days. He draped his jacket over his chair, planning only to call Uspensky to give him what little information he had and to plead for an end to the hostilities. But the flashing light on his phone told him there might be more pressing matters. He had two messages and one of them might be from Cindy. Feeling just a little anxious, he pressed the button.

"Mr. Jones. This is Eric Van Buren, down at UVA. We spoke on the phone in Detective Rissik's office."

"Damn," Hannibal said.

"Listen, I've been thinking about my old student, Hamed Barek. I've remembered some details that might be of interest to you in your investigation. If you're still interested, give me a call."

Hannibal wasn't sure there was any reason to learn more about Barek, AKA Roberts AKA Gana. He pushed the message button again.

"Jones, this is Orson." Sigh. Again, not the voice he was hoping for. "I just got a call that Hamed Barek's mother is in Washington. She's here from Morocco to pick up her son's body, which they moved to Baltimore expecting to do an autopsy, which, of course, she put the kibosh on. She's interested in talking to somebody who can tell her what happened to her boy, and I thought you'd like to talk to her too. Give me a call."

This was more interesting. She might have some insight as to where he left the money, and Van Buren might have some good conversation starters to offer, so he'd return that call a bit later. But first, he needed to get hold of a certain Russian mob boss.

It proved easier than expected to get through to Uspensky. Hannibal simply called the office and gave the receptionist his name. When Uspensky picked up his phone after a surprisingly short wait, Hannibal heard a mixture of impatience and gratitude in his voice. Even without knowing what Hannibal had to say, he seemed to appreciate the fact that he called at all.

"Jones. You got something for me?"

"I've come across some information you might find of value," Hannibal said. "But it's not the kind of news that belongs in a telephone conversation."

"My day's already pretty full. Be here tomorrow around 4:30."

Knowing the fates of Nikita Petrova and Boris Tolstaya made mobsters less intimidating. "You asking me or telling me?"

Long pause. Hannibal could almost feel Uspensky's mind working. Weighing options. Considering possible outcomes. Cost-benefit analysis.

"Can you be here tomorrow around 4:30?"

Better. "Why, yes, I think my schedule is clear at that time. I'm sure I can make it. And it will be worth it to you. See you then."

Hannibal felt a little better when he hung up the phone. In his world, one relished one's small victories. He checked his watch and decided that he didn't want to deal with either Rissik or Van Buren so close to the end of their workdays. Seeing the time also made him realize how hungry he was.

He had missed lunch entirely and dinner time was coming up. And that made him think of Cindy. His Cindy, on her way to dinner with a slick real estate salesman. Unless they decided to dine later. But he knew she liked to eat early.

His right hand moved of its own accord, snatching the phone off its cradle again. While he held it, he used his left to tap computer keys. In a few seconds he had the phone number to Bobby Van's. He dialed and took a deep breath, knowing that he was crossing some invisible line.

"Yes, I'm sorry, but I've forgotten what time my reservations are for tonight."

"Sorry sir," the hostess said. "Your name?"

"Johnson," Hannibal said. "Reggie Johnson."

"Yes sir. Johnson, party of two, for 6:30."

"Great. Thank you."

Now, what did his hands expect him to do with that information? He looked out at the hazy, indecisive sky. The rain had stopped, but the eaves still dripped in front of the big windows. Was it clearing, or just taking a breath before another burst of rain? Would it become really light before the darkness set in?

Could he just sit there and watch the darkness take over?

* * * * *

Early evening was the worst possible time to be driving into the District, especially if you were struggling up from Southeast to the opposite corner of the city. The only good point from Hannibal's point of view was that he would not be holding anyone up if he cruised down the street slowly. The rain had stopped and sharp sunbeams came in from the west, giving the sidewalk and the asphalt on the street a sparkling sheen. Even the air looked cleaner, and the Washington Monument glowed like a ghostly signpost.

The steakhouse sat in an old bank building practically around the corner from the White House. Hannibal wasn't sure where he would park and was even less sure of what he would say to Cindy when he arrived. Would it be less rude to join them or to ask Reggie to excuse them for a moment?

Then he saw her, sooner than expected. Despite the evening cool they were at one of the outdoor tables, talking to their waiter. Opposite her, Reggie sat in a purple suit and orange shirt. A starburst of light flashed off one of his diamond cufflinks.

Cindy was lovely as always, wrapped in a camel coat. Her skin was smooth teak. He thought she had added an auburn tint to her dark brown tresses and left it down, just touching her shoulders, feathered in front. High cheekbones accented her Cuban roots. Her black heels had to be more than two inches high, force-flexing her shapely calves. He had not seen this suit before. The navy skirt looked a couple of inches higher on her perfect thighs than her usual length. A single string of pearls around her neck was the perfect accent, echoing her perfect teeth as she smiled and chatted with a man who could be a professional athlete and had the kind of style that allowed him to pull off wearing a purple suit without effort.

Hannibal took in the whole scene in a few seconds as he rolled past, unnoticed.

She looked so damned happy.

-32-
Wednesday

The sun was just flashing in from the eastern edge of the horizon when Hannibal came within sight of his building and slowed to a brisk walk. The pain lancing through his right side told him that he had held his speed a little high that morning. His heart was drumming triplets in his chest and each inhalation was a dagger in his lungs, almost bringing tears to his eyes. His jogging suit dripped with his sweat, but the early morning breeze cooled him quickly after he unzipped his top.

He had pushed himself for five miles at a pretty strong pace, but he could not outrun his self-loathing for the night before. He dragged himself up the sandstone steps into his building and managed to get back into his apartment without having to say hello to anyone. That was his first success feeling of the day.

During the time he stripped, showered, and ate two hardboiled eggs, Hannibal thought only about Cindy, sitting at an outdoor café table, unaware of his presence. He wondered why he had needed to see that sight, and how he could have just kept driving, never stopping to speak to her.

He wondered, but he knew.

Then he got dressed. He pulled on a white cotton dress shirt, not significantly different from the others hanging in his closet except that it had French cuffs and a designer label and that it was a gift from Cindy. He had said thank you at the time, then since he had no idea who or what an Ermenegildo Zegna was, he had looked it up online. He still didn't understand what could make a white cotton shirt worth $235. He wore the shirt only because it made him feel closer to her.

While putting his cuff links into place he considered where he would go that day. By the time he was tying his tie, his mind was entirely on the business at hand. This was the day he expected to wrap up the whole mob business that had him going in circles like a roulette wheel, chasing a stolen fortune.

Hannibal's day would start with phone calls. Once he was dressed, he went across the hall to make them. There was nothing wrong with his home phone. He just liked to make business calls from his desk. His first important call was to Rissik's office. He pushed the speed dial button, set the phone on speaker, and reached for the coffee beans overhead.

"You're up early," was Rissik's first comment.

"Just couldn't wait to hear your voice, Chief. Now, what's this about Barek's mother?"

"She wants to see you," Rissik said. "Maryland law couldn't answer her questions, so they put her on to me. I didn't want to disappoint an important citizen of one of our allies, so naturally I told her I knew the ace detective who had been following her son's movements."

"Thanks," Hannibal said, pouring water from a carafe into the coffeepot. "That will probably get me killed."

"Actually, she'd like to find out all she can about her little Hamed's American adventures, and she'll be stuck in the Moroccan embassy all day waiting for the murder victim formerly known as Dani Gana to be driven down to Washington from Baltimore. When I didn't hear from you last night I took the liberty of making you an appointment. What the hell is that noise?"

"Sorry," Hannibal said. "Grinding the beans. Someday you're going to have to come over here and get a decent cup of coffee. Now, you were saying about an appointment?"

"You are to meet with Mrs. Fatima Barek at the Moroccan embassy at ten a.m. And don't be late. She's pretty important people over there."

"Fatima? Really? Like the seven veils?"

"Hey, do I make fun of your name?" Rissik asked. "I could, you know."

"Good point," Hannibal said, filling a mug and pausing to inhale the sweet, rich aroma he loved. "I'll be there."

After chatting with Rissik, Hannibal carried his mug around to his desk where he settled back into his chair. He wasn't sure why the black leather felt different that day; softer, somehow. Then he realized what was different. It was really his again. Smiling, he punched buttons to ring the number left in his other message.

"Dr. Van Buren? This is Hannibal Jones. Is this a good time to talk?"

"Fine," Van Buren answered. "But it's just Professor Van Buren for now, or better yet, Eric. In a couple months I'll finish my doctorate and you can talk to me like I'm an old man."

"Noted," Hannibal said, pulling out a note pad and pen. "Eric, then. I appreciate you getting back to me."

"I had to, after hearing from an old colleague," Van Buren said. "Dr. Krada said he knows you too."

"Krada?" Hannibal sipped again, savoring the taste as he organized his thoughts. "Interesting. Why was he in contact with you?"

"Oh, he called about a student we had in common. You guessed it—Hamed Barek, who apparently went to Howard under a different name."

"Yes," Hannibal said, thinking Krada wanted to warn his pupil about the crowd of people searching for him. "Did you have something to tell me about him?"

"Actually, we discussed the boy's history somewhat. That got me looking at his file and remembering old conversations. I know you were trying to trace him back to his roots, as it were, and they are indeed in Algeria."

"Hold on," Hannibal said, jotting notes. "I have information that he really is from Morocco."

"I meant his family," Eric said. "Barek's grandfather was an educated, well-to-do businessman in Algeria. He had position and status, things that mean a lot in that part of the world. But his business interests apparently took him to Morocco where he ultimately went broke."

"I see," Hannibal said, "But I'm sure Dr. Krada was more interested in where his old student is now. I'm rather surprised he found you."

Eric's laughter crackled through the static of a bad connection. "Nothing mysterious there, Jones. I knew Dr. Krada when he was here at UVA. In fact, I was one of his students."

This news came as an unexpected treat, cheering Hannibal like the welcoming aroma of his coffee. "You don't say. Tell me, did he have parties for his students down there like he does up here?"

"You bet. And after he moved to Howard I used to drive up there for them. In fact, I was there the night Hamed Barek was introduced to the Russian girl, Vicki Petrova. He fell for her that first night. Everybody could see that."

"You don't say." Hannibal snugged back into the warm leather, notebook in hand. "And what made Krada move up to Howard? I doubt it was more money, since it's kind of a smaller school."

"Hardly for the money." Eric paused and Hannibal waited through the silence. Interruptions were bad for people's memories. Finally, Eric asked, "Have you met Mrs. Krada?"

Hannibal took his time savoring a mouthful of coffee before he answered. "Nina? Sure. Nice girl. Seems a little young for him."

"Yeah, well she was his student too. The faculty didn't take too kindly to it when Dr. Krada took up with her. Then when Nina came down with a bad case of pregnant, Krada had to leave in disgrace."

"Fascinating, but a little off the topic," Hannibal said, checking his watch. "I do appreciate the background on Barek, though. I'm actually meeting with his mother today. If nothing else I can tell her that he had loved the woman he married for years. Now, I've got to get myself to Embassy Row."

-33-

Comparisons between Embassy Row and his own neighborhood in Southeast seemed unavoidable. The buildings were old and crammed together too closely for comfort. Many of the streets were too narrow for two cars to pass, let alone for cars to park on them. And like Hannibal's neighborhood, city police did their best not to go into the area.

Fortunately, his destination was not clustered with the other embassies on or beside Massachusetts Avenue. Officially "The Chancery of the Embassy of the Kingdom of Morocco," the building was just outside the area generally thought of as Embassy Row, on 21st Street off Q Street, just a couple of blocks from Dupont Circle. He found a parking garage to store his Volvo in, and walked past the bored looking protesters and beggars to the massive stone edifice that could hold clues to the answers he needed.

He could hear a team of bongo and conga drummers in the outer circle of a fountain, sending their energy out from Dupont Circle. Like so many of the buildings in this part of the city, the embassy had round towers at its corners, like pointed-roofed minarets. It must have appealed to the Moroccans who chose it, most of whom were Sunni Muslims.

Inside, the décor was quite contemporary and more Americanized than he expected. Hannibal walked up to the receptionist, who looked like a teenage Tyra Banks.

"Hello. My name is Hannibal Jones, and I have an appointment with Mrs. Barek."

"Of course, sir," the girl said with a smile. "We have been expecting you. You may have a seat in our waiting room but before you do, I am afraid I have to ask you if you are carrying anything that you might need to leave with me before going further into the building. This is simply for security reasons, you understand."

"Of course." Hannibal presented his private investigator's badge. "I show you this, so you will know that I carry this legally." He then showed her his pistol.

"Thank you sir," the receptionist said, betraying no reaction at all. "Please leave that with me while you are in the embassy."

Hannibal was happy to comply. After stowing his pistol in a safe behind her, the receptionist showed him to a comfortable chair in the adjacent bright and airy waiting room. He was on time, but he knew he would have to wait. This was how important people let you know they were more important than you. He didn't mind. Like the quarters he had to toss at gates on the Dulles Toll Road, waiting was part of the cost of getting to where he needed to be.

After Hannibal demonstrated his patience for twenty minutes, the receptionist ushered him into a cozy sitting room and seated him at a small table. A dark and alluring young woman appeared from an alcove, poured tea from a flowered pot, and left. Then the door opened again and a mature yet striking woman entered the room. Hannibal snapped to his feet.

"Mr. Hannibal Jones? I am Mrs. Fatima Barek."

He was struck by her perfect posture and elegant bearing as she floated across the tiles toward him. He had expected traditional Muslim garb, but she wore a very American black evening gown that covered her feet without quite touching the floor. Only the click of her heels told him that she wore shoes at all. White kid gloves covered her hands and reached to her upper arm. It was a canny way to keep her entire body covered while giving the appearance of Westernization.

She presented her right hand, at arm's length, and raised it to shoulder height. Hannibal took just her fingertips between his black-gloved first finger and thumb, gave them a gentle jiggle, and released them. She sat. He sat opposite her. He reached for the pot but she waved his hand away and filled her own cup. He supposed that even when she was the important person in the room, the woman was supposed to pour. She sipped and smiled. He followed suit. She looked at him. He waited.

"Mr. Jones, this is awkward for me. I am still mourning a great loss, and yet I will only be in your country for one day and I need to learn all I can. I understand that you may be able to help me."

She was heavy, but not fat. Her round face was kindly and loving. Hannibal saw that her son had inherited her obsidian eyes and dark wavy hair. Her skin was maybe a half tone darker than Hannibal's, but to a casual observer this could be the result of beach time rather than genetics. In some way he could not define, she reminded him of his own mother. It may have been the smile.

"Ma'am, I am very sorry for your loss," he said, using the words he learned in the Secret Service. "I don't know what you want to know most, but I will gladly share all I do know. I hope you won't blame our nation for your son's misfortune."

"Don't worry," Mrs. Barek said. "Our two governments have a long history and this certainly won't affect it. Did you know, Mr. Jones, that the Kingdom of Morocco was the very first country to recognize the new United States in 1777?"

"I didn't, but it's good to know. It's good to have old friends. I wish I had known your son better than I did."

He fell silent again, and Mrs. Barek stared at his face for a time. He wondered if her formality, and the ice breaker history lesson, were all avoidance behavior for her. She sipped from her teacup, then said, "Mr. Jones. Would you please honor me by removing your sunglasses so that I can see your eyes more clearly as you speak?"

Had he been rude? As Hannibal thought about it, it seemed obvious that he had, but wearing his shades was a habit. He apologized, pulled his glasses off, and tucked them into an inside jacket pocket. Mrs. Barek noted his eyes and nodded.

"I see you are not entirely a son of Africa yourself," she said.

"No, ma'am. My father was African American but my mother was German"

"You speak of both in the past tense," Mrs. Barek said. "You too have known loss."

"Yes, ma'am. But to survive one's parents, while painful, is natural. We are not meant to survive our children."

This time he was certain that her smile was just like his mother's used to be. "You are very kind," she said. "Now, please tell me about my son's death."

Hannibal examined the portrait of some Moroccan ruler in a military uniform while he gathered his thoughts. He was grateful that this woman was patient. He wanted to get the story right the first time and there were other people's feelings to consider in addition to hers.

"Here's what I know," he said, placing his palms together on the table with his fingers pointing toward her. "Your son apparently entered the country some years ago illegally. Using some very well forged papers and an apparent gift for storytelling, he enrolled in the University of Virginia."

"I had such plans for Hamed," Mrs. Barek said. "But he did not want to attend the private school I wanted to send him to, and he wanted to see the world. So, he ran away from home, ran away to America."

"From all reports he did well academically," Hannibal said, wanting to say something positive. "But perhaps he was concerned that he would be found out if he stayed in one place too long. He transferred to Howard University. His transfer kept him in touch with a professor he met at UVA who had befriended him. The professor was also an African native. Algerian in fact."

"This is Dr. Jamal Krada," Mrs. Barek said.

"Yes ma'am. I didn't realize you knew of him. Anyway, your son changed his name then, and claimed Liberian citizenship to deepen his cover. Later, when he returned to the States he changed his name again and, I think with Dr. Krada's help, passed himself off as Algerian. But I'm getting ahead of myself. A couple of important things happened while he was a student at Howard. First, he met and fell in love with a Russian girl named Viktoriya Petrova. When she dropped out of college he got a part-time job at the Russia House here in the city, where her family socialized. There he met a money launderer for the Red Mafiya named Boris Tolstaya."

Mrs. Barek made a dismissive noise by puffing air through her lips. "This is an evil man. I cautioned Hamed when he came home. But a woman cannot choose her son's friends."

"Well, Mr. Tolstaya involved your son in his schemes, which involved moving cash out of the U.S. and effectively making it disappear through the use of foreign banks."

Mrs. Barek slapped a palm on the table. "This is when Hamed came home. He was a new man, ambitious and smart. Mr. Jones, I would not normally reveal so much to a stranger, but I feel that the more you know, the more likely I am to get to the truth. So you should know tht I used what influence I had to move Hamed into a diplomatic position. But then, on a scheduled trip back to the United States he disappeared again."

"Right," Hannibal said. "I figure he must have purchased false documents in advance. He left home as Hamid Barek headed for this building, but he arrived as Dani Gana from Algeria. He also arrived with a quarter million dollars. Someone killed him for that money, but I don't know who."

"Did he suffer?"

"Ma'am, the murderer shot him twice with a small-caliber handgun."

"But was it quick at least?"

Hannibal felt he owed her the truth. "I'm sorry, but it was not quick. It was mean and amateurish. After being shot once, your son left the house he was in, apparently to lead the killer away from his wife and the money, which he had withdrawn from the bank. This was money that Boris Tolstaya had given him to launder. It appears that his only reason for returning to the United States was to win this girl he was in love with. The girl, Viktoriya, would not marry him without her mother's blessing. He stole the money from Tolstaya to show his prospective mother-in-law how prosperous and successful he was. I believe now that he intended to take his new wife home with him."

"Thank you," Mrs. Barek said. "I appreciate your frankness. However, I'm afraid you are wrong on one point. My son is not a thief." Her face was set in stone. It was like staring into the visage of the sphinx.

"I'm sorry ma'am, but where do you think he got such a sum?"

Her black eyes burrowed into Hannibal's. This was what he felt when he faced her son days ago. When she spoke, it was clear that it was to be the final declaration on the subject.

"I do not know. He is gone now, and cannot defend himself or explain his actions. But I know the money was not stolen because my son was not a thief."

Hannibal thought maybe he understood. There was the truth and there was the truth. Whatever was said about Hamed Barek after this conversation would become the truth. She was now the childless woman of a childless son. His reputation would live as his only legacy forever and would represent his family forever. Hannibal sat back and sipped his tea. Her eyes were hard but they were also pleading. He had to stand his own obsessive dedication to the truth against her obsessive dedication to her family's public image. Plus, he knew that offending her would end his chances of getting any further information from her. When he spoke, it was with unusual delicacy, stepping through a minefield of words, looking for safe footing.

"It could be," he said, "that matters have become confused. After all, Hamed Barek was an honored member of your foreign service. It could be that in fact an Algerian named Dani Gana stole money from the Russian mob. But somehow your son was killed for that money. If the funds were recovered, this mystery could be put to rest."

Mrs. Barek nodded and smiled, the sphinx transformed to Mona Lisa. "You are unusually wise for such a young man. But still, you don't know all. Hamed was not killed for this money. This money is not lost."

It took Hannibal a moment to wrap his brain around her words. "You?"

She smiled again.

"How?"

"A large package arrived at my home, delivered by diplomatic courier. American bills, one hundred dollar denominations, totaling more than two hundred and fifty thousand dollars. Hamed sent the money home through the embassy."

"Yes, but Viktoriya…" Hannibal cut himself off. Viktoriya had implied that Hamed/Dani left with the money after he was shot or that the killer took the money. But did she ever actually see a suitcase full of cash? A few thousand on top of a duffel bag full of clothes would have looked the same to her. Hamed may have kept that much for show money, and simply led her to believe that he had all of it with him, rather than tell his new bride that he had sent his fortune home to mama.

"Yes, Viktoriya, that tramp," Mrs. Barek said.

"He told you about her?" Hannibal said. "I'm sorry, I didn't realize."

"I know little," Mrs. Barek said, her pain and sorrow temporarily morphing into anger and resentment. "Hamed loved her, and said he needed to take her away from the bad influences here in America. Bad influences. This girl was not good enough for my son."

"I understand," Hannibal said. What woman is ever good enough in a mother's eyes?

"Do you?" she asked, her voice rising. "Do you? Do you know that Hamed saw her father beaten to death by this gangster Tolstaya? This man was married, but he wanted this Viktoriya for himself. One of her jilted suitors was a hired killer. Hamed even suspected her of having an affair with one of her college professors. Hamed is as likely to have been killed over this slut's affections as he is to have died for money."

Hannibal closed his eyes and silently counted to ten. When he opened them he was looking past the outraged mother facing him. The random bits swirling in his mind had just settled into a pattern as puzzles always do if you push the pieces around long enough. But this time, the pattern had little to do with organized crime.

"Viktoriya Petrova has been at the center of this whole affair from the moment I was dragged into," he said, almost to himself. "but men rarely kill for a woman's affection. Besides, I can assure you, just from the methodology, that your son's death was not the work of any professional assassin. And the gangster, Boris Tostaya, is in the end stages of a nerve disease called ALS. He simply is not strong enough to have chased your son down and shot him, even if he could have somehow found him."

"And the professor?" Mrs. Barek asked.

"Actually, he has no morning classes," Hannibal said, "And his schedule appears to be pretty flexible. It hardly makes any sense. But the pattern. The pattern is there." Hannibal jumped to his feet, an abrupt move that caused Mrs. Barek to draw back. "I'm sorry ma'am, but I need to go now. I have no proof but if what I suspect turns out to be true, then the Russian Mafia is the biggest red herring in history, and the danger might not be over after all."

"You mean this girl Viktoriya, don't you?" Mrs. Barek said. "If she's the reason my Hamid is dead, then I would be glad if the worst happened to her. But it is more important that my son's killer be brought to justice. If you manage this, the government of Morocco will be very grateful. And this mother will be personally grateful and will reward you for your diligence."

"Let's talk about that after we've proven who the killer is," Hannibal said. He hesitated, not sure of the proper way to end this interview. Should he take her hand again? Bow? Maybe if he simply asked to be excused, that would do.

Fatima Barek solved his problem by simply waving him out of the room. "Go and do what you have to do. I hope that if you are able to find the truth, you will contact me through the embassy. I need to know."

Hannibal nodded, pushed his Oakleys back into place, and hurried out of the embassy, stopping only to collect his Sig Sauer automatic. He had a feeling that he might need it soon.

-34-

Hannibal's tires squealed as he locked up his brakes and jerked to a stop in Jamal Krada's driveway. In the thirty seconds or so after he pushed the doorbell, he tapped his foot and his body shook as if it was idling roughly. His thoughts during the short drive had been dark and chaotic, as he reviewed and fumed about the many tiny clues he had walked past in the last few days.

When Nina Krada opened the door, her eyes flared wide. Hannibal realized that she had never seen him in any state but calm and friendly. Well, that was a pattern he was about to break.

"I'm sorry," she said in her meek voice. "I'm afraid Jamal is not in right now. Is there a message?"

"Don't worry," Hannibal said, pushing the door open. "You're the person I really want to talk to anyway." He took five or six steps toward the living room before he realized that Nina was still standing at the door. He turned to see her flushing, her eyes darting left and right. His eyebrows rose, forming a question.

"Mr. Jones, I am not permitted to have visitors when my husband isn't at home," Nina said. "Please, if you could come back when he is…"

Hannibal stepped toward her and she shrank back against the door. "You put up with that bullshit?" he asked. "He's really got you, hasn't he? Well, you answer my questions and help me get the story straight, and maybe, just maybe, I can free you from him."

"Free me? No, Mr. Jones, I love Jamal."

"Do you?" He went into the living room and dropped onto the sofa. "Well, what I want to know is, how much does he love you? Tell me about Jamal's relationship with Viktoriya Petrova."

Nina followed but stopped at the center of the living room floor. Barefoot, in a shapeless neutral color shift, she could have been a Nigerian child in a television commercial asking for donations. She raised her fists in front of her chest but they were too small to provide much defense.

"There is nothing to tell. She was one of his students."

"I see," Hannibal said in a softer tone. "And weren't you one of his students?"

Nina nodded, her lower lip covering its upper sister in what looked like a childish pout.

"And what happened? Is what Eric Van Buren told me true?"

Her head snapped up. "You spoke to Professor Van Buren at UVA?" After Hannibal nodded her shoulders seemed to drop farther than shoulders can. "Then you know what happened."

"Maybe, but I need to hear it from you. Did you...fall in love?"

"You don't know Jamal," Nina said, as if that explained something. When she saw it didn't, she said, "Jamal is a very intense man. He loves a woman so much that she can't help but love him too. He was a powerful, influential man on the college faculty and I was just a lowly freshman come to America from Algeria."

"You dated," Hannibal said. "And things went too far, maybe?"

"No, I wanted it. I wanted him. I wanted his..." the next word caught in her throat, choking her. With her elbows still pressed to her ribs she pointed toward the kitchen. "May I get some water?"

Hannibal waved toward the kitchen and she shuffled off with short, quick steps. He stood and followed at what he hoped would seem a safe distance to her. He stood at the entrance to the room while she pulled a bottle of water from the refrigerator and drank a few swallows.

"Stop me if I go wrong," Hannibal said. "You two were together, but not officially. Professor-student relationships are rather frowned on. But it's impossible to keep such things secret. When you became pregnant, everyone knew who the father was."

"He did the honorable thing and offered to marry me," she said, standing a little straighter than before. "But to the college that was no solution. They cast him out."

"Imagine that," Hannibal said. "So he found a position up here but still made you get rid of the baby?"

Nina spun on him with grief and hurt fighting for space on her small face. "No! He could never. It was me. I could not carry the baby. I lost it. I failed him."

Her legs seemed weak, making Hannibal realize how raw the wound he just touched still was. He helped her into a chair at the table. He wanted to comfort her, to protect her, to make her feel safe, but he also knew that if his guesses were right, time might be short.

"You've done your best to make a good home for him, I can see that," Hannibal said. "But you need to be honest with me. He couldn't stop looking at his younger students, could he?"

Her eyes met his and for the second time that day he felt the need to remove his glasses. He wasn't sure what she was looking for in there, but she appeared to find it.

"The black-haired girl," she said with unexpected venom. "She was so... white. But he loved her from the first."

Hannibal sat facing her, holding one hand. "But you were stuck here at home, alone, right? He came and went as he pleased. You knew nothing of what he did when he left here."

"Ahh, but I knew his students," Nina said. "I saw them all at his parties when they all but ignored me as you would a serving girl. But I saw them. And anyone who saw her with him could see what was between them. At least, until she met that other student, Gartee. I guess she wanted an African man, but this one was closer to her age."

"By then it was too late," Hannibal said. "He did to her what he did to you, but she decided not to keep the baby. I know she had an abortion. But there was no way for anyone to know who the father was."

"There was no doubt in her mind," Nina said.

"Why would you say that?"

"She said so when she called the other day," Nina said, smiling at some private joke. Hannibal sat back, mouth open.

"She called here?"

"Oh, those two have never lost touch," Nina said. "I know that if he could ever make her his, he would leave me. He can't, but they still talk."

"They talk, and you listen."

Nina leaned in very close. Hannibal could smell her sandalwood scent and something else. Was that alcohol on her breath?

"She called after she learned of her mother's death. She accused Jamal of killing her parents to cover it all up. They knew the baby was his. She thought he would be thrown out of a second college if it became public knowledge that he had misused another student, this time while he was married. She thought he would kill for that."

"I'm not so sure he wouldn't," Hannibal said. "But how could her parents know? No way she'd tell them."

Nina leaned even closer and this time he was sure of the smell. She was a lonely daytime drinker, one who could keep her secrets but could share them at the right time. He knew a fraction of a second before she said it.

"Me," she said, waving a finger at him. "After she had the abortion, I called her father and told him his precious daughter had just killed his grandson." In response to Hannibal's shocked expression she added, "Didn't he have a right to know?"

"What did he say?"

"Well, he was not a stupid man, for a Russian." Nina said. "He said he already knew who the father was, and that the bastard should be ashamed of touching a girl that young at his age. Say, would you like some sherry?"

Once she broke through her normal screen of secrecy, Nina was getting quite relaxed. Hannibal shook his head no, still considering her words. Did Nikita ever know the truth? Or had he assumed that Boris was the culprit? That would explain Nikita flying into a violent rage at the suggestion that Viktoriya go traveling with Boris. Boris would respond with equal violence. Nina's helpful selfishness may have been the catalyst for Nikita's death.

"You don't think there's any way Jamal had anything to do with Nikita's death, do you?" Hannibal asked, watching Nina stretch up on tiptoe to reach into a cabinet above the refrigerator. When she came down she was clutching a long-necked bottle.

"I don't really know. But I did hear that Vikki's father died the very next day."

"Well, at least he probably didn't have a chance to share that awful news with his wife," Hannibal said.

"Oh, she didn't know," Nina said, pulling down two water glasses. "She was completely surprised when I called her."

That news, shared so casually, chilled him to the marrow. "You needed to tell her too?"

"Her own fault," Nina said, carefully filling two glasses. "The little whore shouldn't be calling my husband. This time I think she called to tell him she might get married, just to make him jealous."

"So for that, you called Raisa Petrova and told her that her daughter had an abortion."

"Oh, I think she knew that much," Nina said, sipping her sherry. "But she had no idea that Jamal was the father. She didn't sound all that upset, but she swore she would be talking to him. And in fact, she did call him the very next day. I heard them talking."

"What day was this?"

"Well let me see." Nina swallowed half her drink, and seemed to be counting some objects floating in the air in front of her. "Saturday."

Raisa Petrova had called Jamal Krada on the day she died. Hannibal could imagine the scenario. After Nikita's death, Boris gave her money, and later Dani Gana had set up regular payments to her from his African bank to impress her and please Viktoriya. But both those income streams had stopped. Raisa had a flair for blackmail, and she must have tried to put the screws to Krada. Hannibal's breathing stepped up its pace and he could feel the hair on the back of his neck rise.

"And has Viktoriya called again?"

"She calls almost every day," Nina said, waving the glass in his face. "She gets scared, she gets worried, she calls my husband to make sure he knows how to get to her."

Which would explain how someone could find Dani Gana when he would not have told anyone his whereabouts. Money or no, Jamal would have wanted to eliminate the competition. And in Hannibal's experience, once a man has killed, it gets easier to find an excuse to do it again.

"She called here again this morning," Nina said, and the creepy feeling on the back of Hannibal's neck grew more intense.

"Nina, does your husband own a gun?"

"Oh, yeah," she said, taking a sip from the glass she had poured for Hannibal. She looked startled when he grabbed her arm, making her spill the drink.

"Show me. Now."

The fear returned to her eyes. She moved with haste, as she had been trained to do when a man spoke to her. She led him to the linen closet just outside the bedroom. Under a stack of towels lay a brightly colored cardboard box. Hannibal absorbed all of the copy. This was the original box for a Ruger Mark III pistol chambered for the Hornady .17 Mach 2 rimfire cartridge. The gun had a stainless steel frame, an 8-inch stainless steel fluted heavy barrel and checkered cocobolo thumb rest grips. This was a target shooter's toy.

Only an idiot would buy such a thing for personal defense. But in an emergency, any concealable gun would do the job.

"Son of a bitch," Hannibal said. "The murder weapon." But when he pulled the lid off the box, he found only the empty impression of a pistol. The chill was back, walking his spine. He turned to Nina, almost panting as fear crept up on him.

"Where is Jamal Krada now?"

-35-

During the high-speed drive to Viktoriya's motel, Hannibal was locked in a heated argument with himself. The smart money was on calling the police. Of course the smart money put Ivanovich in jeopardy and might scare Krada enough to drive him underground. Hannibal had to see that man in jail. Actually, if what he believed was true, he had to see that man in the electric chair.

The lot was almost empty at midday, but he knew three people who would be home. After shutting off the car he sat for a minute to center himself and bring his blood pressure down. It wouldn't do to rush in, agitated and short-fused with a man like Ivanovich standing guard.

Cooler, his story clear in his mind, Hannibal got out of his Volvo. He took three steps toward the motel building before he realized that someone else might have already made the mistake of approaching the room in some unacceptable manner.

Hannibal could see a man on the second-level balcony, standing at the door to the apartment where Viktoriya and Dr. Sidorov were supposed to be hiding in safety. The man raised his hand as if to knock but before he could, Aleksandr Ivanovich popped out of the door to the left and in three long strides was beside the newcomer. He drove a fist into the man's side, bounced the man's forehead off the door, and shoved him inside.

Hannibal had a pretty good guess of who it was, and sprinted up the stairs to the second floor. When he reached the door he called out his own name before trying the knob. It was unlocked and he pushed in, to find himself staring into the barrel of Ivanovich's pistol.

"Be cool, Aleksandr," Hannibal said, raising his hands. He stepped back, using his shoulder to push the door closed, then paused to take in the situation. Yakov Sidorov was in the chair beside the round table, almost exactly where Hannibal had left him. But now his veined hands gripped the arms of the chair. Viktoriya crouched on the far side of the far bed, looking over the edge of it, half her face hidden from view. At the front of the room Ivanovich stood with his pistol thrust toward Hannibal and his left foot on Jamal Krada's throat.

"It's me, and I'm alone," Hannibal said. Ivanovich relaxed a notch and lowered his gun so that it pointed at Krada's face. The Algerian went pale and Hannibal saw a wet stain begin to spread on the front of his pants.

"You don't want to kill him," Hannibal said, slowly lowering his hands. "Well, maybe you do, but you shouldn't. Do you know who you got there?"

"All I need to know is, he's the man who came here to kill Viktoriya," Ivanovich said. He reached into the back of his waistband and flipped a small handgun to Hannibal. It matched the picture on the box Hannibal saw at Krada's house. "He killed her mother and her husband with that, and here he is to finish the family."

"Not likely," Hannibal said. "She's the reason he killed the other three."

"Three?" Viktoriya asked, standing and walking just far enough around the beds so she could see Krada. "Jamal, did you kill them all?"

"Wait a minute," Ivanovich said, sitting on the bed. He kept his gun on Krada even though he was looking at Hannibal. "I thought Boris Tolstaya killed Nikita Petrova."

Hannibal wondered why these people always used first and last names. "For a while so did I. Boris sure thought he killed Nikita, and Dani Gana held it over him to get what he wanted, a trip to North Africa. They both described a fight and a beating Nikita took. But nobody said anything about throwing him off a roof. I think he was still alive when they left. And when they left, they didn't know that someone else was looking for him and had followed them to the building."

"This is silly," Viktoriya said, leaning back against Sidorov's arm for support. "Why would he kill my daddy?"

"Because he found out that his wife told your father about your pregnancy," Hannibal said. "She gets talky when she drinks. See, he couldn't afford for the word to get out that he had gotten another student pregnant."

"Another?" she whispered.

"He followed your father from the Russia House that night, hoping to persuade him to remain silent. What he didn't know is that his wife never named him as the father. She just wanted you yanked out of school, and figured that letting your dad know you got knocked up would do the trick."

Now Krada sat up. "He didn't know it was me?"

"No, asshole," Hannibal said. "Actually, he accused Boris. That's what set off the fight they had before you got there. But you didn't see any of that, did you? You just hid in the shadows like the coward you are until Boris and his boys were gone. Then you went up, expecting to talk to Nikita, maybe threaten him, I don't know. But instead you found him beaten, battered, maybe unconscious. Your problem was 90 percent solved."

"Nikita was helpless," Ivanovich said, poking the side of Krada's head with the muzzle of his pistol. "So you pitched him off the roof, you heartless bastard. You even took his watch off and took his wallet."

"And you said he killed Mama too?" Viktoriya asked. "That's impossible."

"No, girl, it ain't," Hannibal said, pulling a chair over and dropping into it. "Aleksandr just took the murder weapon off him, an exotic caliber you don't see much around here."

"But there was no reason," Sidorov said, holding Viktoriya's arm as if she might faint and fall.

"You've got to understand," Hannibal said. "When Nikita died he left far less than anyone expected, and the mob did nothing for her. Boris sent her money out of guilt, but had to stop when the half million disappeared and he had to go underground. Dani Gana sent her money from a bank back home, kind of a bribe to get her to keep other men away from Viktoriya here. But that stopped once he was certain the girl would marry him. So things were getting a little tight for Raisa. She had no more pockets to tap. But then Viktoriya called this bum again."

"You were calling him?" The hurt in Ivanovich's voice was palpable. To her credit, the girl met his eyes without blinking.

"I'm thinking she told him every time anything important happened," Hannibal said. "But again, Mrs. Krada heard it and figured she'd try the same trick twice. Only this time, when she called Raisa, she told her who the culprit was. Raisa was more desperate than angry. Her daughter was about to leave her in the dust."

"Oh dear," Sidorov said. "She tried to blackmail him."

"Bingo," Hannibal said. "She called him to demand money, and let him know why. Now, Krada here is no killer, but once a man kills another human…"

"For some, it gets easier each time," Ivanovich said.

"So he took his little, quiet, easily concealed target pistol over to Raisa's house, plugged her, and ran off. And you never even suspected it was him, did you?" Hannibal turned to Viktoriya.

"Daddy and Mama?" she said, looking at Krada as if he was a new kind of lizard she had not seen before. "How could you? I love you. I loved you."

Ivanovich looked at her face, now with tears streaking down it, and then looked at Sidorov's shocked expression and Hannibal's look of contempt. Then he looked down at Krada, who forced a terrified smile. Ivanovich nodded and grinned back.

"Smiling in their faces," he said, "while filling up the hole. So many dirty little faces, in your filthy little, worn-out, broken-down, see-through soul."

Hannibal knew he was the only person in that room who recognized the Nine Inch Nails lyric, and he knew what came next. Ivanovich pulled Krada to his feet.

"Where do you think you're going?" Hannibal asked.

"You are not a killer," Ivanovich said in a very level, businesslike voice. "I will take this one to a good place and dispose of him. He won't be found for days and even when he is, he won't be identifiable."

Krada's eyes flared wide, as if it had never occurred to him that such a thing could happen to him. He turned to Viktoriya, who looked at the carpet. Hannibal got to his feet.

"No, Aleksandr. I have to take him to Rissik. He deserves the collar for bending the rules for us the last few days, and this man needs to face justice."

Ivanovich dismissed Hannibal's words with a puff of air. "Your justice system isn't worth shit. My way, the world is rid of a cockroach for good. Your way, he probably goes free."

"Come on, Aleksandr," Hannibal said. "I've got the murder weapon in my pocket. Besides, he's going to confess to everything. Won't you, dickhead?"

Krada looked from the pistol in Ivanovich's hand to his eyes, swallowed hard, and moved his head up and down like a drinking bird. Hannibal wrapped his hand around Krada's arm. He hadn't seemed so small when Hannibal was sitting in his house.

"Let me take him, Aleksandr," Hannibal said, ignoring the gun and fixing his attention on the real danger, Ivanovich's eyes. It was one of those times when six seconds felt like a lifetime and Hannibal forgot to breathe.

"All right," Ivanovich said. "But not without me."

Hannibal let out a long breath, filled his lungs again, and nodded. He pulled the door open.

"You can't just leave us here," Sidorov said. Hannibal had forgotten the other two were in the room.

"I must go with you," Viktoriya said. "Aleksandr will kill him if he gets the chance, but not if I am there. And I need to hear Jamal confess to his murders so there can be no doubt."

All eyes turned to Viktoriya, showing varying degrees of surprise.

"All right, I guess my car can hold us all. It's a fitting way for this to end, anyway."

"The only fitting way for this to end is death," Ivanovich said.

* * * * *

Rolling west on Capitol Street en route to Rissik's office in Fairfax, Hannibal had Sidorov in his rearview mirror. His face jiggled as they bounced over potholes, but he stared straight ahead, his hands on his knees. He probably felt useless, but he served an important purpose. He separated Viktoriya, behind Hannibal, from Krada. This was good, because from the way Viktoriya was staring at Krada, she would be touching him if she could. And then Ivanovich would kill him.

Ivanovich sat beside Hannibal, literally riding shotgun. He held his automatic pressed against the deep tan upholstery of the seat back, its muzzle just below the top edge. He sat turned toward Hannibal with his eyes locked on Krada's face. Krada sat with his hands folded in his lap, perspiration dripping down his mahogany face.

"I thought you were taking me to Fairfax County," Krada said to Hannibal in the rearview mirror. The smell of his fear filled the car. "Isn't that where you said the detective was that you could trust to keep me alive for trial?"

"Waste of time," Ivanovich said.

"We should be on the beltway, then," Krada said.

"Just making a little detour," Hannibal said. "Dr. Sidorov doesn't need to ride with us into Virginia. I offered to take him home, but he asked to be dropped at the Russia House."

"How could you?" Viktoriya asked, seemingly out of nowhere. "How could you kill my parents?"

The traffic lights on C Street gave Hannibal ample opportunities to turn and talk to his passengers. "You got an answer for that one, Krada?"

Krada broke eye contact with Ivanovich long enough to turn to Viktoriya. "You think it was selfishness? No. I had to protect my job so that I would be able to make a life for you."

"For this you pushed my father off a roof," Viktoriya said. But why did you take his watch off him? Why take his wallet away? "

"I'm sure he heard somewhere that suicides often leave their valuables behind," Hannibal said. "Not that he'd have been very worried about that. He knew damned well that if the suicide story didn't stick, someone else was already set up to get the blame. In fact, even Boris Tolstaya himself thought he was responsible for Nikita's death."

"You imagined that a woman would love you after you destroyed everything she loved?" Ivanovich asked. Then he turned to Viktoriya.

Hannibal couldn't see what Viktoriya's face might have told Ivanovich. He was fully occupied scanning his three mirrors and traffic ahead. The hair on the back of his neck tingled and stood erect. He crept up on a yellow light on Constitution Avenue, and then pressed the accelerator to the floor, pushing the Black Beauty through the intersection as it turned red. He changed lanes without signaling and lodged his car between two slow-moving vehicles. Ivanovich never looked at Hannibal, but he did draw a second pistol and turn around to watch out the passenger window.

"How many?"

"What's going on?" Sidorov asked.

"We've picked up a tail," Hannibal said. Even as he said it, he spotted what he believed to be a second car pacing him just a little ahead of his car. "My fault."

"Not the time," Ivanovich said. "Get us someplace private."

But passing between the National Mall and the Museum of Natural History, Hannibal knew the sudden danger was his fault. He let his guard down after he was certain he had the murderer. They could all die for his carelessness.

"I've picked up the second car," Ivanovich said. "Silver Honda Civic, right? The backseat man is holding an auto pistol."

"They're serious," Hannibal said.

"Who do you suppose?" Sidorov asked, with a calm that surprised Hannibal.

"Mob," Ivanovich said. "Still looking for the money. If they think Viktoriya has it they will take her. And kill me and Jones for interfering."

"I have nothing to do with any missing money," Krada said. "Let me go."

"This was your choice?" Ivanovich asked Viktoriya. "At least Gana tried to protect you. And I have always been here." Hannibal could hear the depth of the pain in Ivanovich's voice. He tried to focus on driving through downtown DC at the start of rush hour, the two cars pacing his own.

"I'm not willing to let you go, Krada," Hannibal said, driving a little faster. "You're the prize at the bottom of the box. But the doc here, they don't need him any way."

"Agreed," Ivanovich said.

"Can't you just call the police?" Viktoriya asked.

"Maybe," Hannibal said, easing to a stop at a light. "But there's no point getting Dr. Sidorov mixed up in that either. I'm going to pull over at that next corner. We'll just let you out and let them follow us all the way to a police station."

Hannibal had cut left on Fifteenth Street and followed it around, keeping the Washington Monument on his right. Part of him wished he was out there with those camera-carrying tourists, or the homeboys involved in some fierce Frisbee tossing. He figured the closer he stayed to the monument area, the safer they all would be. What kind of an idiot would start trouble just a few blocks from the White House? The loop segued into Seventeenth Street, which was a traffic squeeze with cars that had just come into the city over the Memorial Bridge. He no longer saw either of his chase cars.

"We might have caught a break, gang," Hannibal said, turning right to get back on Constitution, which at that point was a wide two-way street. There were three lanes going each way but the cars parked on both sides made the two outer lanes useless. After another five blocks he pulled over to double-park in front of the Federal Reserve Building and issued instructions to each of his passengers.

"Viktoriya, sit tight. Krada, get out and stand by the car with your hands on the trunk. Dr. Sidorov, get out and walk straight into the Federal Reserve. There are armed guards in the lobby, and there's also a phone. Wait ten minutes and call a cab home. Aleksandr, watch Krada. If at any time he loses physical contact with this vehicle, shoot out his right knee. Everybody got it? OK, move."

The door opened and Krada moved with care to the side of the car, resting his palms on the trunk. Sidorov patted Viktoriya's knee the way an uncle would. Then he leaned forward to address Hannibal.

"Thank you for everything,"

Sidorov stepped toward the building at a normal pace without a backward glance. Hannibal took those few seconds to consider where he was. The black granite Vietnam Memorial stood just over the hill in the park across the street. It was designed like a slash in the earth. If he walked across the street and down the path he could point to the exact spot where his father's name was engraved on that wall. And that led him to consider the nature of devotion.

"You're still hooked on her, ain't you?" he asked the back of Ivanovich's head.

Without turning, Ivanovich replied, "Sometimes, when nothing seems worth saving, I can't let her slip away. All right, Krada, back in the car."

Hannibal knew the sound that came next, although most people would mistake it for a loud cough. Krada's body snapped backward as if pulled by invisible wires. Before

Hannibal could turn he heard Ivanovich's elbows hit the Volvo's roof and two guns roared as one. When Hannibal did see the black BMW moving down the road, its back window was spider webbed from the impacts of two bullets. Then Ivanovich bounced back into his seat.

"Move!"

"Not without the prize," Hannibal said.

Ivanovich said something rude in Russian, snatched Krada off the sidewalk, and tossed him back into the car. Viktoriya was lying across the seat, so Krada landed partially on top of her. She screamed and sat up, slapping at blood in her hair.

Hannibal ground the gas pedal into the floorboard and pulled out into traffic the instant Ivanovich was back inside, letting his forward momentum slam the doors shut. His jaw was clenched tight as he spurred the car forward.

"You have them again?" Ivanovich asked.

"Black Beemer ahead. Silver Civic behind. They're a lot ballsier than I thought. Gunfire in broad daylight in front of the Federal Reserve Building? A couple blocks from the Lincoln Monument? What's the matter with these morons? And why the hell shoot Krada?"

"He was with us," Ivanovich said. "Guilt by association. And I'm sure he never saw it coming. Will you call the police now?"

Hannibal grinned. "They'd hang you up by your thumbs, buddy. I'm pretty sure you don't have licenses for those two handguns you just discharged in the middle of the city. Besides, we got to keep on the move. If these guys find us waiting for the cops, they won't hesitate, they'll just shoot. So by the time the cops found us, it would all be over anyway. Unless…"

"Yes?"

"Unless we find a safe place to sit for a while."

Hannibal hit the ramp to I-66 with everything the Black Beauty could give him. As he reached the top of the curve he was staring at a bank of dark, forbidding clouds. Hannibal rarely prayed, but he did at that moment. He prayed that they would not be hit with another cold rain that afternoon. He expected to be outdoors for quite a while.

Traffic was only moderate, so on the downhill run he was able to slide into the farthest left of the three lanes as they hit the Roosevelt Bridge.

Behind him he heard Krada coughing and Viktoriya sniffling. In his rearview mirror he saw her stroke Krada's head in an affectionate way. Then she slammed her fist down onto his right shoulder and shouted, "You bastard!"

"Hang onto something," Hannibal said. The bridge was less than a half-mile long and the first exit was coming up on the far end. The BMW was not far in front of him, the Civic only one car behind. Traffic was moving at a smooth seventy miles per hour, despite the fact that they were driving directly into the setting sun.

"Come on, baby," Hannibal said under his breath. Then he slapped the shifter down into second gear, popped the clutch, and yanked the wheel to the right. He could almost hear the other drivers cursing him as he shot across two lanes of traffic onto the off ramp. In the past, in New York or even in Germany, his maneuver would have raised a chorus of horns, but for some reason Washington drivers rarely honked at idiots.

Hannibal's tires squealed only a little as he pulled into the parking area and rolled to the far end. When he cut the engine he noticed that Ivanovich was staring out the back window.

"I think that worked," the assassin said. "Between your speed and driving into the sun, neither of them could get to the ramp in time to follow us."

"They'll be back," Hannibal said. "Uspensky doesn't pay these boys to quit. Come on."

He got out of the car and opened the back door to help Viktoriya out.

"Where is this?" she asked, looking around at the parkland surrounding the parking area and the welcome center at the far end.

"Welcome to Roosevelt Island," Hannibal said. "Ninety acres of woods and marshes and swampland. By the time those clowns figure out how to turn around and get back here, we'll be well hidden in those woods and waiting for help to come."

"We might not be moving too quickly," Ivanovich said. He had Krada out of the car, but the Algerian was leaking life into a little pool. Lucky for him, he had passed out. Lucky for him, but real bad news for Hannibal.

"How bad?" he asked, walking around the car.

"Two inches high and to the left of the heart," Ivanovich said. "Without care real soon, he will never be able to confess to anything."

"Shit!" Hannibal's eyes darted around. The parking lot was empty but for the cars he assumed belonged to the employees. Roosevelt's memorial was not very popular during the week, especially after summer ended. The island officially closed at dark anyway, which wasn't all that far off. Taking Krada with them seemed pointless. Leaving him to die seemed inhumane. The Russian mobsters had stolen his neat, tidy ending and Hannibal wanted to hate someone for that. He chose Krada.

"Sit his ass next to that Land Rover," he said, pointing at a nearby vehicle. "If he's still alive when the owner comes out, maybe he'll get medical care. If not, he gets the sentence you'd have given him anyway."

Ivanovich was quick to comply, wiping his hands on the dead man's jacket afterward.

"And now?"

"Now we head for the trails," Hannibal said, moving off at a slow jog. "There must be a couple miles of trails wandering all over this place. It will take your pals hours to find us in here."

The trails were mostly wooden boardwalks over the wet earth, about four feet wide. Tall, narrow trees overhung the paths, almost shutting out the waning sunlight, despite the fact that most of the leaves had deserted their posts. The group walked at a brisk pace while Hannibal opened his cell phone.

"Rissik."

"Hey, Chief, it's Hannibal. I got a long, fascinating story to tell you, but it will have to wait. Right now, I need some help and I'm pretty sure I'm on your side of the Potomac."

"What kind of help?" Rissik asked. "You sound kind of out of breath."

"That's because I'm out here hiking with a couple of friends, including Viktoriya Petrova."

"The girl you said you were protecting."

"That's right," Hannibal said, "but it's turning out to be more challenging than I thought. Right now a couple of cars full of Russian mob muscle is chasing us and I could really use a little police assistance here."

Hannibal heard Rissik's chair squeak as he stood. "Moving now, buddy. Where are you?"

"We're trying to lose them on Roosevelt Island. Make lots of noise when you get here, okay?"

As Hannibal ended the call he heard Viktoriya say, "I'm cold," to no one in particular. He turned long enough to see Ivanovich, bringing up the rear, holster his weapons long enough to pull off his sport coat and hand it to the girl. Then he drew his Browning Hi-power from the holster under his right arm, and pulled a smaller Colt Commander from a holster in the back of his waistband.

"Hannibal, I wonder if you realize the irony."

Right then all Hannibal could think of was turning at random points in the trail so there would be no pattern for their pursuers to guess. "Something here strikes you funny?"

"Not funny, my friend, ironic," Ivanovich said. "We Russians, we are very sensitive to irony."

"Oh yeah," Hannibal said, his breathing getting deeper as they hiked into the gathering darkness. "Dostoyevsky and Chekov and all those guys were into it. But we're not being chased by wolves we think are friends coming to save us."

"No, but consider this," Ivanovich said. "Jamal Krada murdered three people. "Two of his victims died slowly of gunshot wounds that would not have been fatal if they'd gotten immediate medical attention. And he didn't hate these people; they were just in his way."

"I see. He got his comeuppance in a similar way. I suppose that's ironic. Or maybe it's just fitting, in a karmic kind of way. Like my dad used to say, what goes around comes around."

They lost the hollow sound of their feet on wooden planks as they moved onto a branch of the path that put them back on hardpacked earth. A bench invited them to stop and rest for a while. Hannibal declined.

"All right then, consider this," Ivanovich said. "We have come to Roosevelt Island to find peace and avoid war."

"Going to have to explain that one to me," Hannibal said.

"You Americans are so ignorant of history," Ivanovich said. Hannibal could hear a smile in his voice. He was enjoying this. "Just after the turn of the century, my country was at war with Japan," Ivanovich went on. "Your President Roosevelt offered his good offices as mediator between Russia and Japan to negotiate the conditions of peace. With his help, they worked out a peace settlement in a couple of months."

"OK, that is ironic," Hannibal said. "Was it a fair settlement?"

"Well, I'm sure the Americans thought so. It led to a loss of face for us, and eventually to the downfall of the czar, but it saved many lives."

"Do you think we'll be able to negotiate a peace here, between us and the Red Mafiya, and maybe save a few lives?"

"With Roosevelt's own island helping us, maybe."

After covering about twenty minutes of trails, Hannibal came to a crossroads with a large tree at its center and walked into a heavy branch hanging over the road. He stopped and tucked his sunglasses into his jacket. A bench on the other side of the trail offered a comfortable resting place. He turned to face his followers. It was getting dark now, but he could still make out the maroon stain on Viktoriya's dress below the sport coat she had wrapped around her. Behind her, Ivanovich didn't seem to mind the chill at all. Unlike Hannibal, he was bred for this.

"This is a good place to leave the trail," Hannibal said. "Then we just hunker down and wait for the police to search us out. This way."

Again Hannibal led. He stepped down about a foot to the marshy land off the hard packed trail. Five steps off the path the ground became very wet. His feet sank ankle deep into the muck, but six steps later he came to a mound surrounding a tree trunk. The tree was nearly a foot thick, and he figured the mound was the top of its root ball and therefore was relatively solid. He turned to face the trail but could not see it. If he didn't know what direction he had come in, he would never have found it. As he dropped to a seated position, he saw Ivanovich approaching, with Viktoriya in his arms.

"Her heels would have sunk into the marsh so deep she'd never have gotten free," Ivanovich said. Hannibal decided to say nothing. Ivanovich lowered the girl onto the mound on the other side of the tree. After settling her in place he bent and kissed her very respectfully on the cheek. Then he walked around to Hannibal and held out his hand.

"What's this?" Hannibal asked, looking up into the Russian's ruddy face and making out a smile.

"Probably good-bye," Ivanovich said. "I'm going to a better position to watch over you two. When the police arrive you will say, with complete honesty, that you do not know where I am. It is unlikely that we will meet again. So this is my chance to wish you well, and say that it was a pleasure to work with a man I could respect."

Hannibal seized the offered hand in a fierce grip. "Likewise, brother. And if you ever want to find a better path, let me help you."

"Thank you for the offer," Ivanovich said, "but my path is set and I know what lies at its end."

Then Aleksandr Ivanovich took two steps back and disappeared into the darkness.

Now that he was sitting still, Hannibal realized that it was getting cold. Not the cold of his youth, not Berlin-in-the-winter cold, but maybe approaching the freezing mark. It didn't get a whole lot worse than that in what passed for winter in the District. He sat with his back against the tree and his hands on his upraised knees and wished his behind wasn't wet from the marshy ground. But the slip of a girl behind him wasn't whining, so he certainly wouldn't either.

Besides, he knew it wouldn't be long. He figured twenty minutes for Rissik to assemble a team and get on the road. Maybe a half hour to get to the island. They'd search with lights and loud hailers and that would be enough to discourage even rabid Russian mobsters. Viktoriya would support his story, as convoluted as it was. And whatever coroner had Krada would tie the bullet to a Russian mob gun. So he had a few minutes, and only a few more questions.

"Viktoriya," he whispered.

"Yes?" There was a slight shiver in her voice. She was cold too.

"You attacked Krada for killing your parents, but you never mentioned your husband, Dani Gana."

Silence.

"That same weird little gun Jamal killed your mother with was used to kill your husband. You knew Jamal shot Dani, didn't you? You knew before I did."

"Yes." Viktoriya said. It was cold confession, but now that the door was open he could draw more out with less effort.

"How did you know?"

"Because Dani told me," she said. "The doorbell rang and he answered it and when he opened the door, Jamal shot him. He told me when I found him in the living room. Before I called for help."

"How did he even know where to find you?" Hannibal asked. He heard short rapid breaths, the kind that precede sobbing.

"It was my fault," she said, almost too low to hear. "I always called Jamal when I was scared or in trouble. I didn't know that he would…"

Hannibal fell silent as something tiny drifted past his nose. It was followed by a second speck, then a third, and then a steady falling flock of them. White flakes were landing on the back of his gloved hands and disappearing as soon as they touched him, only to be replaced by others.

"I don't believe it. It's snowing," he said, although he knew it was unnecessary.

"Things happen," Viktoriya said.

"Yeah, I know," Hannibal replied. "It's just that I prayed it wouldn't rain tonight. Guess I should have been more specific."

He heard her stifling a laugh and for some reason that made him angry. He let a few minutes pass while he watched the world grow a tiny bit brighter and examined his new information to see where it might lead. After a while he turned his head so that he could at least speak in her general direction.

"You loved Krada, didn't you?"

A long sigh. "Yes."

"So what was the plan, Viktoriya? You could have had his baby, but instead you went to another man. Didn't you want to marry Krada?"

"I loved him, but I could not see myself living on a college professor's salary." Her voice was matter of fact, as if she was discussing stock options or the price of gasoline.

"Did you ever care for Aleksandr?"

She snorted in the darkness. "He was the solution to my problem, that's all."

"Your problem?" Hannibal asked. "You mean the money."

"The mob paid him huge sums to do their dirty work. I planned to marry him. Then, after a couple of years I could

242

divorce him, take half his money, and then live with Jamal in the manner I had become accustomed to."

Sitting on the ground, the smell of decay in the swamp was harder to avoid. "Why didn't you?"

"The fool was accused of killing my father," she said after another snort. "Everybody thought it was him, hired by a rival. Dani and Uncle Boris made sure everyone thought it was him. And I couldn't marry a man who killed my father, could I?"

"I see," Hannibal said. "So you just had to change your target. Dani was plan B." Hannibal thought he heard an animal approaching on the trail.

"Yes," she said. "Plan B. Different man, but the intent was the same. Do you hate me now?"

"Hate you?" Hannibal asked. "I hardly know you. But I got to admit, I can admire your focus. You knew what you wanted and you went after it."

"You mean Jamal."

"I mean the life you wanted to lead," Hannibal said. It sounded as if the animal on the trail was getting closer. "I'll bet you understood what Dani was doing for Boris Tolstaya. Yeah, and you convinced him to steal that money. The whole idea of him going to Africa instead of you, then coming back under another name, that was all you, wasn't it? All that so you and he could live happily ever after. Except you planned to dump him and make off with the cash, and your happily ever after was going to be with Krada. Too bad you didn't share your plan with the professor, because he sure screwed things up for you. Now he's probably dead. And Dani knew it would be easier if he and his fortune traveled separately, so now his mother's got the money."

If she had an answer for all that, Hannibal never found out. A flashlight beam lanced across the ground a dozen feet away, pulling an involuntary gasp from her throat instead. Hannibal sat very still. The police would be shouting for them. That meant that the wolves had arrived before the rescuers first after all.

"We know you are there," a man called. The voice carried a strong Eastern European accent and seemed familiar. "This need not be messy. Show yourselves. We take your weapons, tie you, and leave you here to be found in the morning. We take the girl for questioning. Nobody dies."

Hannibal wanted to respond to that disembodied voice, to say that he knew the kind of questioning his people did, that he could spend the night hidden in those woods without their help, and that anyone trying to take his gun would pay dearly. But he knew the wise course was to stay silent.

Snow was just beginning to stick to the frigid ground around him, and in the distance he thought he saw a ghostly form, or maybe two, on the trail. And then he heard the calm, assured voice of Aleksandr Ivanovich.

"You can leave now."

His voice seemed to come from everywhere, and Hannibal could hear the smile behind the words. He was ready.

"You know better," the other man said. Hannibal waved to Viktoriya to stay still. Then he slowly rolled forward to his knees and began inching toward the trail.

"Vladimir?" Ivanovich asked, his voice drifting through the trees like that of an angel.

"Yes, Aleksandr."

"How many?" Ivanovich asked.

During a pause, Hannibal moved again. The damp ground sucked at his gloves as he crawled forward. He wondered if other men were moving just as carefully around in the muck near him, trying to get better position.

"Seven," Vladimir said.

"You underestimate the black one," Ivanovich said. "And you insult me."

"Is the girl worth so much?" Vladimir asked. Hannibal could now just make out a form, standing near the crossroads. Both his hands were full of pistol. At least two stood behind the front form. Hannibal was not sure which form was talking. Nor could he figure out the source of Ivanovich's voice when he answered the question with a question.

"Must we kill each other, old friend?"

Hannibal rolled to his right side. Now he lay only a few feet from the trail, looking up at the front figure in the darkness.

"I cannot simply walk away," Vladimir said.

"I cannot simply surrender the woman," Ivanovich replied.

"Well then," Vladimir said. "Here we are."

Hannibal heard a deep sadness in both voices. He had heard it before, sitting next to Yakov Sidorov in the Russia House. Grudging acceptance. This is the way things are. Ivanovich knew his path, and he knew what lay at its end. And now Hannibal knew too.

Silence fell with the snowflakes. For a few seconds the night held its breath. And then one cloud shouldered another aside and a moonbeam laid a soft glow on the forest. Tree branches like bent, gnarled fingers reached for the figures on the path.

A concussive burst of sound set off Hannibal's startle reflex as a pair of flame jets burst from the tree at the crossroads. Two bodies sprang off the path and into the marsh as if yanked by wires.

Hannibal pressed his back against the ground as a roar of gunfire answered the first two shots. Five or maybe ten guns lit up the night as their bullets chewed the top half of the tree to kindling. Shell casings bounced along the ground all around him. In the muzzle flashes Hannibal could see no joy in those stern faces, no excitement. This was business. And this was survival.

The gunmen stopped and seemed to be appraising the damage to the tree they had assaulted. Hannibal drew his pistol and aimed at the nearest man, knowing that firing would make him a target. Before he could squeeze the trigger, Ivanovich leaped from behind the tree with both guns blazing. In that seemingly slow motion that Hannibal sometimes experienced at moments of extreme tension, he watched Ivanovich float in a horizontal arc across the path and down into the swamp on the other side. Two more men crumbled to the ground. Hannibal could not see the remaining shooters, but thought he could get close to their last positions based on the location of the muzzle flashes. If Ivanovich would stay down for a moment, they might get out of this whole.

But then, Ivanovich rose up out of the swamp and began walking slowly toward the path again. Someone fired at him from ten yards off to the right. He fired back. A man howled in pain.

"It didn't turn out the way you wanted it to," Ivanovich said. Hannibal wasn't sure if Ivanovich was talking to his attackers or himself. He stepped up on the path and started walking in the direction the killers had come from. As his foot touched the first section of wooden boardwalk, another man fired at him from farther down the path. He raised his left hand slowly and fired back. Again he was rewarded with a shriek of pain.

"It didn't turn out the way you wanted it, did it?" Ivanovich asked. More damned Nine Inch Nails lyrics even in the face of death. Then Hannibal noticed a movement ahead of him. Down off the path on his side, a man raised a gun to shoot Ivanovich in the back.

Like hell! Hannibal ran toward the man, firing at the vague shape in the darkness. His target turned in surprise, dived away from the path and fired at Hannibal. He also missed and suddenly they were too close for guns. Hannibal screamed out as his shoulder hit the man's chest and they went down into the mud.

The other man was bigger, and skilled. He punched Hannibal hard enough to crack a rib. Then he managed to gain the top position, straddling Hannibal's waist. Hannibal managed one solid right cross before his enemy locked fingers around his throat. The starless night sky was a solid deep purple shroud, threatening to cover Hannibal permanently. He heard his own breath rattling in his throat. His hands and feet scrambled for leverage, but the mud beneath him offered no purchase. He could feel the welts rising on either side of his larynx.

Rage shook him when he glanced at the impassive face of the man strangling him to death. Then his right hand hit something that was not mud. A root? No, a stone. It was small, but it made a sickening crunch when Hannibal swung it up and slapped it into his enemy's temple. The fingers weakened and the man fell to the side.

As the stranger crumbled to the earth, Hannibal felt an unexpected joy. He struggled to his hands and knees, gasping to suck in as much of the frozen air as he could. Then he felt around until he found his pistol and clambered up on the path to follow in Ivanovich's footsteps. Ahead of him, two shots came from the right, out in the swamp. Ivanovich jerked to the side, returned fire, and dropped to his knees. As Hannibal reached him, he could see the shooter off to the side, crouching in the mud behind a mound of earth. Hannibal dropped low beside Ivanovich, who wavered and tumbled to his side. Blood poured from his chest and neck.

"Hang on, man," Hannibal whispered. "Help will be here soon."

Ivanovich shook his head, and offered Hannibal a half smile. "Only one left. We saved her. Finish it for me."

"Fuck that asshole, and the girl too," Hannibal said, pressing a gloved hand against Ivanovich's neck wound. "You need to focus on saving yourself."

"No," Ivanovich said, staring into Hannibal's eyes in the darkness. "This time, you know the song. I've held it for my final words for years."

"What are you talking about?"

Ivanovich swallowed hard, clenched his teeth as if accomplishing his next task was vital, and mumbled out, "I try to save myself but my self keeps slipping away."

"Are you crazy?"

Ivanovich continued, as if it was a mantra to guide him into Valhalla. "Try to save myself but myself keeps slipping away. Try to save myself but myself keeps slipping…"

When life slips away, a human body feels different. Startled by the change, Hannibal dropped Ivanovich's head to the path. These were not final words to be remembered by, so he mentally stepped over them to Ivanovich's previous words. Finish it for me. He stood straight up and stared at the last man. He thought it was Vladimir, the man they met at Boris Uspensky's office.

"Just you and me now." He said it softly, but he was sure the other man heard him. "Soon, just me."

He stepped over Aleksandr Ivanovich and off the boardwalk. His foot sank ankle deep in the soft earth but he kept going. Vladimir fired at him and Hannibal had no idea where the bullet went. The clouds jostled each other again and the moonlight vanished.

He could make out the other man's form on the ground in front of him now. Vladimir fired again. Pain lanced through Hannibal's right arm but the bullet didn't throw him down. That meant it had not encountered bone, but just dug a divot of flesh out of the side of his arm. Too bad for Vladimir that Hannibal was lefthanded.

In the distance he heard a loud hailer asking for whoever was in the park to identify themselves. He kept going. Left foot, right foot, like he remembered his father saying when he was small. That's how you get where you need to go. Left foot, right foot.

A dozen feet away, Vladimir raised his gun and Hannibal raised his as well. As Hannibal stepped closer, waiting to be in certain one-shot-kill range, the two men looked down their sight posts into each other's eyes.

A light beam slid between them and Vladimir squeezed his trigger. Hannibal heard the hollow clack of a hammer falling on an empty chamber. It seemed that Vladimir had lost count. Vladimir turned on his back, watching Hannibal between his own feet. Hannibal continued on until he stood inches from Vladimir's shoes. Now he could see that Vladimir was bleeding from his right side. His face was calm, placid, as

Aleksandr's had almost always been. Did this man understand that Hannibal had to finish his friend's business?

"He was already mortally wounded you know," Vladimir said. As if that made any difference.

"You don't want to shoot me," Vladimir said. "You are not like us. You are not a killer."

Hannibal lowered his weapon, took a deep breath, and raised it again.

"You think you know what I am? I'll tell you what I am." Hannibal took another deep breath, and heard Ivanovich's voice in his head. Or Trent Reznor's.

"Broken. Bruised. Forgotten. Sore. Too fucked up to care anymore."

Vladimir nodded slightly, indicating that he recognized the lyrics. Hannibal squeezed, but never felt the trigger let off. The slide rocked back and slammed forward, but Hannibal never heard the blast. Vladimir's forehead offered no resistance to the jacketed hollowpoint on its way into the ground. Then Hannibal dropped to his knees. Some number of seconds later he heard a familiar woman's voice scream. Then a cluster of light beams flashed around him, illuminating the entire swamp. There was a lot of conversation, but it all seemed muddled to him. A coat fell around his shoulders and he heard Orson Rissik's voice.

"Hannibal. It's Orson. I got here as fast as I could."

"Seemed like all night. Is it midnight yet?"

"Midnight?" Rissik asked. "Son, it's barely six. We had daylight until we arrived but finding you out here in the dark was a bitch. Are you OK?"

"I'm fine," Hannibal said as Rissik and another man laid him on a stretcher. "At least, better than anybody else out here except...did you find the girl?"

"Yeah, she's fine. Not a scratch on her."

"Yeah, that figures," Hannibal said, rummaging through his jacket for his phone.

"Hey, we need to get somebody to look at that arm," Rissik said. "Whoever you're thinking of calling, it can wait."

"No," Hannibal said as they bounced him along the boardwalk toward the parking lot, "no, it can't."

Epilogue

There was no way to see in the window at Kinkead's, just a couple blocks from the White House. Watching snowflakes melt as they hit the restaurant's fogged-up bay window, Hannibal spared himself a smile, thinking of the conversation he had on his cell phone while sitting in the emergency room.

"It's your own fault for being in the office so late, Mrs. Abrogast," he had said. "I've already tried her home phone and her BlackBerry. And I've got a feeling you know where she is."

"She left late, Mr. Jones. I believe she had an appointment."

"And that would be where?"

"I don't have her appointment book handy."

"Come on, Mrs. A. You keep it all in your head anyway."

"I'm surprised she didn't tell you. Maybe if you hadn't stood her up for lunch…"

"Look, Mrs. A," Hannibal said through clenched teeth. "I have had a really shitty day."

"Excuse me, young man?"

"I haven't eaten since breakfast, I have huge bruises on my throat from where a guy tried to strangle me, and I'm sitting here watching some guy from Pakistan stitch up a bullet hole in my right arm. The jacket's ruined too. I just need to talk to her, all right?"

There was a long, hard pause. He heard a deeply drawn breath. He was through. If she didn't talk she wouldn't, but he would not ask again.

"She's meeting him for a late supper," Mrs. Abrogast said.

"Terrific. Where?"

And that was what brought him to Kinkead's. He ignored the maitre d's questions and glanced only briefly at the stairs. No, she wouldn't want to go up to the formal dining area. She would prefer the more casual feel of the street-level café and bar. He brushed past the man telling him how long the wait was. He brushed past the congressional staffers and lobbyists who crowded the tables, talking shop and making deals. Their conversation, and the lady churning out predictable jazz on the piano, made it unlikely anyone would hear him approach. No one even looked up until he was standing beside the table.

Reggie Johnson sat to his left. Cindy sat on his right. Both looked perplexed when they noticed him. Cindy opened her mouth to say something he was sure he didn't want to hear, so he focused on the man.

"Blow," Hannibal said, nodding his head toward the door. "We need a little privacy."

"Hannibal, what the hell?" Cindy said. He had been right. He didn't want to hear that.

Reggie stared for a second, his brows knit together in confusion.

"You got a hearing problem?" Hannibal said, just a little louder. "Hit the bricks, bud."

The two men locked eyes. Reggie stood, very slowly, to his full height and looked down into Hannibal's face. Hannibal never flinched.

"You don't want none of this, son. Don't make the mistake of deciding to fuck with me. Not now. Not today."

"Reggie," Cindy said. "Please. It's all right. We do need to…to talk. Let me call you, OK?"

Was it the consoling tone in Cindy's voice? Did he see something behind Hannibal's dark lenses that he didn't want to disturb? Did he notice the bullet hole in the right sleeve of Hannibal's mud-encrusted suit coat, just above the elbow? Did he guess the significance of the twin bruises on Hannibal's throat? Whatever the reason, Reggie Johnson turned his face to Cindy, said "Another time," and walked out of the restaurant. Hannibal let out a long breath and sat in the chair Reggie just emptied. He folded his hands on the table between him and his woman.

"That was rude…"

"Damn straight," Cindy said.

"… but I couldn't be away from you another minute." Then he pulled his glasses off and laid them on the table. Cindy looked closely at his eyes, then looked around the rest of him. He knew his hair was dirty and his jacket was caked with dried mud. He saw her eyes linger on the bullet hole and with the jacket pressed against his arm he knew she could see the white bandage beneath.

Hannibal closed his eyes. He wanted to tell her how much he had missed her in the last week. He wanted to tell her why he had been away. He wanted to ask her what there really was between her and the man who had just left. He wanted to tell her how much he needed her. He wanted to believe she could see all of that in his eyes.

Cindy leaned close, almost as if she was reading his fine print.

"You hurting, baby?"

He nodded. His mouth opened but nothing came out.

"You need some healing," she said. He nodded again. His lips curled in to his teeth. She took his hands and stood up.

"Come on. Let's go to your place so I can get started."

The End

BOOK CLUB INVITATION – PLEASE READ

Gentle Reader,

Authors of Victorian novels used an odd literary device: speaking directly to the reader. You know, that point when they write, "Let us take advantage of this lull to whisper a few biographical details."

This "Gentle Reader" technique is rare in modern fiction. But since you just finished *Russian Roulette* I think it's okay for me to address you directly to ask for an invitation to your next book club meeting.

I know that many of you meet with other readers to discuss your favorite books. If you enjoyed this Hannibal Jones mystery I would love to discuss my book with your book club. If you are within the Washington, DC metro area I would be happy to attend a meeting of your book club so you can ask all the tough questions about my plot, the setting, the clues and the characters.

If you are farther away, I can still attend your meeting virtually if you have a speakerphone available. We can even make it work as an online chat if you prefer. Either way I would be able to give live responses to your questions and comments.

To invite me to join your book club at a meeting – and I hope you do - just send the information below in an email to dbcamacho@hotmail.com.

1. Book club name
2. Contact name
3. Contact telephone number and e-mail address
4. City and State
5. Date and time of the meeting

I look forward to meeting you!

Austin

Austin S. Camacho

Austin S. Camacho is also a public affairs specialist for the Department of Defense. America's military people know him because for more than a decade his radio and television news reports were transmitted to them daily on the American Forces Network.

He was born in New York City but grew up in Saratoga Springs, New York. He majored in psychology at Union College in Schenectady, New York. After three years, he enlisted in the Army as a weapons repairman but soon moved into a more appropriate field. The Army trained him to be a broadcast journalist. Disc jockey duties alternated with news writing, video camera and editing work, public affairs assignments and news anchor duties.

During his years as a soldier, Camacho lived in Missouri, California, Maryland, Georgia and Belgium. He also spent a couple of intense weeks in Israel during Desert Storm, covering the action with the Patriot missile crews and capturing scud showers on video tape. While enlisted he finished his Bachelor's Degree at night and started his Master's, and rose to the rank of Sergeant First Class. In his spare time, he began writing adventure and mystery stories set in some of the exotic places he'd visited.

After leaving the Army he continued to write military news for the Defense Department as a civilian. Today he handles media relations and writes articles for military newspapers and magazines. He also teaches writing classes at Anne Arundel Community College and is deeply involved with the writing culture. He is an active member of the Mystery Writers of America, International Thriller Writers, Sisters in Crime, Washington Independent Writers, and the Virginia Writers Club.

Camacho has settled in Springfield, Virginia with his wife Denise and Princess the wonder cat.

Also in the Hannibal Jones Mystery Series

The Troubleshooter

A Washington attorney buys an apartment building in the heart of the city, but then finds the building occupied by drug dealers. Police are unable to empty the building for use by paying residents. No one seems willing or able to take on this challenge until the lawyer meets Hannibal Jones. He calls himself a troubleshooter, but he finds more trouble in Southeast Washington than he expected. Hannibal soon finds himself facing off against a local crime boss and his powerful, mob connected father.

Blood and Bone

An eighteen-year-old boy lies dying of leukemia. Kyle's only hope is a bone marrow transplant, but no one in his family can supply it. His last chance lies in finding his father, who disappeared before Kyle was born. Kyle's family has nowhere to turn until they learn of a troubleshooter named Hannibal Jones. His search for the missing man leads Hannibal down a twisting path of deception, conspiracy, greed and murder, but with each step the danger grows.

Collateral Damage

Bea Collins is certain her fiancee wouldn't just leave without telling her. Troubleshooter Hannibal Jones is skeptical until the missing fiancee turns up dazed, confused and holding a knife over a dead body. To find this killer Hannibal will travel to Germany, Vegas and through Dean's past, which includes the murder of Dean's father, his first childhood crush and brings Hannibal face to face with Dean's convicted mother.

Damaged Goods

The death of Anita Cooper's father crushed her dreams of a better life. Then a hard man named Rod Mantooth stole both her innocence and her father's legacy, a secret that could have rebuilt her life. Anita was lost until she encountered another hard man - the professional troubleshooter named Hannibal Jones. Like a rolling mass of icy fury, Hannibal follows a trail of corrupted human debris leading to Rod Mantooth and a final showdown in the icy waters of the Atlantic.

Also by Austin S. Camacho

Stark and O'Brien Thriller series

The Payback Assignment

Morgan Stark, a black mercenary soldier, is stranded in the Central American nation of Belize after a raid goes wrong.

Felicity O'Brian, an Irish jewel thief, is stranded in the jungle south of Mexico after doing a job for an American client.

In the first novel of this series they learn they've been double-crossed by the same man: Adrian Seagrave, a ruthless businessman maintaining his respectability by having others do his dirty work.

Morgan and Felicity become friends and partners while following their common enemy's trail. They become even closer when they find they share a peculiar psychic link, allowing them to sense danger approaching themselves, or each other.

But their extrasensory abilities and fighting skills are tested to their limits against Seagrave's soldiers-for-hire and Monk, his giant simian bodyguard. A series of battles from California to the New York lead to a final confrontation with Seagrave's army of hired killers in a skyscraper engulfed by flames.

The Orion Assignment

Retired jewel thief Felicity O'Brien travels to her native Ireland to defend her uncle's Catholic parish. With her is her partner, Morgan Stark, a retired mercenary soldier. The job looks easy until they meet Ian O'Ryan, an IRA terrorist who believes he is the reincarnation of Orion the ancient hunter. He is determined to keep the violence alive in Ireland and to spread it throughout the island.

To avoid bullets, bombs and beatings, Morgan and Felicity rely on a special gift, a psychic link that alerts them to danger. But against O'Ryan they face danger from an entire army of enemies.

Trying to separate patriotic mercenaries from heartless terrorists leads them to a sniper mission on the rocky Irish coast, a deadly high speed motorcycle race in Belgium, and a final confrontation on an island off the coast of France where Morgan could die by slow torture if Felicity doesn't find him in time.

LaVergne, TN USA
26 April 2010
180566LV00001B/1/P